THE *Weight* OF Entanglement

BY MALCOLM IVEY

Consider the Dragonfly

With Arms Unbound

On the Shoulders of Giants

Sticks & Stones

THE MIRANDA RIGHTS SERIES
Year of the Firefly
The Weight of Entanglement

www.MalcolmIvey.com

MALCOLM IVEY

THE Weight OF Entanglement

A MIRANDA McGUIRE NOVEL

Miranda Rights

-BOOK TWO-

tempus fugit ☽ *amor manet*

ASTRAL PIPELINE BOOKS | ORLANDO ★ PENSACOLA ★ SAN DIEGO

Literary works
AI-Free
of natural origin

First Astral Pipeline Books Edition, April 2022

Astral Pipeline Books LLC
1317 Edgewater Dr., Ste 2023
Orlando, Florida 32804
astralpipelinebooks.com

ISBN: 978-1-953519-06-1 (paperback)
ISBN: 978-1-953519-07-8 (ebook)
Library of Congress Control Number: 2022937006

Cover design by Astral Pipeline Books

For Shonda. Air and Water.

"In the field of quantum mechanics there is something called quantum entanglement. It is what happens when two particles interact, vibrate in unison, and are separated. They remain connected by something that defies logic, something science has yet to explain. If one particle vibrates, no matter the distance, the other particle reacts in unison. Even if there are oceans between them, even if there is a universe separating them."

—TYLER KENT WHITE

PART ONE
Orientation

1

Her N95 was confiscated, replaced by a stifling triple-ply polyester mask that appeared to be cut from the same material as her state-issued blue uniform. She tied the straps behind her ears and around her neck as she followed the rest of the new arrivals out of the receiving building and into the September humidity.

Gleaming coils of razor wire spiraled endlessly over the tops of the interior fences that separated the compound into four equal quarters. Sunshine played on sharpened steel. She made an awning of her palm and scanned the landscape. There was more of it across the yard, nailed to the eaves of dormitories, and still more climbing drainpipes on the sides of buildings like thorny silver kudzu.

"Eyes straight forward! No talking!" barked a voice over her left shoulder. "Stay inside the yellow line."

Miranda risked a glance—mirrored shades and a Lara Croft braid with a can of pepper spray the size of a small fire extinguisher dangling from her belt. Her name tag read *P.K. Napier.*

"Problem inmate?" the guard snarled.

Busted, she looked away. The woman behind her tsked, the woman in front of her shook her head.

She seems pleasant, her inner narrator observed. *Much nicer than the chick with the flashlight . . . But then so does the guy up there with the machine gun.*

The tower rose from the center of the compound like a massive concrete fist. An armed silhouette paced the catwalk. She shivered, swallowed, willed herself forward. It was all so stark, so suffocating. The strip searching, the razor wire, the gun tower. Not a tree or flower in sight. Even the rec yard grass appeared to be eking out a brittle existence. The vibrant life and color of nature seemed to stop at the prison gate. She wondered if she could ever get used to it.

Hey, you're the one who signed the plea agreement.

Did she? The weeks after Cameron was ripped from her arms were a tear-streaked blur of hurt. It was difficult to recall any single instance with clarity. She just remembered the trauma, the guilt, the shame, the powerlessness, the hopelessness. These echoed in her heart even now. But she really didn't have a choice. She *had* to sign the deal. It was either that or 25 to life. Her public defender said so.

You didn't have to do anything. No one made you, her inner narrator insisted. *You gave up. You could've fought.*

Up ahead an older woman was struggling with her property—two overflowing mesh bags and a pillowcase. The line snaked around her as she knelt on the sidewalk.

Miranda glanced at the officer before stopping and reaching for what appeared to be the heaviest bag. "I don't have much to carry. Let me—"

"Don't touch my shit!" The woman swatted her hand away. Her speech was slurred, the left side of her face was slack. "I don't need no damn help. Now git!"

The guard smirked. Laughter trickled across the yard. Miranda realized there were women under the pavilion.

"Welcome home Ms. Tussie," one of them shouted.

"Yeah. Fuck you!" she shouted back.

"Jones, that's enough," said Officer Napier.

"Tell *them* that's enough. They the ones that called this shithole my home. My home is Fairhope, Alabama." She ran her tongue along her toothless gums and spat through the fence.

"You do that again and your home will be disciplinary confinement."

"What'd I do? Spit?" Her eyes were different colors—one gray, one green. Her mask hung from her neck like a bandana. "This place is getting stricter and stricter. Everybody spits. It's like pissing."

"If your mask was covering your mouth like it's supposed to be . . ."

"I can't breathe in this damn thing."

"Put your mask on, Jones. Now. That's a verbal order."

Miranda turned to catch up to the back of the line.

"Stop right there, inmate. Nobody told you to move."

With a sinking feeling, she halted by the fence and looked out across the rec yard toward the pavilion, hands instinctively clasped behind her back. A girl doing squats blew her a kiss.

"Okay Jones," Napier glared over her shades. "Real simple. Three choices and three seconds to make up your mind. One, you carry all that excessive property to quarantine."

"Quarantine?" Her slurred voice was muffled through the mask. "I ain't sick."

The officer ignored her. "Two, you allow this nice young lady here to help you."

"Hell no."

"Three, you leave it right here on the sidewalk as abandoned property and I'll make sure it's properly disposed of. But what we're *not* going to do is stop twenty times between here and Alpha dorm. I've got other things to do."

The older woman ran gnarled arthritic fingers through her limp gray hair. "Why do I have to go to quarantine?"

"Because you're a new arrival."

"I ain't new," said Tussie Jones. "I've been in prison for thirty-four calendar years."

Thirty-four years? her inner narrator blurted. *Did she just say thirty-four years?*

"Well you're new today." The guard signaled the tower to hold up the line. "And everybody coming in, whether on a county van or from another prison, has to be quarantined for fourteen days. Those are CDC guidelines, not ours. Now what's it going to be? You want to just leave one of those bags right here? It's just a bunch of garbage anyway. I'll make sure it gets to the dump."

"No!" The old woman stepped in front of her property, shielding the bags as if they were small children. "I'll . . . I'll let the redhead carry one."

Miranda turned from the fence and stepped forward, again reaching for what appeared to be the heaviest of the three.

"But not that one." Tussie squinted at her suspiciously. "She's had her eye on it all afternoon. Haven't you girlie?"

"Not at all," said Miranda.

"Take the pillowcase." Her frown lines hardened into a menacing scowl.

Ooookay.

"But I want you to know something—if I catch you digging around in there, I'll gut you like a fish."

"Inmate Jones!"

"I was just playing, Officer Napier."

Her eyes told a different story.

2

Of the eight dormitories on the compound, none were as depressing as Alpha and Bravo. Located in the most remote quadrant of the prison, their slatted plexiglass eyes and steel door mouths looked out over a desolate strip of sun-cracked concrete and an acre of empty track. The other sectors at least showed some evidence of life—exhausted inmate work squads from food service and inside grounds were staggering back to neighboring Charlie and Delta dorms. Some were yelling over the fence at Echo and Foxtrot who still lounged under the rec pavilion. Directly across the yard, the women of Gulf and Hotel waited in line at the canteen window. But aside from Officer Napier with her fire extinguisher pepper spray cannister and the ragtag group of new arrivals filing into the Alpha dorm hallway, there was nothing going on in this far-flung corner of the facility.

At least not on the outside of the buildings.

Thump . . . thump.

Muffled pounding, dull and persistent, filled the narrow corridor as the door slammed behind Miranda. The guard pushed her sunglasses up her forehead and massaged the bridge of her nose. The women toward the front began to stir.

Thump . . . thump.

Miranda glanced at Tussie. The old woman had removed her mask again. Her gray eye glinted defiance, her green glimmered madness.

"What's that sound?"

The door buzzed. The line pressed forward. The banging grew sharper, louder, more insistent.

Bam . . . bam.

"Somebody's pissed off," Tussie slurred. "They're mule-kicking their cell door. Sounds like wing three. Disciplinary confinement, the last time I was here."

"Crazy bitches," muttered Napier.

"Naw, crazy bitches is next door in Bravo. Psyche dorm." She lifted her bags and staggered forward. "TCU. I been there. A few times. CSU too."

"Why am I not surprised?" The guard waved at a musclebound coworker in the officers' station.

Bam . . . bam . . . bam.

"They're just letting her tire herself out." Tussie yanked her mask down around her neck again. "They'll run in there and spray her in a minute, if they haven't already. You'll hear 'em coughing. The whole damn wing'll be choking on the gas. It gets in the vents. After that, if she still won't cuff up, they'll bring in the shield . . ."

The women in front of them were herded into the quarantine wing like cattle. "In you go ladies," said Officer Napier, just as the cell extraction team stormed past; five beefy guards in turtle suits behind a shield followed by a white shirt with a video camera. She nodded at her superior. "Captain."

Miranda hefted the pillowcase over her shoulder watched them pile through the door of the next quad.

"Don't get too comfortable, girlie."

"Oh sorry." She walked over to a bench in the dayroom and set the property down. "Here you go."

A thunderous rumble penetrated the walls, followed by shouting and screaming. Tussie shot her a *told you so* look. "I've been on the wrong end of that shield a few times. Ain't no party, I can tell you that."

Miranda attempted Amity's havening technique for the second time that day. Didn't work. Between the screaming and slamming of doors in wing three and the bustle of inmates dragging mats into newly assigned cells all around her, it was impossible to concentrate. Her senses were overloaded, her nerve endings were fried.

Tussie licked her gums and frowned. "You all right?"

She nodded and continued rubbing her arms. Two mesh bags and a pillowcase. That's what 34 years of accumulated property looked like. She did the math in her head as her eyes wandered over the dayroom benches, the television on the wall, the second-tier railing. *1986*. The old woman had been in prison since Reagan was president. Her dad was ten years old when Tussie Jones lost her freedom.

A buzzcut blonde with a thumb ring and a clipboard leaned over the rail and pulled her mask down around her chin. "Y'all two! Little red riding hood and grandmother wolf. You been assigned cells yet?"

The slack skin of the old woman's face began to quiver. "*Grandmother?* Who's this dyke calling—"

"No ma'am," Miranda answered. "Not yet."

Napier clicked her handcuffs behind them. "Can we get them in the same cell, Sarge?" There was a smile in her voice. "They're besties."

3

Tussie Jones snored like a drunken sailor. She had barely stuffed her beloved property in her footlocker before the walls began to vibrate from the raucous chainsaw in her nasal passages. She didn't bother making her bunk or even removing her shoes. Two minutes after moving into the cell, the old woman was out; hands at her sides, mouth wide open, zzzing louder than Patrick McGuire.

Dad . . . She could only hope he was somewhere snoring. It took fully functioning lungs to suck down one of his snores and it was common knowledge that Covid was the mortal enemy of the respiratory system. She blinked away gathering tears as her mind scrolled through snapshots and mental video. There had to be a way to find out if he was okay, if he was alive. She looked around the cell as if the answer would appear on the cinderblocks.

The room was larger than the one she shared with Amity in the county jail. Instead of bunkbeds, two single racks ran parallel to the wall. Her head would be inches from Tussie's feet. Tussie's head was next to the toilet. At the back of the cell, a narrow window looked out over the empty yard. At the entrance, no bars, just a reinforced steel door painted correctional blue.

As if on cue, it rumbled open, along with the rest of the doors on the wing. She glanced at Tussie before poking her head out. Other women were making their way to the dayroom. Some bolted for the phones, some for the kiosk, some to secure seats on the benches. The television zapped on. *World News Tonight* was already in progress. Her cellmate's snoring trailed her like a swarm of hornets as she hurried to find a spot.

Kamala Harris smiled over the top of a plain black mask and waved at the camera. Miranda vaguely remembered someone—*Amity?*—telling her that Biden had tapped the California senator to be his vice president. She wondered what else had happened since her baby was born.

You mean besides you signing away ten years of your life?

A middle-aged woman with a shock of white hair that spiraled down a cascade of otherwise brown curls slid next to her on the bench, tapping away on a tablet.

Miranda didn't want to appear nosy, but it was difficult to restrain herself. As the news turned to California wildfires, she stole a quick glance. *Unbelievable.* "Um, excuse me, are you texting?"

"Yeah," the woman answered without looking up.

"And that's allowed?"

She shot Miranda a sideways look. "I wouldn't be doing it out here in front of the officers' station if it wasn't."

"Right." She glanced over at the wall of windows and the computer-lit terminal on the other side.

"They sell them to us," said the woman. "Actually, they're giving them to us now. But for the last two years they've been selling them. One fifty a pop. They're really pieces of shit. I'm on my third. But they're better than what we had before."

"What was that?"

"Nothing," she laughed. "The U.S. Mail and those collect call phones over there . . . You should have seen it when they first came in. Some of these old lifers that have been down thirty, forty years, stumbling around looking confused as hell, jabbing and mashing the living shit out of those touchscreens."

Miranda thought of her cellmate. Maybe there was a tablet in one of Tussie's precious bags. Maybe that's why she was so uptight about people touching them.

"They're pretty cool though. Check it out." She held up the screen. "Movies, music, pictures, videos, games . . . They've definitely changed the way we do time. It ain't cheap though. Even the emails cost money. Somebody has gotten extremely rich off this little thing."

"Prison profiteers usually do." Miranda studied her screen saver; a black woman waved from a fishing pier. "That's why they sink millions into lobbying firms, and why they campaign for politicians who claim to be tough on crime. Strict laws equal less empty cells. More customers."

The woman set her tablet on the bench. "Are you, like, some type of activist?"

"Kinda," said Miranda. "Once . . . Who was the lady on the pier?"

"Tina. My girlfriend. She got out two months ago. I'll be joining her next March if I can stay out of trouble. She got us an apartment in St. Pete."

The television went dark. The women on the benches instinctively turned toward the officers' station. The intercom crackled. "This is your one and only warning, ladies. Masks on in the dayroom. Class A on the kiosk. If I have to tell you again, the TV's staying off."

Miranda looked around. Many of the women were wearing their masks around their necks like Tussie. Others wore none at all and had to get up and retrieve them from their cells. The woman next to her wore hers like a chinstrap. She rolled her eyes as she pulled it up over her mouth.

"This is so lame. We're all in this little bubble together, using the same phones, touching the same kiosk, touching *each other*." She looked pointedly at a couple on the next bench who were holding hands. "The air in this bitch is recycled, the windows don't open. If somebody is sick, we're all catching it. Masks or no masks."

Miranda glanced at the kiosk. "What's *Class A* mean?"

"You're wearing it." The woman reached out and brushed a speck of dust from her shoulder. "It's this wrinkled blue uniform they gave you. Once you hit the compound, you can buy nicer clothes. I'd wait if I was you though. I doubt you'll be here longer than a couple months."

Miranda shook her head. "I've got ten years."

Minus time off for good behavior, her inner narrator added.

"I meant at this camp, love. This is a reception center. Aside from a handful of permanents that work food service and inside grounds, the only girls who stay here are in the TCU next door and the faith-based dorm across the compound. Everyone else is on their way to Lowell or Gadsden."

"Where are you going?"

"I'm here for Hep C medication. A few of us from Gadsden are. I heard it takes a couple months. I should be pretty close to my release date by then. They might just keep me until I *e.o.s.*"

Miranda glanced at the woman's arms, noted the tell-tale track marks.

"Yeah," she shrugged and smiled. "I like to play with pointy things. What's your downfall?"

Spineless losers? her inner narrator suggested.

"Pills," said Miranda.

"Ahh, pills . . . That's how I started. In the golden age of the Central Florida pill mills. Fifteen years ago everybody was taking road trips to Orlando pain clinics and coming home with their pockets rattling with prescription Oxy bottles. Xanax and methadone wafers too. Whatever you wanted. But then the attorney general shut 'em down almost overnight. Created a gigantic hole in the market. Everybody was strung out on opiates, dope-sick with nowhere to score." She paused, patted her tablet. "You think prison profiteers are stacking money hand over fist? Imagine the heroin dealers after the pill mills shut down."

There was a time when the mere mention of opiates was like a struck match flaring in the innermost sanctum of her heart, where ravenous shadows flickered against arterial walls. She braced for that familiar hunger now but was met with only stillness. The last of that dark time and that lost soul of a girl vanished down a hospital hallway with the fading screams of an infant child. At least she hoped so.

"What, were you crushing 'em up and banging 'em?"

Miranda blinked. "Huh?"

"The pills. Were you shooting them?"

She shook her head. "I was snorting them."

"Yeah, weren't we all . . . once." Knowing smile. "Pop, snort, shoot. The evolution of a junkie. You just get to the point where anything else is a waste. But I'll tell you this from experience: If you have a taste for opiates, look around. Get used to this. You'll be in and out of these places for the rest of your life."

4

That night she dreamed that Cameron was locked in a freezer. Tiny blue fists pounded the frosty door as he cried for someone to save him. She was six feet away, naked and bent before a guard with a flashlight. If she could only cough loud enough, the strip search would be over, and she could rescue her baby. But each attempt came out prim and ineffective. *Ahem.* Meanwhile the pounding grew weaker, less urgent. *"Let's go McGuire! Louder damn it! I wanna see those vaginal walls shake!"*

She exploded from the dream realm in a bronchial blast. The thunderous cough echoed from the surrounding cinderblocks like a gunshot. Relief washed over her as the nightmare slithered back into a cave in her subconscious. She sat up and searched the darkness for familiar landmarks. Everything was wrong. The toilet was at the back of the cell. The bars had been replaced by a steel door, and Amity's bunk had disappeared. Then the light from the tower dragged across the window slat, illuminating an old woman curled up on the blue plastic mat behind her. The final cobwebs were cleared with the sledgehammer of reality. Conflicting emotions alternately caressed and depressed her. First a dazzling ray of relief that Cameron was not trapped, suffocated by the dense black cloud of knowledge that she *was*. At least for the next 3000 days.

Minus any time off for good behavior, her suddenly optimistic inner narrator reminded.

She pulled at the drawer beneath her bunk. Ungreased metal groaned as it slipped open a few inches. Tussie mumbled something in her sleep and rolled over. Miranda reached inside and felt for her lone piece of personal property.

The manila envelope was creased from the journey and curled at the edges. She lifted the flap and removed its contents with reverence, as if handling some sacred parchment. It was too dark to see in the cell. She stood and walked over to the door. His footprints destroyed her. Hot tears streamed down her face as she slid down the wall and mourned in silence by the light coming under the steel.

"You ain't gonna kill yourself, are you?"

She looked up. "No."

Tussie was a jagged shape in the darkness. "I had a bunkie do that in the box at Broward Correctional. Back in the late eighties before they shut it down. I slept right through it. Woke up to the guards beating on the door. Blood everywhere." Her slurred words filled the cell. "What you got down there?"

The inky impressions of Cameron's feet measured less than three inches from heel to toe. She traced the maze of swirling black lines with a gnawed nail.

"Hey girlie, I'm talking to you." She leaned over and spat in the toilet. "What are you reading?"

"Huh? Oh, I'm not reading, not really. I was just looking at my son's birth certificate."

"Is that right? A son? I ain't got no kids." She rose unsteadily from the bunk and staggered over to where Miranda was sitting. "Probably for the best. Can't be no momma from in here. Let me see that thing."

The fingers of her outstretched hand were gnarled and bent in odd directions. Reluctantly, Miranda held out the precious document.

She licked her gums as she studied it by the dim light coming through the plexiglass. "June?" Maniacal eyes bulged from skeletal sockets. "Hell, that was just a couple months ago."

"Three." Miranda hugged her knees.

"You had him in the county?"

"Mm hmm."

She passed back the certificate. "Least he wasn't born in this godforsaken place. What are you in for?"

"Heroin," said Miranda. "Armed trafficking."

"Well, well." Her garbled voice was thick with saliva. "Ain't we hot shit. Who's was it? Your boyfriend's? Your pimp's? Your daddy's?"

She shook her head. "It's a long story."

"Yeah?" Tussie smiled a crooked smile. "Well, I've got a life sentence to hear it. How much time do you got to tell it?"

"Ten years," said Miranda.

Minus any time off for—

"Minus any time off for good behavior."

The old woman limped back to her bunk and sat down. Bones cracked in the darkness. "Armed trafficking carries a ten-year minimum mandatory. Day for day. You won't get no time off for good behavior."

Miranda frowned. Maybe she misheard something in the slurred speech. "I'm sorry. I'm not sure I—"

"No gain time on mandatory sentences! It ain't rocket science, girlie."

"How do you know?"

"Oh, I know. You want the statute? It's 778 something. Or is it 775? Can't remember. I'm a little rusty, but I was a law clerk for the first fifteen years of this sentence. Damn good one too. Right across the street at Lowell until they banned me from the library."

"Well, my public defender assured me that I would receive time off for good behavior."

"He did, did he?" She spat at the toilet again. Missed. "You're lucky. He lied. That's grounds for reversal on your 3.850. Now all you gotta do is prove it."

The overhead fluorescent ticked, flickered, then bathed the cell in electric light. Miranda flinched, momentarily blinded.

"Five o'clock," said Tussie. "Breakfast oughta be here soon. What day is it?"

"Wednesday," she mumbled, lost in thought.

"Good. Coffee cakes and oatmeal. I don't need my teeth. Damn dentures hurt."

"What were you saying about *grounds for reversal?*"

"I already said all there is to say." The old woman glared at her. "And I ain't gonna be repeating myself for the next fourteen days just because you're homesick for your baby and can't do ten years. Not while I'm sitting in here with a life sentence."

The cell door rolled. A few early risers padded out into the dayroom. She heard the television come on.

Tussie yanked open the drawer and rummaged through her bags until she found a dirty brown coffee cup. Then she limped past Miranda, wincing with every step.

"Damn gout. Killing me . . . Keep an eye on my shit, girlie. I'm gonna see if I can scrounge us up a cup of coffee."

Miranda leaned back against the wall, absently worrying the corner of the certificate between her thumb and forefinger. *Grounds for reversal?* Someone raised the volume on the television. She was ripped from her reverie by the somber voice of a morning news anchor.

"*. . . and today the nation mourns the recent loss of iconic Supreme Court Justice Ruth Bader Ginsberg, affectionally known as* The Notorious RBG. *The second woman to serve on the court was the leading voice of its liberal minority and a fierce advocate for gender equality . . .*"

A woman stomped past her cell and called into the dayroom. "Y'all turn that stupid shit down!"

The world was unraveling stitch by stitch. She climbed into her bunk and pulled the blanket over her head.

5

The following Tuesday, a week into quarantine, she sat on the back bench in the dayroom, wedged between Tussie and the woman with the shock of white hair, watching the first presidential debate.

Her cellmate elbowed her in the ribs. "This is gonna be good!"

She was not alone in her expectations. Every bench and table was packed. There were even women sitting on the floor. As Miranda looked around, she experienced an electric connection to her fellow prisoners. For the first time since she was arrested, she did not feel like a tourist, a stranger in a strange land. She was just like every other woman in the unit—trapped in the system, missing her baby, worried about her dad, longing for freedom. The election was five weeks away and the stakes could not be higher, not for women or people of color or prisoners. All the picketing and protesting of her former life, all the vigorous debates with campus conservatives, all the late-night twitter wars . . . It was finally rocketing toward its dramatic conclusion. Homesick as she was, she was grateful that the postpartum fog had lifted enough for her to experience this pivotal moment in history, and humbled to be witnessing it alongside her incarcerated sisters. Now Biden just needed to come through . . . for all of them.

A hush fell over the dayroom as moderator Chris Wallace introduced both men. Miranda was fidgety with excitement. She reached for Tussie's hand. *What the hell are you doing?* She snatched it back. She wondered if the women on the sixth floor of Grayskull were watching. She hoped Amity was. The president received the first two minutes. With lips pursed, he looked into the camera and began congratulating himself on the wonderful job he was doing. From his Covid response to immigration to his trade war with China to his bold and decisive pick to replace Ruth Bader Ginsberg on the Supreme Court, it had truly been a historic four years, possibly the best ever. Don't forget how Wall Street was smashing records before the *China Virus* hit . . .

Then it was Biden's turn. Though he lacked the liquid wordsmithery of Obama, he could still run circles around a blowhard like Trump. Miranda leaned forward as he began to speak. *Come on Joe, you've got this.*

He was tentative out of the starting gate. Shaky. Trump must have sensed this too because he waded in belligerently. The moderator admonished him but he kept coming, kept attacking. The strategy was obvious: interrupt, insult, overpower. His *bull in a china shop* style was on full display.

Biden stammered, recovered, then recited a prepackaged line about health insurance during a global pandemic. A woman on the front row scoffed, others shook their heads and rolled their eyes. Tussie pretended to snore. Trump made a crack about the size of his mask, and the dayroom exploded in laughter.

Tussie elbowed her again. "Look how he's got him all tongue-tied."

"He used to stutter as a child," said Miranda softly. No one heard. They were too busy giggling at the podium-pounding president. Giggling as the death toll surpassed 200,000. Giggling as wildfires ravaged California and hurricanes decimated the Gulf Coast, as children wept for their mothers in cages on the southern border, as hate groups were emboldened and city streets burned, and allies were abandoned, and Supreme Court seats were filled. Giggling. As if none of it mattered, as if it were all one big reality show. Miranda gnawed on her pinky nail.

Trump was imposing his will on the debate, fully dictating the pace. The moderator's repeated feeble attempts to gain control—*Mr. President!*—were barely acknowledged, trampled like every other norm since he moved into the White House and effectively grabbed America by the pussy. *". . . and when you're rich, they let you get away with it."*

She clenched her fists. Her breath was shallow, rapid against her mask. The president thundered on pompously about Hunter Biden and Hillary Clinton, socialism and the radical left, mail-in ballots being dumped in rivers, and rigged elections. She remembered him declaring the process rigged in 2016 too . . . until he won.

This was one of the more deflating consequences of the Trump era: the devaluation and outright assault on the truth. Facts and science and evidence were only accepted to the extent in which they painted the president in a positive light. Everything else was dismissed as fake news, liberal media bias, and deep state propaganda.

Miranda wished Biden would call him out on this, but aside from a few well-timed zingers, his words either fell flat or were drowned out by his bellowing opponent. At times he seemed befuddled by the utter lack of decorum, squinting into the lights and cameras beyond the moderator as if to say, *"Is this really happening?"* Other times he came off as a career politician, practiced smile in place, as he dodged the question on expanding the Supreme Court then flip-flopped on the Green New Deal. At one point, he was so rattled by the interruptions that he blurted, *"Will you shut up, man!"* This, of course, provoked another ripple of laughter and another elbow in her ribcage.

"Crafty bastard knows how to flustrate 'em, don't he?" Tussie licked her gums and shook her head in amazement.

Miranda felt sick to her stomach. Presidential debates were supposed to be battles of ideas between dignified and intelligent people. Not whatever *this* was. Trump did everything but stick his fingers in his ears and hum *La La La* while Biden was speaking. She was disgusted but not surprised. Was she really expecting substance? Obama versus Romney? This was the same man who suggested that moderator Megyn Kelly was menstruating during the 2016 debates. Enough was enough.

"Where you headed, girlie?" Tussie cackled as she worked her way between the benches and out of the suffocating dayroom.

She could not get her mind around the fact that these incarcerated women—possibly the most oppressed and voiceless demographic in America—were cheering on Donald Trump. It made no sense. But then what did in 2020? Between Covid, her sick father, her baby drifting around the foster system, and the ten-year sentence she was just beginning—without any time off for good behavior according to her grumpy homicidal cellmate—could things possibly get any worse?

"Stand back," the president boomed from the television, "and stand by."

6

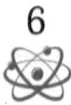

Master roster count was conducted at 10:00 p.m. every night. Unlike the other various counts performed throughout the day, master roster demanded that she display her inmate identification card and recite her six-digit DC number so the guard could check her name off.

"McGuire, 070419, ma'am!"

"Jones, 046842."

They wanted you to say *ma'am, sir* or at least the gender-neutral *officer* after relaying your information, but Tussie never did. *"What do I look like calling a woman fifty years younger than me* ma'am?" she would say, pretty much every night. *"That ain't happening."* Miranda admired the old woman's defiance, her tenacity. Thirty-five years in prison and she remained unbroken. The guards must have had a grudging respect for her as well because none ever demanded to be addressed by rank or title.

After master roster on the night of the debate, Tussie ordered Miranda to stand at the door.

"What for?"

"Cuz I gotta use the damn bathroom, girlie." Those eyes bore into her, wolf-gray and Destin-green. "That all right with you?"

The distance from her bunk to the door was two small steps. She pressed her forehead against the plexiglass slat and looked out into the empty dayroom.

Clothes rustled behind her. Old bones creaked and popped. "Goddamn, this seat is cold!"

Miranda was expecting light rain, but instead heard rolling thunder.

"Sorry about that." Tussie flushed the toilet. "So, I see you got yourself a dead man's number."

The smell was overpowering. Like dog poop. Miranda breathed through her mouth. "A what?"

"Your DC number, 070 whatever it was. You're too young for that. Mine is 046842 and I got it back in the mid-eighties. What year was you born?"

"2000." Her breath fogged the window.

"Aw hell." The toilet flushed again. "You just came off the damn porch. One thing about Florida—they love locking up their young'uns. Yeah, that number don't fit you one bit. It's funny just hearing you say it. What is it again?"

"070419."

Ma'am! shouted her inner narrator.

Tussie cackled and spat. "Long time ago when they first started passing out these numbers, some pitiful bastard stepped up and got five zeros and a one. Next in line got a two. Once they burned through one short of one million unsatisfied customers, they switched over to letters. Well, one letter and five numbers. *P12345*, like that." She grunted, exhaled, flushed. "Each letter covered a city. M for Miami, T for Tampa, X for Orlando for some weird reason, P for Pensacola . . . That was in the mid-nineties. Now they've went through most of them and they're back to the numbers again. But the only ones they reuse are prisoners they know are dead. Mostly lifers that died in custody and whoever they kilt on death row."

Miranda frowned at her ID card.

The sink water trickled behind her. "Got any extra soap?"

"Just the bar I use to bathe with."

"Aw hell," said Tussie. "Damn corona's got everybody so terrified they won't even share state soap. Soap cleans itself!" She snatched open her drawer and turned one of her treasured mesh bags upside down. A cascade of belongings spilled out. A stack of time-worn, rubber-banded photo albums with ocean scenes on the covers accounted for the bulk of the deluge but there were also orange dining-hall sporks, flex pens, and tubes of Freshmint toothpaste. "I know I've got a bar in here somewhere."

Calling the thin, two-inch sliver of cheap motel soap a *bar* was a stretch. Still, Miranda grabbed hers from the foot of her bunk, snapped it in half, and held out a piece for the old woman.

Tussie muttered a thank you and walked back to the sink. "How do you know Kat Bailey?"

Miranda pulled back her blanket and did her best to fluff her flat pillow before *lights out.* "Who?"

"You know good and goddamn well who I'm talking about, girlie. Store bought titties and that streak of white hair like a damn skunk. You sat next to her during the debate."

"Oh, her. I don't really know her. I just met her the other night. She was telling me about the tablets and stuff."

"Mmm." Tussie dried her hands on her pants and sat down on her bunk. "Two things I ain't got no use for—tablets and lesbians."

Miranda glanced at the pile of overturned property in her open drawer. "You don't have a tablet? She said they were giving them away for free."

"Don't have one, don't want one," said Tussie. "I ain't got nobody to email anyway."

"What about games?"

The old woman shot her a withering look.

"Or music and movies?"

"All that costs money. I ain't had a dime in my account since I got banned from the law library. But even if I did, I wouldn't waste it on that shit."

Miranda couldn't wait to get off quarantine so she could begin the orientation process, blow through whatever tests they gave her, and get transferred to her permanent camp. The sooner she landed at her final destination, the sooner she would be assigned a tablet. Just the promise of email capability was a beacon of hope.

"Look here," said Tussie, "I know this is your first time in prison so I'm gonna give you some free advice—don't get caught up in these lesbian soap operas playing out in every dorm on every compound."

Miranda shook her head. "I'm not—"

"Yeah, yeah." Tussie licked her gums. "You ain't gay. Neither is anyone else when they first come in. But it's lonesome in here. It wears on you, wears you down."

"Did it wear *you* down?"

"None of your goddamn business!"

Miranda didn't flinch this time. After a week in the cell with the old woman, she was growing accustomed to her volatility. There was a sweetness to her grumpy outbursts anyway. Something almost grandmotherly in her no-nonsense tone.

I know, right? her inner narrator gushed. *So sweet . . . Remember when she threatened to gut you like a fish?*

Tussie studied her wrinkled hands. "I loved a woman once. A long time ago."

"What happened to her?"

"Don't matter what happened," she growled. "That ain't the point. I'm 72 years old with a life sentence. All my appeals have been denied. Ain't nothing left to do but die. How old did you say you was?"

"Almost twenty."

"Twenty years old." She leaned forward, spat. "With a baby out there that needs you, probably crying for you right now. You need to get home."

"I know," said Miranda, her heart suddenly a thousand pounds.

"Remember what I told you the other day about your 3.850? If your attorney promised you gain time on a mandatory sentence, you can get back to court. There might even be some more mistakes."

"Like what?"

"Who knows? You'd have to research it. That's what I'm telling you. You've got one shot at an ineffective counsel claim and two years to file it. Your clock is already ticking. Don't be like these other little bimbos and miss your window because you were too busy swooning over some stud on the yard."

"I won't," Miranda vowed.

Gross, said her inner narrator.

"Hmmph," said Tussie, unconvinced.

Miranda sat cross-legged on her bunk, hugging her pillow. "Can I ask you something?"

"Not about her," Tussie bristled.

"What did you do to catch a life sentence?"

"Catch it?" The old woman cackled. "You make it sound like Mobile Mardi Gras beads. Oh, I caught it all right. Caught it like a terminal disease. It ain't much of a story. I was working at the Waffle House, midnights, and had a crush on a customer. Jimmy Sutton. Worked at the shipyard. Ten years younger than me with a confederate flag tattooed on his forearm."

A picture formed in Miranda's mind, of a crowded eighties-era Waffle House, the air thick with cigarette smoke and the smell of greasy hashbrowns. Silverware clanked against ceramic and country music played in the background as a younger Tussie cleared tables, took orders and made nervous eye contact with Jimmy Sutton.

"Did the tattoo bother you?"

"Bother me? Hell no, it turned me on . . ." She frowned. "Why would that bother me?"

"It's a symbol of hate."

"It is? I always figured it was a Southern thing." She paused, licked her gums. "Well, there's worse things in the world than symbols, I guess. Anyway, we started hanging out. He lived with his aunt over in Spanish Fort, Alabama. Turns out he was on parole. I should've run like hell when I found out, but I didn't. That just made him more handsome in a dangerous sort of way."

"Well, at least he gave you his real name."

Tussie looked up. "Huh?"

"Nothing."

"Jimmy taught me how to freebase cocaine. I never even heard of it till he came around. Worst I ever done was smoke weed with my cousin Rufus. You ever tried it?"

Miranda shook her head.

"Good. Don't. That shit had me crawling around on the floor for crumbs, going through Jimmy's pockets, stealing from the register at work . . . until one morning Jimmy gets this bright idea that he wants to rob a credit union, just over the state line in Perdido Key. All I gotta do is drive. That was my last day of freedom. March 16, 1986."

"What happened?"

"He killed the branch manager and a security guard. I had no idea until the cops surrounded us a few miles outside of Gulf Shores. Idiot bailed out of the car and made a beeline for the Gulf like he didn't know there was a big-ass ocean on the other side of them sand dunes. They had to pull him out. I just put my hands up."

"Wait a minute," said Miranda. "You got life in prison for that?"

She nodded. "Sure did. Hell, he got the death penalty. They fried him back in . . . 99?"

"Yeah, but he killed two people! All you did was drive the getaway car. You didn't know he was going to do that."

"You're preaching to the choir, girlie. Florida has a felony murder law that says if somebody gets killed during the commission of a crime, everybody involved is getting a minimum mandatory of life in prison. From the master-mind to the lookout to the getaway driver. That's just the way it is."

"I can't believe you've been locked up over three decades for something you didn't do."

"Yeah . . . I didn't drive that damn Mercury Cougar fast enough!" She threw her head back and cackled until she coughed. "Naw, the icing on the cake is that we drove all the way to Florida to get hemmed up. If we didn't cross the state line, and just robbed a bank in Fairhope, I probably would've been home years ago. Alabama has parole."

If . . . thought Miranda. Fertile soil of alternate realities, scaffolding of daydreams. If she didn't hurt her back she would have never been prescribed opiates. If she didn't pull into that apartment complex she would have never been arrested.

If you weren't suffering from postpartum, her inner narrator asked, *would you have signed away ten years of your life?*

Miranda looked over at Tussie, eyes wide.

"What is it?" said the old woman.

She opened her mouth to speak then pulled back at the last moment. Knowing her cellmate's story, it felt inhumane to continue to pepper her with legal questions about her own comparably light sentence. Like complaining about the temperature of a meal while eating in front of a starving woman.

She changed the subject. "Are those pictures?"

Tussie followed her gaze and grabbed a tattered photo album from her drawer. "Come see." She pulled off the rubber bands and gently flipped open the decomposing cover.

Miranda scooted to the end of her bunk for a better view. Beneath the laminate overlay, yellowed and faded with time, was a picture of . . .

"Meatloaf?" said Miranda.

"Skillet meatloaf." Her dichromic eyes twinkled. "That's the recipe right there under it."

She turned the page. Tomato Feta Bisque with Garlic Toast, Twice Baked Potatoes stuffed with Broccoli, Sheet Pan Chicken with Roasted Plums and Onions . . .

"You collect them?"

Tussie nodded at the pile of photo albums in her open drawer. "Yeah, I got better'n a thousand of them. I quit counting a few years back. It got tiresome trying to remember what number I was on."

She thought back to her first day, to the walk down, how violated she felt in the aftermath of the strip search, how paranoid the old woman was about her property. Was this what she was protecting? Water-stained photo albums packed with recipes? Recipes for meals she would never get to cook? Miranda oohed and mmmed, feigning hunger as Tussie proudly flipped through pages. But inside, her heart was breaking for her cellmate.

7

On a soggy morning in early October with Tussie snoring like a blender full of gravel and Maury trumpeting paternity test results from the dayroom television, Miranda lie awake in her bunk, staring at the cell ceiling, her inner narrator babbling neurotically, oppressively.

You were so terrible to Amity. Vicious, really. You're no different than any of her other tormenters on the sixth floor. She's probably still on suicide watch because of you. Is that mold? Up there in the corner, the black stuff. You don't even know. Lucky for Cameron, his new mom knows. She can spot mold and choking hazards and diaper rashes. He's so much better off without you. Why do you keep itching under your arm? What is that? I hope you didn't catch scabies already. You probably got it from the lady in receiving. You couldn't even out-cough her. Louder! I wish she would stop snoring.

Suddenly a godlike voice boomed from the dormitory PA system. "Jones, Davis, Sanchez, Parker, Bailey . . . pack up! You're moving to Foxtrot. Everyone else is going to Echo dorm for orientation. Ten minutes, ladies. Let's go!"

A cheer erupted from the dayroom. Quarantine was officially over. Tussie swung her legs over the side of her bunk, stretched and yawned, then began stuffing loose items back into her mesh canteen bag.

"I'll help you with that," said Miranda.

"You can't." She crammed a stack of photo albums down the side. "We're headed to different dorms."

Miranda quickly stripped her bunk and placed her extra uniforms and underwear in her pillowcase along with the few hygiene items she managed to scavenge over the last 14 days. The birth certificate came last. She slid it inside her wool blanket and carefully set it on top. Then she looked around the cell for a final time as she waited for Tussie to finish, willing herself to not be too emotional in her goodbye.

While she was silently rehearsing this equanimous farewell, her cellmate stood, hefted her property and walked out the door.

Miranda stared after her for a long moment before grabbing her pillowcase and following.

A crowd of women gathered in the dayroom, with more streaming down the staircase and dragging property across the dorm. She noticed the woman with the spindle of white hair near the door, a combination lock conjoining the handles of the two canteen bags slung over her shoulder.

Kat Bailey, her inner narrator observed. *Tussie's favorite.*

The old woman had already located an open seat on the back bench of the dayroom, a protective arm draped over her property as suspicious green and gray eyes surveyed the crowd.

Miranda smiled and walked over. "We didn't say goodbye."

"Waste of words," said Tussie. "Do you know how many has come and gone since I've been here? You get tired of all those hellos and goodbyes. It's all bullshit anyway."

"Well . . ." Miranda glanced at the bags piled next to her. "Thanks for showing me your recipes. I had fun."

The door buzzed. Women began filing out into the hallway.

"Never mind fun." Tussie licked her gums. "That's the problem with these girls coming in nowadays. They're too focused on having fun when they oughta be focusing on caselaw. One shot, girlie. That's all you get to file that 3.850. Don't blow it."

Kat Bailey tapped on the glass and waved.

Miranda waved back.

Tussie rolled her eyes and stood. Calloused arthritic fingers wrapped around the dirty nylon handles of her bags.

"And for godsakes steer clear of these lesbians and their love triangles."

8

Echo-one was an open bay housing unit on the opposite end of the compound, the furthest point from Alpha dorm on a diagonal line running straight through the gun tower at center court. It might as well have been on another planet.

Instead of sharing her living space with one woman, she lived in a warehouse with eighty of them, five of whom resided within arm's reach at all times. The cramped alleys between the steel bunk beds on either side made for awkward encounters with her new neighbors. But not nearly as awkward as the communal showers. Eight nozzles were aligned on a tiled wall in the back of the bathroom, in direct view of the officers' station as well as the cattle-shoot hallway where women loaded up for meals and callouts.

Some of the more seasoned inmates disrobed without a care; panties on the wall, slinging suds, shaving their legs, belting out slow jams at the top of their lungs. Miranda bathed quickly and quietly, in her underwear and crocs. Preferably in shower eight.

Other bathroom activities were equally humiliating. She would never forget the first time that she was relieving herself when she glanced over the chest-high stall and locked eyes with a male guard. *"You plan on flushing that anytime soon darlin'?"* Even brushing her teeth could be an adventure when, in the mirror's reflection, there were two girls making out on the toilet.

Aside from a handful of *permanents* who were assigned to the dormitory to clean and assist staff with the orientation process, the women housed in Echo-one were mostly *transits*, meaning they were only passing through. It was not difficult to discern the former from the latter. Permanents wore form-fitting tailored blues with *Access Catalog* tennis shoes and Covergirl makeup from the canteen. Transits wore ragged ill-fitting blues with state-issued crocs and were lucky if they had any lotion from the county jail.

The same guards who barked orders at the transits and treated them with hostile indifference seemed to almost dote over the permanents, engaging in friendly banter, sometimes openly flirting.

Miranda was assigned to E-1105-Lower. Her bunkie was a thirty-year-old stud from Jacksonville who everyone called "Duval." Rangy and long-legged with light skin and lighter eyes, Duval was the exception to the shabby transit cliché. Along with a couple of other studs in the dorm, she lived like a monarch. Every day some hungry-eyed permanent would show up at the bunk with honey buns and cookies from the canteen, followed by another with a coveted cigarette. It got to the point where she ran out of space and started using Miranda's empty drawer for the spillover. *"Eat whatever you want, Red . . . Take that deodorant too, I know you need one . . . You don't smoke, do you?"*

Her inner narrator warned her about strangers bearing gifts. She told her inner narrator to lighten up.

Okay, said the voice in her head, *I just wish Tussie could see this. You do remember what she said about steering clear of lesbians, don't you? This is not steering clear. This is the opposite of steering clear.*

Her neighbors in bunk 1104 were both Latina and both transits. Between her limited Spanish and their limited English, she managed to ascertain that Senora Valdivia—the older Cuban woman in the bottom bunk—was serving five years for running marijuana grow houses down in Naples, while Rojas in 1104-Upper was a Mexican laborer from a town called Immokalee, doing six for assault.

On the other side of her, in 1106-Lower, lived a permanent named Charlene Boyd. She only knew her name because every night at master roster, the neighbor would sound off, "Boyd, Charlene! T21749 Officer!" Other than this, she never spoke. But she emitted a vibe that seemed to scream, *Don't fuck with me!*

1106-Upper was the diametrical opposite, a diminutive transit with taped horn-rimmed glasses resting crooked on her freckled nose and a bracelet of runes tattooed on her wrist. There was something in her energy that reminded Miranda of Amity.

"Mother of Dragons!" she blurted on the first day. *"Your hair. It's . . . crimson. May I call you Sansa?"*

"Who?"

"Sansa Stark of Winterfell. Ned's oldest daughter. You've never seen Game of Thrones?"

Miranda shook her head.

"Blasphemy! I bet they have the books in the library. Wait. Do they even have a library here?"

Miranda shrugged. "I just got off quarantine. I haven't been given the grand tour yet. But I think I'll pass on the nickname, although Sansa does sound much cooler than Red. My friends call me Miranda."

"Daphne Throckmorton!" Her legs dangled from the side of the bunk, dangerously close to the scowling face of Charlene Boyd. "My friends call me Throkkie. Like the Dothraki? You'll see when you read the book."

For the duration of her time in Echo dorm, whether in the dayroom, the classroom or the bathroom, it was a rare occurrence if Daphne Throckmorton was not in the next seat, babbling away.

9

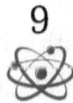

"Throckmorton?"

"Yes ma'am."

"Shut up!"

"Yes ma'am."

The guard folded her hands over her substantial stomach and glared in their direction for the remainder of the timed test. Miranda smiled behind her mask as she filled in answers.

The front of the booklet said *T.A.B.E.*, an acronym for *Test for Adult Basic Education*, but there was nothing basic about it. The questions began harmless enough with word problems, multiplication and division of fractions, and equations, but then quickly crossed over into more advanced algebra and geometry.

She felt bad for many of the older women in the classroom who hadn't converted a fraction to a decimal since high school, much less attempted to find the hypotenuse of a triangle. The Pythagorean theorem rarely came up in drug transactions, most women were more concerned with being robbed or sexually assaulted. And even those who didn't indulge in substances were probably not out there solving quadratic equations. The calculus of single parent child rearing was mentally exhausting enough.

A quick glance around the classroom revealed Rojas taking a nap, Senora Valdivia frowning at her test booklet, Duval passing notes with a blonde from Panama City named Morgan, and Throkkie Christmas treeing her answer sheet in the next desk over. The only sounds were the labored breathing of the guard and number two pencils etching graphite into bubbles.

The teacher silently paced the aisles, hands clasped behind his khakis with one eye on the clock. He exuded smugness, as if he was proctoring a college SAT. It was almost comical the way he sniffed the room for impropriety, missing everything. As Miranda worked through the tedious steps of the final problem, she wondered if he could solve it.

Doubtful, her inner narrator smirked.

She raised her hand. "I'm finished."

The teacher raised an eyebrow.

"Me too," said Throkkie.

"How convenient." The guard shifted in her chair. Springs creaked and twanged. "Well, y'all just sit still and shut up till everybody's done."

10

A line of bedraggled women were being escorted down the sidewalk, past the tower at center court, to the quarantine unit across the compound. The same miserable journey she had made a month before, the first day in prison, like staring up the side of the mountain. She watched them until they faded beyond the layers of chain-link, wondering if Amity was in the group. She knew it was impossible. Covid had delayed all jury trials indefinitely. Still, she kept an eye out for her friend.

"Hey Red!" her bunkie called from the dayroom. "It's on you."

She spun around, almost tripping as she hurried past the officers' station.

"You ain't gotta run," said Duval, one arm slung over the back of the chair, her tapered blues like skinny jeans that disappeared into Xanny-bar-white sneakers. "I told you I got you."

Miranda had been waiting two days to get on the kiosk. Ever since she received her password in the mail. The line was not really a line, but a fluid situation where one woman finished her fifteen-minute session and then called for the woman behind her. Many times this did not happen, and a new line formed behind whoever sat down instead. This led to frequent misunderstandings and sometimes fights. Studs and permanents were the exceptions. "*These bitches do what they can,*" Duval told her one night. "*I do what I want.*" Miranda was grateful to have such a powerful ally.

She arranged her body in the plastic chair and stared at the screen. *JPay,* the logo read, *Stay connected.* That was the plan. A floppy shield sagged behind her, velcroed to the chair for privacy. Her hands brushed across the metal keyboard, locating the home keys naturally. The braille-like ridges on the *F* and *J* were old friends, as familiar and comfortable as a fretboard to a guitarist.

She typed her DC number from memory then unfolded the paper and entered her password. *51LVs49q.* A disclaimer appeared. She clicked *agree* without reading and watched the blue loop chase its digital tail while information was uploaded. Suddenly the home page popped up, a no-frills screen tabbed in institutional blue with a dash of green for variety. By programming standards it was minimalist bordering on fundamentalist, if there was such a thing in the world of tech. Didn't matter. All she cared about was email capability. Instant messaging would be better, but beggars couldn't be choosers.

There was a single message in her inbox. Her heart pounded as she opened it. *"Find Hope . . . a message from the Secretary of the Florida Department of Corrections."*

Throkkie munched pork skins beside her. "I got that one too. Seems like he really cares about us, right?"

Miranda glanced at her neighbor. "Where'd you get the chips?"

"Duval." Another noisy crunch. "I washed her socks for these and a soup. Want one?"

She shook her head. "How do I send an email on this thing?"

"Click on *write a message.*"

"I just did. See? Nothing."

"You don't have anyone on your contacts list."

"Exactly." Miranda willed herself to be patient as precious seconds ticked away. Fifteen minutes evaporated quickly. "How do I *add* people?"

"You don't," said Throkkie. "They have to sign up."

"There has to be some way to . . ." She clicked each tab frantically. "My baby . . . he's in foster care. My dad is sick."

A small hand rested on her shoulder. "I don't have any contacts either."

11

Hot dogs for dinner. They made her think of Amity in those dark and hazy days after Cameron. Amity, force-feeding her when all she wanted was to die. It almost felt like she got her wish. Like the Florida Women's Reception Facility was the port of entry to hell.

"Shut the fuck up and eat!" roared a musclebound guard with rolled sleeves and tight pants.

Throkkie rolled her eyes and nibbled the corner of her mustard packet. After squirting a small amount on her hot dogs, she carefully set it near the edge of the table.

Miranda quietly picked at her rice and cabbage, her appetite still not back to full strength.

"Row one, pick up your trays and get out," announced the guard. "Row two, you're next."

As he neared their table, Throkkie grinned mischievously.

"What are you smiling about, four eyes?" His mask inflated with his breath.

"Nothing, sir."

"If you're smiling, that means you're happy. If you're happy, that means I'm not doing my job. This is not supposed to be a happy place, people. Prisons are miserable by design . . ."

Once he passed, she planted her palm on the mustard packet and a splat of yellow ejaculated from the table to the back of his tight pants.

Miranda's eyes widened. She glanced at the other guards. None appeared to notice.

Throkkie held a finger to her lips.

He whirled on his heel at the end of the aisle and surveyed the dining hall suspiciously.

"Row three, get out!"

They dumped their trays and spilled out into the twilit October evening in a trail of giggles. For once, Miranda was grateful for the stifling mask.

"Are you crazy?" she hissed as they stepped inside the yellow line.

"Totally," said Throkkie. "You should see me when I'm off my psych meds."

The gate popped and buzzed. The line began to move. They passed the women of Foxtrot on the way back, heading to the dining hall. Due to Covid protocol, dormitories had to eat separately.

She spotted Tussie near the end of the line. Two younger girls were badgering her about Trump. She wasn't having it.

"What makes you think the Democrats are gonna do something for prisoners? They're the ones that come up with all the tough laws! I was in here last time Florida had a Democratic governor. 1995. Lawton Chiles. Walkin' Lawton. Know what he did? He got rid of early release and helped Chain Gang Charlie sign '85 percent' into law. There's your bleeding-heart liberal, girls."

Miranda waved as she passed.

The old woman yanked her mask down and spat.

"Who was that, Ms. Tussie?" one of the girls asked.

"How the fuck should I know?" Her voice faded into the night. "I don't even remember who *you* are."

12

Midnight. The first officer zipped by, her uniform swishing with every step. Although the clock was not visible from Miranda's bunk, it was easy to tell time after lights out because counts were every hour on the hour.

She wondered if they were really counting or just going through the motions. Nobody had gone anywhere since master roster. Why bother?

The second guard to walk through was around her own age. Crystal meth-thin with a dyed black pixie cut. She was definitely counting, methodically, meticulously. At one point she lost it and had to start all over. Miranda identified her as a trainee by the empty holster on her belt. Only certified officers were allowed to carry pepper spray. Duval taught her that.

They conferred by the water fountain, apparently agreeing on a number because moments later they disappeared through the dayroom door into side two.

Once they were gone, music from nearby radios began to play and conversations reconvened. Throkkie dropped from her bunk and padded off to the bathroom. When she returned, she plopped down next to Miranda and set a Chapstick cap on the floor in front of her.

"Think we'll transfer tomorrow?" she said. "It's Friday. Lowell."

Duval's face appeared above her, hazel eyes glimmering in the dark. "I wish. I'm so sick of this boot camp shit. But I doubt we're going anywhere. We ain't done with orientation yet."

"What is there left to do?" Throkkie used a pen top to stir the contents of the Chapstick cap. "We've seen laundry, dental, education, mental health, the chaplain . . ."

Duval yawned. "We've still gotta see medical, classification, seems like there was one more."

The yawn was contagious. Miranda stretched and rolled onto her side. "I think I'd rather go to Gadsden than Lowell."

"I'll bet you would." Her bunkie smiled. "Air conditioning, good food, soft toilet paper, guards that call you ma'am and Ms. McGuire. Everybody wants to go to the private prison."

"Don't you?" said Throkkie.

"Can't." Duval's voice was suddenly far away. "I got shipped from there my last time down. Special review. They busted me with a jack. I probably would've only did sixty days in the box but the phone was loaded with naked flicks of my girlfriend . . . She had just made lieutenant. She never showed her face but her tattoos were easy to identify. They fired her and shipped me."

"That's awesome." Throkkie pushed her glasses up on her nose and squinted into the Chapstick cap.

"I just want to get closer to home," said Miranda. "Gadsden is less than three hours from Pensacola."

"We're probably all going to Lowell." Duval dropped from her bunk gracefully, liquid and feline in her movements. "I just hope we don't get stuck at the main. I'm surprised they haven't shut that old dump down by now. It's ten times worse than any project building I've ever lived in. Roaches, rats, mold. The annex might be cutthroat but at least you ain't gotta worry about bugs crawling all over you in your sleep."

Miranda shivered from the image.

"I hope we all go to the same place." Throkkie lifted the cap to her nose, tilted her head back, and quickly snorted its contents.

Charlene Boyd mumbled under her breath and rolled over. Throkkie looked at Duval and smiled her gap-toothed smile.

"What did you just snort?" Miranda whispered.

"A strip." Throkkie pinched her nostrils and sniffed a final time, then tried to lick the inside of the Chapstick cap. "A little piece of Suboxone."

"Little my ass," said Duval. "That was a twenty."

Miranda could not believe it. "But . . . why?"

"Um, because they don't have any heroin." Throkkie frowned at her. "Are you okay? You look pale."

Duval squeezed her leg through the blanket. "Want me to break you off a piece, Red? I've got plenty."

13

The Ocala noonday sun was relentless. Her arms were beginning to burn. At least an hour had passed, possibly longer. The center court officers chatted in the shade, chain-smoking cigarettes and guzzling Monster Energy drinks, occasionally shouting, "Next five!" which meant that five more women at the front of the line could head over to the medical building. Not occasional enough.

"See what I'm saying," said Duval, six feet in front of her. "This is the same petty shit I've been talking about. They only do this here at the reception center. Ain't nobody at Lowell standing in line for no two hours. Unless it's the canteen line."

"I just wish we didn't have to be socially distant," said Throkkie, six feet behind her at the end of the line. "It's harder to talk without getting caught."

Miranda glanced up at the tower. A hundred feet above her, an armed guard slowly circumnavigated the catwalk. "They can't tell who's talking with these masks."

"It's still stupid." Throkkie removed her glasses and gave her nose a thorough, opiated scratching. "We all live within inches of each other. We all pile in the dayroom every night for the news and squeeze into the hallway three times a day for chow. Yet when we're out here in line, we've gotta *maintain social distancing*. For what?"

"Girl, your teeth are social distancing!" Duval laughed at her own joke.

"Good one," said Throkkie, "but seriously, we're stuck in that overcrowded dorm with zero ventilation all day, but when we come out here we've gotta stand six feet apart? Look at Kim and Stacey over there. Six feet apart in line, but in the laundry room in the afternoons they're not even six centimeters apart. Hands all over each other."

"You're just jealous," said Duval. "I see the way you look at Stacey with your little freaky self."

"I do like her boobs," Throkkie admitted.

"I'm with you on that, Rocky." Duval was either unwilling or incapable of calling Daphne Throckmorton by her preferred handle.

Miranda was sunburned by the time she made it to the medical building. And her nerves were raw from listening to Throkkie's incessant chatter. For two grueling hours she was subjected to a lengthy synopsis of the first season of *Game of Thrones*, the pros and cons of the lesbian lifestyle and why she was considering it, and how Eric—her boyfriend since the eighth grade—betrayed her by never writing or visiting after he was released from the hospital. *Yes, she attacked him with his grandmother's fire poker, but it never would have happened had he not vindictively killed her character while larping Dungeons and Dragons.*

"What's larping?" said Duval.

"Live action role playing." Throkkie blinked. Tiny pupils vanished and reappeared, her face all glasses and mask.

"Live action," Duval repeated. "I feel that."

They sat on steel benches in a small waiting room while the officer in the bubble violently chomped gum and argued on the telephone.

The door opened. A nurse in tight pink scrubs with a matching mask was laughing at something down the hall. She waggled her fingers at the guard and glanced at her clipboard. "Um . . . is it Throckmorton?"

Throkkie stood.

"Excuse me. May I ask you a question?" said Miranda, unable to restrain herself.

The nurse glanced at her watch. "Quickly."

"As a health care professional, do you think it's right that they make us stand in the sun for hours?"

"Well . . . look at the bright side," said the nurse, "at least you're getting a tan while you wait."

"I don't tan." She held up her arm. "I burn. Redheads account for sixteen percent of the world's Melanoma cases. I've been protecting my skin since—"

"Ask the doctor for sunblock when you get your physical." The nurse waved Throkkie into the hallway.

"—since I was six years old," Miranda forged on, "and they say that just one bad sunburn can do irreparable harm."

The door shut.

She glanced over at Duval. "You know, the operative word in the term *health care professional* is care."

"I thought you was gonna say *professional.*"

"That too." Miranda tentatively touched her arm, neon white fingerprints pulsed against scalded lavender skin.

"You're right though," said Duval. "Don't nobody in here care about us. That's why we gotta care for ourselves."

The door reopened. The remaining transits in the waiting room looked up expectantly. A lanky woman in faded jeans and a starched white button-down scanned their faces with piercing blue eyes. Her gaze settled on Miranda. "You. What's your name?"

"Miranda McGuire," she said, before hastily adding, "ma'am."

"Thought that was you. Come, let's have a little chat in my office. I'll make sure you don't miss your physical."

The hallway reeked of industrial bleach. Nurses carried files from the triage to exam rooms. Somewhere above the hum of activity she could hear Throkkie's Suboxonized voice recounting her entire medical history. *"And when I was nine, I fell out of a tree and broke my collarbone . . ."*

"This will only take a few minutes," she said, opening the door to a cramped office and flipping on the lights. "I wanted to speak with you about your test results."

Miranda took in the rows of books on the shelf behind her desk. *The Road Less Traveled by M. Scott Peck, The Four Agreements by Don Miguel Ruiz, The Untethered Soul by Michael A. Singer, The Possibility Principle by Mel Schwartz* . . . "Which test? The Covid test? Tuberculosis test? TABE test? Seems like I've had a different test for every day I've been in orientation."

"Your TABE test results certainly warrant discussion. I spoke to Mr. Rush, the head of education. He said you scored 800s across the board. You only had one incorrect answer in the entire mathematics portion."

Slacker, her inner narrator stirred.

"Well, I'm an English Lit major," said Miranda.

"According to him this has never happened at this institution. He's seen it only once in his career. And that was down the road at Marion, the male prison. A former NASA employee was serving a life sentence there for murdering his wife and faking his own death."

NASA! Her inner narrator whistled. *Good company except for the whole murdering his wife part.*

"But I want to talk to you about the test *my* department administered last week. The intelligence quotient test. I'm Leah Avery by the way. Resident quack." She motioned to a chair across her desk. "Please . . ."

Miranda sat across from her and folded lobster-reddened hands in her lap.

"Have you ever taken an IQ test before?"

She shook her head. "But I was in the gifted program in middle school and took honors classes in high school. I scored a 2300 on the SAT test. Good enough to get into the University but not on an academic scholarship. I had to apply for financial aid. I was only a couple months into my freshman year when this happened."

"2300 on the SAT?" The doctor sat back in her chair and made a steeple of her fingertips. "My nephew barely eked out a 1900. And Ernie is a highly intelligent young man. But believe it or not, the IQ test has nothing to do with education—"

Her phone rang, shrill as a fire alarm. Miranda jumped.

"One second." She picked up the receiver. "Mental Health, Avery . . . Hey Caroline . . . I heard. Listen, can I call you back? I'm with an inmate right now . . . Okay, talk with you then." She hung up the phone. "Sorry about that. So, as I was saying, the IQ test has nothing to do with education or knowledge acquired through life experience . . ."

A phone! Her inner narrator gasped. *She can dial out, call the jail, find out if Dad is alive!*

Dr. Avery paused, frowned. "Are you okay?"

"Yes ma'am."

"The intelligence quotient," she continued, "deals more with cognitive skills. Logic, reasoning, problem solving. Things we are largely born with."

Miranda glanced at the phone. *Would she?*

"The test is scored on a bell curve. 100 is average, 115 is above average, and anything over 130 is considered a high IQ. The highest on record belongs to Terrance Tao, 220. He entered high school at age 7, earned his BA at 16, and his doctorate at age 21."

She might even be able to find out about Amity. What was the doctor at the jail's name? The one who put her on suicide watch?

"Albert Einstein and Stephen Hawking both had IQs of 160."

I wish I had a number to check on Cameron. He's almost five months old. I wonder if he remembers me? I need to get out of here.

"So are you interested in knowing what you scored on the IQ test?" The doctor smiled as if holding an Oscar envelope.

A light on the phone was blinking, syncopated with her hammering heartbeat. She chewed her lip, nodded.

"135. The highest in the history of this facility! You could apply to Mensa if you wanted to. Isn't that exciting?"

Miranda nodded.

"I checked your release date. 2029. I know that seems like a long way off. But you're fortunate. So many young women have sat in that same chair with life sentences." She tugged at a *#1 Mom* charm on a small gold chain that hung from her neck. "And because your test results are so high, while you're here in the Department of Corrections, any job you're interested in will be open to you. Orderly, clerk, education tutor, impaired assistant . . . you name it. Is there something in particular you'd like to do?"

"Maybe work in the law library," said Miranda. "So I can research my case. I have a son who I'd like to get back to. Preferably before 2029."

"Well, I'm sure you'd make a fine inmate law clerk." She stood, closed the file. "I just wanted to tell you personally how impressive your scores are. Come, let's get you back out front so you don't miss your physical. Maybe they can give you something for that sunburn too. It looks painful."

Miranda looked longingly at the phone once more.

Now or never, her inner narrator urged. *Don't tell me you're afraid to ask. What's Dad always say? Closed mouths don't get fed. She can't help you if you don't ask. She's a psychologist not a psychic . . .*

"May I ask a favor?"

The doctor froze. Guarded smile. "A favor? Hmm. You can ask."

"My dad contracted Covid at the Escambia County Jail." As soon as the first words were out of her mouth, the rest tumbled forth unabated. "He's smoked cigarettes his entire life, he's almost fifty years old, he suffers from mental illness. Last I heard he was on a ventilator. Is there any way you could call—"

She shook her head. "I'm sorry."

"I don't need to talk to him. I just want to know if he's alive. Please . . ."

"I can't make personal calls for inmates." She opened the door. "You'll have to ask your classification officer."

14

Her face was two-toned. From midway across her nose up to her hairline, the skin was a deep red, bordering on purple. Magenta. While the southern hemisphere beneath the mask was an alabaster white. Had it not been so painful, it would've been funny. Corona tan.

"Damn Red, that shit looks like it hurts," said Duval. "I've still got a few of these Subs. They're supposed to be good for pain. You know I fuck with you, girl. Just say the word and I'll break you off a little piece."

The promise of instantaneous relief beckoned. Not from the fleeting pain of a sunburn, but the unrelenting pain of life.

It would be a nice vacation, said her inner narrator. *Maybe just once, since it's free. It's not technically an opiate anyway. It's an opiate blocker. People use them to quit opiates . . .*

Somehow, she stood firm. "No thanks. I'm good."

Throkkie shrugged. "I'll take her piece."

"I bet you would," Duval laughed. "Slow down Rocky."

Miranda looked out over the dorm, at all the cliques and the couples and the loners, the mumbling mentally ill. Most of the women were unscathed by the sun. A few were pink and peeling. The blond permanent doing lunges in the corner had a farmer's tan. No one was as blistered as her. Her two Latina neighbors were playing a variation of Rummy in the next bunk. Senora Valdivia smiled at her while Rojas studied her hand.

"Ahem."

Miranda looked up. Officer Napier was standing at the foot of the bunk, a white FDC emblem silkscreened on her black mask.

"You ladies speak English?" She toyed with her gas cannister. "Habla Ingles?"

Slowly, they shook their heads.

"Convenient." She turned and addressed the dorm. "Somebody in here needs to let these transit immigrant women know my rules. One bitch to a bunk and no games in the bedding area."

"We got you, Officer Napier," said a voluptuous middle-aged permanent who slept against the far wall. "Hey Marlo! Tell Sanchez to come out here and translate. She's in the dayroom watchin' the stories."

Satisfied, the guard moved on, then paused at Miranda's bunk and glanced at the number stenciled on the steel. "McGuire?"

"Yes ma'am."

"Classification just called for you. Get Class A and pick up your pass from the window. Officer Floyd will buzz you out."

There were two doors and four gates between her bunk and the classification building. She had to wait to be noticed at each before the tower popped her through. This stretched a five-minute walk into a half hour. She utilized the time to rehearse what she was going to say.

"Can you please help me find out if my father is still alive?" *Too desperate.* "My father was on a ventilator when

I left the county jail. He's my only living relative." *Don't you have a son?* "I gave birth to a little boy on June second of this year, and I have no idea where he is. Somewhere in foster care. Due to postpartum, these last few months have been a daze. Is there any way you could—" *Snore. Look around. All these women are moms. Nobody cares, Miranda.* "Please help. I just need to know if my dad is alive, and my son is safe. I'm a long way from home and I'm worried about my loved ones." *Hmm. Concise, honest, not too needy. This approach might work . . .*

The door to classification banged open and a squat woman in green polyester pants with cruel eyes scowled into the lobby.

Whoa, said her inner narrator, *unless we get her.*

"Who's McGuire?"

Shit. Miranda raised her hand.

"Took your sweet damned time, didn't you?" She picked something from between her teeth. "Well don't just stand there like a sunburnt idiot. Let's get this over with."

Her office smelled like feet and root beer. A snot-crusted mask dangled from the doorknob. A computer-generated stop sign was taped to a dented file cabinet in the corner, and below it were the words, *"A lack of preparation on your part does not constitute an emergency on mine."*

She sniffed a half-eaten sandwich before taking a substantial bite. "Whar wor yar barn?" she garbled through a mouthful of tuna fish and white bread.

"I'm sorry?" said Miranda.

Big swig of root beer. She swallowed and wiped her mouth on her sleeve. "Where were you born?"

Miranda stared at the residue. "Pensacola."

She tapped a couple of keys, frowned at the computer screen. "Last grade completed?"

"Twelfth."

"I said *completed*," she snarled.

"I graduated from Washington High School. Class of 2019. I was in my first semester of college when I was arrested."

"Hmphh." She grudgingly pecked at the keyboard. "Don't see that too often."

Abort mission, her inner narrator warned.

"All right, what's your relationship like with the inmates in your dorm? Good, fair or poor?"

She thought of Throkkie and Duval. "Good."

"What about your relationship with staff? Good, fair or poor?"

She shrugged. "Good, so far."

"Family relations."

Deep Breath. "Actually, I wanted to talk to you about that. My father contracted Covid in the county jail and I was wondering if—"

"Good, fair or poor?"

"Please," she said, "I just had a baby and—"

"Are you refusing to answer, McGuire? Because if you're not going to cooperate, we can terminate this interview now. Lord knows I've got better things to do. Last chance. Family relations. Good, fair or poor?"

Miranda stared at her. "Poor."

She took another bite of her sandwich, another swallow of root beer. "How would you rate your attorney's performance? Good, fair, or—"

"Poor."

"Your outlook for the future."

"Poor."

"Excellent." She belched. A wave of Barts and Bumblebee tuna wafted across her desk. "Now we're getting somewhere. Are you interested in any faith-based programs?"

"Poor."

"I'll take that as a no. How about our vocational—"

"Poor."

She stopped typing and leaned back in her chair.

Miranda hands were trembling. Lava boiled in her heart. "Same goes for your professionalism. And your job performance. And your . . . hygiene!"

They stared at each other over the top of the computer. Neither blinking, neither moving. Heels clicked down the hallway. Someone in a nearby office sneezed. When she finally spoke, her tone was icy.

"Get out of my office."

She havened all the way back to Echo dorm, rubbing her sun-blistered arms with maniacal desperation. Despite her fervent efforts to console herself, she could not generate oxytocin, only adrenalin and cortisol. Her mask was damp with tears of rage by the time she reached her bunk.

Throkkie was braiding Duval's hair when she collapsed face down on her pillow.

"How did it go?" said her bunkie.

Poor? her inner narrator offered.

She rolled onto her side. "I'll take that Suboxone now."

15

Adrift. Day melted into night as she faded in and out of consciousness, wrapped in the warm embrace of an old lover. All the hurt, all the longing, all the anxiety; each of these decelerated with her plummeting heart rate. Disintegrating clouds in a marble sky.

She got up to vomit sometime after lights out. Throkkie followed and held her hair back. She felt even better after puking. As if what she expelled from her body and flushed down the toilet was not oatmeal and chow hall chili mac but stored tension and trauma from the past year. When she washed her face and looked into the bathroom mirror, the girl looking back at her was smiling. Not a full-on McGuire smile but a wry smile, a confident smile. Life was not so complicated minus the shrill and crippling emotion. Even prison life.

Suddenly, like Scenic Highway winding over the bluffs of Escambia Bay, bending through East Pensacola Heights and crossing Bayou Texar before morphing into

Cervantes, the way home unfolded before her. She would commit every shred of intelligence, every ounce of will, every moment of every day to learning the law as it applied to her case. She would research minimum mandatory sentences as Tussie implored her to do, but also police searches and postpartum plea agreements. She would find every error made by her public defender and she would meditate on how to attack them. Then, once fluent in the information and corresponding caselaw, she would assemble the facts like an English Lit major and write a Pulitzer-caliber brief that would not just get her back into court but get her home. And if it took a synthetic opioid to keep her surgically focused and emotionally detached until she made this happen, so be it.

The next day she had Throkkie cut two more slivers from the strip Duval gave her, and they snorted them after lunch.

"I can't believe I threw up last night." Miranda pinched her nostrils and tilted her head back, ensuring that nothing was wasted. "Especially from something so small."

"Well, your tolerance is way down," said Throkkie. "But yeah, just shows how little we really need."

"How much does it cost?"

"On the street? Around ten bucks," said Throkkie. "But in here they go for a hundred."

"A hundred dollars?" Miranda's jaw dropped. The fine print of her plans for opiated legal wizardry contained a small financial oversight. "I can't afford that."

You're broke, her inner narrator pointed out. *What* can *you afford?*

"Just chill." Duval looked over the side of the top bunk. "That was on the house. You don't owe me nothing."

Throkkie smiled her gap-toothed grin and pushed her glasses up her freckled nose. "I think she was talking about the next one."

"Ain't no more." Duval shook her head. "The chick I was getting it from next door shipped to work release this morning. Maybe when I get to Lowell, I'll be straight. But just so you know, I cut fifteen dimes off a hundred-dollar strip. And it sells like heroin."

Great, her inner narrator smirked. *Heroin.*

Miranda massaged her temples and willed the elixir to hurry up and work its magic. So typical of the voice in her head to lobby for a bump of Suboxone in one breath and then castigate her for succumbing in the next. One of the serendipitous perks of opiate life, synthetic or otherwise, was the way that dope jammed gauze in the mouth of her prattling inner narrator.

"What I'm saying is that it pays for itself." Duval reached down and hooked a strand of red hair, tucking it behind Miranda's ear." Long as you got somebody that'll front it to you."

Throkkie's eyes were growing heavy. "Mmm."

Duval smiled. "You still with us Rock?"

"Yeah." She scratched her nose.

Miranda was feeling it too. The outer bands of serenity arrived in rolling waves of warmth. Such an incredible chemical compound, this *opiate blocker*. When she was up and talking, she moved with single-minded precision; yet when she allowed herself to relax, she sank into a nod so deep and blissful that it rivaled the effect of the pills she once coveted. "Did you ever try this on the street?"

"The street?" Throkkie opened an eye. "I was never on the street. I lived with my boyfriend . . . that chinless bastard."

Miranda smiled. "You know what I mean. Did you ever use Suboxone to kick heroin?"

"Nah." She leaned her head against Miranda's and said dreamily, "I was a Methadonian."

Later that night she wandered into the dayroom and watched Jim Carey play a slightly senile Joe Biden on *SNL*. She was still feeling it the next morning during the powerhouse roundtable on *This Week with George Stephanopoulos*. But witnessing Chris Christie perform the political contortions necessary to defend a bully like Trump made her want to snort another strip. She cut the last three slivers on Monday morning. Orientation was officially over and there was nothing to do but gawk at Maury and Jerry Springer with the rest of the sheep. She snorted one, hid one, and gave the third to Throkkie. Tuesday night, she put her final piece in a Chapstick cap and melted it with warm water.

Most of the other women were breathing rhythmically beneath their wool blankets, soft shapes that rose and fell in the dim dormitory lighting. The guards had already passed on the 1 a.m. count, and their annoying flashlights would not return for another hour. She planned on being enveloped in cozy oblivion by then.

Carefully, she raised the cap to her nose and suctioned off the fluid in a quick efficient sniff. Then she licked the pinkish residue that stuck to the bottom. Her tongue was still in the cap when she happened to glance over at the next bunk. Senora Salazar was staring at her. They held each other's gaze for a moment. Miranda let the cap fall from her mouth but could not resist checking once more to make sure there was nothing left.

The old Cuban woman made the sign of the cross and rolled over.

16

She spent Wednesday in a groggy dream-like state; unhurried, unworried, but mourning the last of the Suboxone like an old friend come to visit and gone again.

That last piece was too big, her inner narrator arose and stretched. *You could've cut it into two and had another one for today.*

Throkkie was glowering in her bunk. Her downstairs neighbor was rocking back and forth while reading her Bible and the motion was clearly agitating her. A woman across the dorm erupted in a shriek of laughter and Throkkie glared heat-seeking lasers at her too.

"Hey Rock," said Duval. "You good, baby?"

She muttered something under her breath and pulled the blanket over her head.

Miranda frowned at her friend. She seemed annoyed with everyone and everything. *Why so grumpy? Homesick? PMS?*

On Thursday she was reminded of a universal truth: the world was an irritating place when the dope ran out. She spent the majority of the day in her bunk pretending not to see the pitiful parade of emotionally needy women that came to fawn over Duval; some bearing notes, some bearing gifts, some begging to buy Suboxone.

"Come on Duval. I'll give you twenty for a dime."

"Ain't nothing baby. All gone."

The second hand circled the dormitory clock like the guard on the catwalk of the gun tower. Her nose was en-flamed and stuffy from a week of snorting. She snuggled with a roll of scratchy single-ply toilet paper.

Duval climbed down from the top bunk, took one look at her, and shook her head.

"What?" said Miranda.

"You look like shit, Red."

"Have I ever told you how much I hate that name?"

She smiled. "You probably hating everything right about now. You and Rocky both. Your sunburn is all gone though."

Miranda blew her nose.

"Well, I just bought this." She grabbed a digital radio and headphones from her bunk. "Wanna ride out for a little while? The stations 'round here ain't all that but you might find something you can vibe with."

It had been a year since she listened to a radio. The last time was in her car with Nick, or whatever his name was, on the day she was arrested. It all sounded the same: homogenized, auto-tuned synth pop. She scanned for the local NPR affiliate and found it toward the bottom of the dial. *World Café* was on. Some artist named Elle King was singing about "The Let Go." She could have been singing about Miranda's life. Blindsided by an onslaught of tears, she sank beneath the blanket and cried herself to sleep.

She awoke to Throkkie shaking her shoulder. The BBC News bumper music was pummeling her eardrums. A woman with a British accent announced, "It's coming up to eight o'clock, GMT." She tried to remember what time zone she was in.

"Miranda, wake up!"

The dormitory was lit up like a convenience store. In the next bunk, her Latina neighbors had pulled off their sheets and were stuffing their property into pillowcases. Many of the other women were doing the same thing. She removed the earbuds and squinted at the clock.

An incoherent belch of an announcement blasted from the PA system. Miranda fell back onto her pillow and looked at the overhead steel, her head pounding. "Did you get all that?"

"He said we've got five minutes to pack up and get in the sally port." Throkkie seized her wrist with both hands and pulled her back up. "We're transferring."

"Everyone?"

She shook her head. "Maybe half the dorm."

"What about Duval?"

"She's in the bathroom. All three of us are going!"

Miranda wiped the sleep from her eyes. "What day is it?"

"Friday!" Throkkie's face was flush with excitement. "Lowell!"

They ate breakfast just before dawn—runny eggs, raw potatoes, and tortilla wraps—with guards barking at them to hurry up the entire time. Once finished, they filed into the receiving area to be strip searched and loaded onto the Blue Bird for the short trip to Lowell.

The crew working was the same that handled her intake. Since she knew what to expect, disrobing and spreading her genitalia was a little easier the second time around. But not by much. It was still tremendously awkward and humiliating. When it was her turn to cough, she hacked like an emphysema patient with all the volume she could generate. The guard with the flashlight smirked and waved her though.

"Damn, I hate that shit," said Duval, as they returned to the cage where they left their property. "I've probably been through a hundred strip searches, and they still make my skin crawl . . . Rocky! What is that on your ass, girl?"

"A dragon, you can't tell?"

"I thought it was an alligator."

She twisted her torso and stretched the skin to see. "Alligators don't have wings, Duval."

"I thought those was really big claws. My bad."

"That's stupid," said Throkkie, indignant. "Why would I get a tattoo of an alligator?"

Miranda dressed quickly and joined the flood of women staggering toward the metal detector. She thought she heard Tussie's Alabama drawl somewhere behind her and stood on her tip toes to see.

"I don't know," Duval was saying. "Maybe you're a Florida Gators fan . . ."

No sign of Tussie. The voice she thought belonged to her old cellmate was broadcasting from the dry and cracked lips of a leather-faced woman with a lopsided bun.

They squeezed back into the crowded cage. Chains rattled. The hangar door groaned as it rolled slowly up. October dawn splashed gray light on the oily concrete. The Blue Bird shuttered, brakes beeping, as it backed into the loading bay.

"Shut up!" Flashlight yelled as she unlocked the front of the holding pen.

"Get me on this fucking bus," said Duval as they made their way to the bench where they left their property. "I'm so sick of this petty-ass boot camp shit."

"Hey slim, with the braids." The guard singled out Duval. "You got something to say?"

Her jaw muscle twitched. She shook her head.

"Don't make me make an example outta your little narrow dyke ass." She waited to see if a response was forthcoming. When it was clear that none was, she rolled her bloodshot eyes and cleared her throat. "All right, when you hear your name, you gonna come up here and tell me three things. I want your DC number, your date of birth, and the city where you was born. Then you gonna get on this bus and shut the fuck up." She pulled the first two files from a wobbly red cart. "Ward! Stevenson!"

Two women shouldered their property and moved forward. Miranda turned sideways to allow space for them to pass, frowning at the empty spot on the bench where she left her pillowcase of belongings.

"Put your damned masks on!" ordered the maskless Flashlight, hand on massive hip.

Her heart began to slam against her chest as her eyes darted beneath the bench and over the mesh canteen bags of nearby women. She even glanced up at the exposed rafters. Was someone playing a cruel joke on her? Not only did that pillowcase contain the overflow of ramen and coffee that she was carrying for Duval along with the few health and comfort items she was able to scrounge during orientation—it contained Cameron's birth certificate. Her north star, her anchor, her lifeline.

The cage began to tilt. She felt as if she'd been punched in the stomach. It was difficult to breathe.

"Hey Red," said Duval out of the side of her mouth. "You good?"

Throkkie tugged at her shirt sleeve.

She ripped her arm away and spun toward the women making their way to the bus. Ward and Stevenson. The chubby one with warts on her elbows was dragging a dirty white laundry bag behind her. Miranda could see a manila envelope inside the nylon. Her heart leapt. With single-minded focus, she pushed through the crowded cage and went after her.

"Excuse me, I think you have my—"

"Go sit your little dizzy ass down till I call your name!" roared Flashlight.

Miranda ignored her and lunged for the bag.

The woman backpedaled and pulled away. "Hey! What are you doing?"

Miranda bit down on her own lip until her teeth broke the skin, her mask darkening with blood. All the anguish of losing her child, the recurring image of her father on a ventilator, the guilt over crushing Amity's spirit, the frustration of sitting in prison for someone else's crime, the cluelessness of her public defender, the rudeness of the classification officer, the armed silhouette in the tower, the flashlight on her genitals, the razor wire, the sunburn, the nightmares, Suboxone, Covid, Trump . . . All these were fingers pressed against a festering sore within her, pushing and probing, forcing the poisonous puss to a head, and in that moment—it popped.

"Get her off me!" the woman screamed as Miranda uncoiled and pounced like a mountain lioness; scratching, ripping, slapping, mauling.

"Inmate!" an authoritative male voice commanded. "You will cease your unruly behavior this instant!"

She only wanted the birth certificate, the one piece of property that mattered to her. It was hers.

"Yeah!" Throkkie's voice lifted above the chaos. "Kick her ass, Miranda!"

"Stand back," Flashlight ordered. "I got her."

The gas cannister roared like a blowtorch. Three consecutive blasts. Suddenly 10,000 fire-breathing wasps attached to her face and her lungs were packed with sandspurs.

Beyond the wail of thrumming pain, she was aware of the sound of violent hacking. It came from every angle—the guards standing over her, the women in the cages, the thief . . . Miranda retched and rolled blindly on the concrete, attempting to put out the chemical fire that tore across her skin. During these wild gyrations, she bumped against something soft. Through burning eyes smeared with gas and tears, she caught a glimpse of nylon mesh and clung to it like a life raft, pulling herself on top of it.

Then a boot nudged her in the ribcage and the bag was snatched away. "We need to get her in the decontamination shower. Both of them. We'll let Lowell deal with vitals and preconfinement."

Her arms were pulled firmly behind her back and handcuffs placed on her wrists. "What are we gonna write her up for Sarge? Fighting?"

"Absolutely not." She was pulled roughly to her feet. "This was clearly an assault."

"I'll handle the DR." Flashlight's voice was dripping with venom. "Y'all heard that ugly word she called me, right? I'll give her one for disrespect too. She'll have plenty of time in the box to think about what she did . . . jumping on these people's children."

PART TWO
The Box

17

The sun imposed its will on the window of her confinement cell, filling the slat of plexiglass with radiant light. Yet no warmth made it through. The only heat to be found in the stark and frigid dormitory was in her chemical burns, in the nightmarish memories of gas on her skin and fire in her lungs.

Her room was a 3D printing of the quarantine cell she shared with Tussie Jones at the reception center: steel door, toilet and window in the back, two single bunks along the right-hand wall, and a floor worn from pacing. A cinderblock tomb.

The van ride to the annex came back to her in fragments, flashing images of tower lights, rolling gates, a gentle nurse taking her vitals, the night air pulsating with crickets, the cell door slamming behind her.

Days blended. She picked at the trays that were pushed through the metal flap and stared at the pigeons that lined the roof of the adjacent dorm. Some nights, a pink-faced guard in a sweat-dampened uniform would handcuff her and escort her to the shower, but not very often. Not that she cared. The shower was no field trip. She was given a towel but no washcloth. Once she rubbed the thin bar of state soap all over her body, she would stand under the tepid water until it was time to dry off.

Then she would shiver beneath her blanket for the rest of the night.

The other women on the wing began shouting back and forth between cells every day after lunch. Conversations usually continued until long after lights out. Topics ranged from music to pop culture to fashion to compound gossip to the upcoming election. After a few days of ongoing discussion, her inner narrator began applying names to the voices. The needy chick downstairs who asked, *"Do you guys think Jocelyn is cheating on me?"* multiple times throughout the day was tagged *Jelly* for her insecurities. The woman next door who eagerly indulged Jelly's neurosis with relationship advice was christened *Delilah*. There was also Whistler, Sneezy, Grumpy, and Loquacia, as well as Long Hauler (*"So weird . . . I still can't smell anything."*) and Stalker (*"Yo, who was that redhead upstairs on shower night?"*).

She used meals to track the passage of time since there was no clock. Breakfast arrived before dawn, lunch was when the sun was high outside her cell window, and dinner in the afternoons before shift change.

On the evening of her fifth dinner in confinement—square fish patty, congealed yellow grits, and cole slaw—a key rapped against her door. A small bespectacled man with an airtight mask unlocked the flap and knelt in front of it. Cold inquisitorial eyes bore through the slot. "McGuire?"

She lifted a finger, dropped it.

"DC number?"

"070419."

He waited, staring a question at her.

". . . sir."

Satisfied, he proceeded. "I'm here to investigate your disciplinary reports. It appears that you have two. You can either participate or sign a refusal." He paused for a long moment. His obvious desire to have her refuse was a gravitational force.

"Why would I not participate?"

He sighed and unzipped an FDC gray attaché case. "I don't know. Why do drugs? Why commit crimes? Why have babies you can't take care of? Why do you women do any of the things that you do? It's my job to afford you the opportunity. That's all."

Another one, said her inner narrator. *So hateful. It seems like the people who are trapped in these places would be the miserable ones. Not those who get to go home every night.*

"At any rate . . ." He tested the pliancy of the computer-generated paper and cleared his throat. "The first DR is for 1-18, battery or attempted battery on an inmate. It states, *'On Friday, October 23, 2020, at approximately 5:50 A.M., while assigned to receiving and transport, I, Sgt. Tamara Haines, observed inmate McGuire, Miranda #070419 physically assault inmate Ward, Erica #B21696 by throwing her to the ground, pulling her hair and clawing her face. Inmate McGuire was given several verbal commands to cease her unruly actions, which she refused to obey. I broke the security seal on my department issued MK4 chemical agent cannister, serial #1119. I then administered one continuous application of MK4 oleoresin capsicum chemical for a total of 27 grams in her direction to cease the altercation. Inmate McGuire was placed in administrative confinement pending the outcome of this report.'"*

Miranda stomped her foot. "She stole my property!"

"I'm not finished." He glared through the flap. "When I am, you may then make your statement. Are we clear?"

She chewed her lip.

Tell him to fuck off, said her inner narrator. *What are they going to do? Spray you with more gas? Put you in prison? You're already in prison, inside the prison. How much more locked up can you get?*

"Are we clear?"

She breathed through her nose, exhaled. "Yes sir."

He shuffled paperwork. "The second DR is for 1-4, disrespect to officials. It states, *'On Friday, October 23, 2020, at approximately 5:50 A.M., while assigned to receiving and transport, I, Sgt. Tamara Haines, observed inmate McGuire, Miranda #070419 physically assault inmate Ward, Erica #B21696 by throwing her to the ground, pulling her hair and clawing her face. When I commanded inmate McGuire to cease and desist, she looked directly at me and shouted "Fuck you nigger! I do what I want!" Inmate McGuire was placed in administrative confinement pending the outcome of this report.'"*

It was as if someone punched her in the throat. She was shocked, appalled, speechless. When she finally found her voice, it came out choked and quavery. "I have never used that horrible disgusting word in my life."

"Right." He smiled. "Neither have I. Are you calling any witnesses?"

18

DR court turned out to be a dusty windowless room downstairs. The panel charged with dispensing justice was a giggling classification officer in a sunflower mask and a young lieutenant with his shirt sleeves pushed up to emphasize his bulging biceps.

In rumpled blues with dirty white stripes and a serious case of bedhead, Miranda stood handcuffed before them, pleading her case.

Her only defense for the battery charge was that she was attempting to secure her property which had been stolen.

"That does not give you the right to put your hands on another inmate," said Biceps.

The witness statements did little to improve her odds. Duval declined to write one at all, and Throkkie alleged in all caps followed by an exclamation point that *THE GIRL HIT MIRANDA FIRST!*, an assertion that was clearly not supported by video evidence.

Although the battery DR was the more serious of her two infractions, she was prepared to be found guilty as charged since she did go slightly ballistic on the woman who made off with her property. But the writeup for disrespect and the despicable lie it put forth was something she would never accept. Not only was it an egregious abuse of power and a miscarriage of justice, it was also a deliberate attack on her character. She refused to have her prison record stained by such ugliness.

Eyebrows raised as the lieutenant read the second disciplinary report aloud. When he finished, he dropped it on the desk. "How do you plead?"

"Not guilty," she stated firmly.

"Do you want to make a statement?"

Miranda nodded, swallowed, and began the speech she had practiced in her confinement cell over the weekend. "I . . . abhor that deplorable word. Its history—"

His smart phone jangled like a high school fire alarm. He glanced at the screen. "Hang on a minute. I gotta take this." He raised it to his stubbled face. *"Hey girl. Where were you last night? I was looking for you . . ."*

Her wrists throbbed from the handcuffs. The woman in the sunflower mask pretended to jot official notes in an open file. The phone call dragged on. Miranda went over her statement in her head, making minor revisions each time.

After what felt like ten minutes, he said goodbye and shoved the phone back into a holster on his belt. "Sorry about that," he mumbled to the classification officer who was no longer giggling.

"It's fine," she lied.

"Okay, inmate, uh . . ." He searched the paper in front of him. "McGuire, step outside the door for a minute."

Miranda frowned as she backed out of the room. After all these delays, she feared her statement was going to come off as mechanical and rehearsed. The DR team needed to know how sincere she was, how innocent she was. She would never even *think* such an ugly word, much less say it aloud. She was raised better.

Not sure about abhor. *I could go with* despise *or even plain old* hate. *"I* hate *that word." I'm already using* deplorable *which will be forever associated with Hillary Clinton. Shit! I bet he's a Trump supporter. She probably is too. I need to keep my statement nonpartisan. Just the facts.*

"McGuire," he called. "Come on back in here."

He leaned back in his chair and began reading from the worksheet before she could even return to her square of linoleum in front of the desk.

"So as to the disciplinary report for *one dash eighteen,* battery on an inmate," he said, "the team finds you guilty as charged and sentences you to sixty days in confinement."

Sixty days! Her inner narrator gulped. *Locked in a cell? You'll go crazy!*

"As to the DR for *one dash four,* disrespect to officials, the team finds you guilty as charged and sentences you to thirty days in disciplinary confinement—"

"Wait a minute!" she blurted.

Amusement flickered in his eyes. "Both sentences are to run consecutive to each other for a total of ninety days with seven days credit for the time you've served in administrative lockdown."

"But you didn't even hear my statement."

"Sure I did."

"No, you did not. You were on the phone the whole damn time!"

"Careful, McGuire."

She looked at the classification officer. "Please. I can't be locked in a cell for ninety days. I have to get to the law library. I have a son at home. He needs me."

The woman returned to doodling on her Post-it pad, either unwilling or unable to look her in the eye.

The lieutenant closed her file. "Well maybe you'll think about that the next time you decide to jump on another prisoner or call my employees racist names."

"I have never used that word in my life." She could feel tears of frustration welling in her eyes. "Not then, not now, not ever."

"Based on the officer's statement, you did." He signaled the guard. "Now if you'll excuse us, we have other cases to hear this morning. You have fifteen days to appeal this decision."

"Appeal to whom?" She felt an iron grip seize her arm and begin leading her toward the door. "Another kangaroo court like this one? I think I'll just write my congressman instead."

"You do that." He crossed his arms over his chest. "Maybe he'll come down from Tallahassee and I can show him the video of you attacking that poor girl."

"Show him a video of this joke of a hearing while you're at it," Miranda said over her shoulder on the way out.

"Officer Daniels!"

Her escort paused and turned back. Miranda noticed him for the first time, a tall African American with delicate facial features. "Sir?"

"This one's got a problem with blacks—"

"That's not true," said Miranda.

"—When you get her over to Tango dorm, make sure you house her with her own kind." His eyes narrowed with cruelty. "Matter of fact, I think there's an open bunk in Dixie Adams' cell. Quad two if I remember correctly. Let's put her in there."

Officer Daniels hesitated. "I think Adams is flagged as a *house alone.*"

The lieutenant smiled, admiring his biceps. "Not anymore."

19

The walk from Sierra to Tango dorm was brief. She could hear voices carry from a nearby yard and birdsong overhead. The fresh air, though filtered through her mask, still tasted exquisite. She wondered how long it would be before she breathed any again.

A quick glance over her right shoulder revealed the foreboding tower in the center of the compound, surrounded by razor wire. It occurred to her that Lowell Annex was built on the same architectural concept as the reception center. Only the names of the dormitories changed.

"Listen honey," said Officer Daniels as they neared the door, "whatever you got against black folks is between you and the Lord."

"I'm not a racist," Miranda sighed, "I'm a Democrat."

"Just listen!" he hissed. "I'm about to tell you some good shit girl. It might just save your life."

She frowned up at him. He was tall enough to block the sun, his gloved hand could have wrapped twice around her arm, yet his voice and mannerisms vibrated on a frequency that was pure femininity.

"You're about to go in a cell with a very dangerous woman. Her last bunkie is still in the infirmary recovering."

"Recovering from what?"

He rolled his eyes. "Seriously? You just coming to prison or something?"

She nodded solemnly.

"Jesus." The door buzzed. He held it open. "Look, if anything happens, you scream, okay? Just scream your red little head off. We got audio in the bubble. I'll come running."

The bubble was a windowed terminal that looked out into four quads that ran clockwise around the building. Quad one housed *S.H.O.S.* inmates downstairs—an acronym for Self-Harm Observation Status—while the upstairs was reserved for women placed under investigation and protective management. The first six cells of quad two were designated for death row inmates, although only three were occupied, and the rest of the wing was utilized for disciplinary confinement. Quads three and four were on the other side of the bubble and subdivided for *close management*; mostly women who had received DRs for stabbings, assaults on staff, and other serious rule infractions. Many would spend years behind *the door.*

The tall effeminate guard snapped the radio from his belt. "Confinement to Tango, pop quad two please."

Another buzz. He pushed the door open and they stepped inside, letting it bang shut behind them. Plexiglass smiles and scowls appeared in window slats with more materializing as they moved deeper into the unit; some alone, some cheek to cheek, many of the faces were pale from lack of sunlight. Miranda surveyed the surrounding steel and concrete, her home for the foreseeable future. Her hands reflexively moved to haven but were stayed by the bite of the handcuffs.

"Twelve!" someone shouted.

"Aww . . . check out Officer Daniels y'all," one of the women teased, "all starched and creased in his little FDC tie. He looks so cute."

"Hush up, Jenkins." He glared playfully at the corner cell on the second tier. "I know your damn voice."

"Did you bring me a cellmate?" asked the woman in 2101.

He smiled. "Nah, Ms. Tina. Not today."

His grip on her arm loosened as he led her up the stairs.

"Wait a minute, where are you putting her?" An alarmed voice rang out from the bottom tier. "Ain't no open cells up there. I know you ain't putting her in with Dixie Adams!"

The molecules in the confinement unit instantly changed. The entire wing seemed to pulsate with nervous energy. Muffled and excited conversations seeped through steel doors, morphing into one expectant hum.

"That's fucked up Daniels," another voice shouted. "You know what's gonna happen. Why do y'all keep putting people in there with her?"

At the top of the stairs, an older woman with hollow eyes and mumbling lips shook her head. A pretty black girl in the cell next door mouthed *don't go in there* as she passed.

"They need to charge *y'all* with the murder when she kills that girl," yelled another voice. "Y'all know what the fuck y'all doing!"

"All right, that's enough!" Daniels lisped. "I don't like it any more than you do, okay? I'm just doing my damned job."

The hum rose in volume, factions formed, arguments broke out.

"Y'all leave Officer Daniels alone!" shouted a woman at the end of the wing.

Miranda looked up at him. "I swear I'm not a racist. You can put me in that first cell downstairs if you want. With that nice lady who asked if you would let me be her roommate. I don't care what color she is. That's so stupid."

He shook his head. "She's on death row. I can't put you in there. And anyway, the lieutenant wants you in 2212."

She looked up at the stenciled numbers over the doors. It was the next cell.

"You're gonna be all right." He reached for his keys. "Just remember what I told you."

Every woman on the wing was now standing at her window.

"Don't do it, Red."

"Refuse."

"She ain't 'posed to have no cellmate no way."

Daniels unlocked the flap. "Inmate Adams. Come over here and cuff up. You've got a new roommate."

Miranda snuck a glance through the scratched plexiglass slat on the door. The woman who was going to kill her—or at the very least, beat her sadistically until help arrived—was doing pushups with her feet propped on the toilet. *Extremely large feet.* Everything about her was large, from her thick legs to her wide back to her powerful shoulders to the knuckles on her massive hands. Although her head was down and her face concealed, there appeared to be no trace of estrogen in Tango 2212. Her hair was buzzed like a boot camp Marine and sweat dripped into a puddle below her.

She ignored the verbal order and continued to pound out reps.

Daniels glanced at Miranda and shrugged. "We'll just let her finish up."

This is your karma, said her inner narrator as the pushups persisted. *You put violence into the universe when you attacked that girl and now violence is returning to you. You could've waited till you got on the bus then firmly demanded your property back. You've never even been in a fight! What were you thinking? Where was your Mensa-level IQ on that one, Ms. Suboxone? You weren't thinking, that's the problem. For every action, there is an equal or . . . Holy shit!*

With an animal growl, Dixie Adams finished her set, going down on a knee before rising to her full height. She was easily six feet tall with knotted muscle and ropey veins covering the landscape of her towering frame. Yet it was the hellscape of her face that was most intimidating. Baleful charcoal eyes glared out from a mess of scar tissue and bunched molten flesh.

Refuse! said her inner narrator. *Do not go in that cell. Listen to these women. They know what they're talking about. Fake a medical emergency. Demand to see the warden. Whatever you have to do. This is way worse than I thought. You're in danger!*

Somehow Miranda managed to keep her facial expression impassive. Not as a show of courage but one of kindness. It felt important to meet her gaze and resist the urge to recoil, even as Dixie approached the door and stuck her scarred and calloused hands through the flap.

Daniels removed an extra set of cuffs from his belt and gently clicked them over her wrists. Then he reached for his radio. "Tango, roll 2212 please . . . 2212."

20

Her bunk was two feet from the toilet. Not an ideal situation but it had its benefits. Located beneath the window in the back of the cell, she could see down into the rec cages below and further out over the perimeter fence where wildflowers splashed purple and yellow on an empty field. More importantly, at night she could see the stars.

So much had happened in the space of a year. Tragedy and hardship had whittled away most of her lingering innocence. But deep inside her still lived the girl who used to pull the mattress close to her East Hill bedroom window and fall asleep looking at the stars.

Her cellmate did not speak. Miranda was uncertain whether this was by choice or if her tongue was a casualty of whatever destroyed her face. Either way, she was respectful of the silence and did nothing to attempt to draw her out.

This silence, however, did not translate to her eating habits. Dixie grunted and smacked her way through every meal, devouring her tray within seconds, tilting it back to slurp off any remaining carrot juice, then carrying it back to the flap under her arm like a book.

Miranda quietly offered her leftovers that first night, a cold quivering lump of beef noodle casserole and some rubbery uncooked green beans. Dixie inhaled this in similar fashion, all the way down to the discarded crust from the white bread Miranda still nibbled.

As she watched her cellmate eat, she wondered about her life. Not just about the trauma that disfigured her face and the pain she must have endured, but who she was before, how she grew so strong, why she attacked previous cellmates, why she came to prison. Perhaps somewhere inside her also lived a little girl who once looked up at the stars with wonder. She was more than the monster she appeared to be. At some point she was someone's heart, someone's miracle, someone's Cameron.

The memory of her baby's scent flared like a struck match in her hippocampus, the soft crown of his head tickling her nose in the hospital bed. He was now five months old. She wondered how much he had grown. Was he crawling? Sitting up? Smiling? Was he calling someone else *Mama?* Was he safe?

The clock was ticking. Every day that she sat in prison was a memory missed. A lock of hair, a new tooth, an inch grown, a first step. She had to get to the law library and begin her research. How infuriating that she had dug herself a ninety-day hole!

It wasn't all your fault, said her inner narrator in a rare moment of kindness. *They lied on you.*

"Based on the officer's statement." That's what the court used to find her guilty. That's how they justified locking her in disciplinary confinement for the next three months. Did it really matter that she was unable to give her version of the events? Would it have made a difference if the lieutenant pretended to listen instead of talking on the phone? Doubtful. *Based on the officer's statement,* she was guilty before she ever entered the room.

A concussive sound reverberated through the wall that ran parallel to her bunk, disrupting her thoughts. She glanced at Dixie. No help there.

The orderly who was picking up trays stuck her plump face in the slot. A cracked heart was tattooed beneath her left eye, just north of her mask. "Your neighbor wants you to come to the door."

Miranda frowned, unsure whether it was her being summoned or Dixie. As if reading her mind, her cell-mate leaned back in her bunk, interlacing her thick fingers over her sternum.

Tentatively, Miranda approached the flap. "Yes?" Her voice floated down the tier.

"Hello there," came a silky replay, vaguely familiar. "We were in S dorm together, weren't we?"

"Probably," said Miranda, "I just went to DR court this morning." *Where do I know that voice from?*

"I came over last Thursday," said the woman. "Unauthorized physical contact. I was hugging my girlfriend. It's amazing how much energy these people waste trying to outlaw intimacy. The first DR only carried ten days so of course they lied and said I disobeyed a verbal order, then gave me thirty more for that."

"I know the feeling."

"Are you back here for the same thing?"

Delilah! her inner narrator exclaimed. *I knew I recognized that voice.*

"Um, no." Miranda glanced back at Dixie. "It's a long story. Someone stole something of mine and I got in trouble for battery."

Dixie raised a scar-tissue eyebrow.

"Right on girl!" said Delilah. "You've got to stand up for yourself in here. These bitches will walk all over you if you don't."

"They gave me sixty days for that." Miranda knelt in front of the flap. "But then the officer lied and said I called her a . . . a racial slur—which I absolutely did not—so they gave me thirty more."

"Ninety days." Delilah whistled. "Ouch. Do you have anyone on the compound to look out for you?"

She thought of Duval and Throkkie. "I've got a few friends here. We were actually transferring from the reception center when all this happened."

"Oh, so you haven't really experienced the annex yet?"

Miranda flicked a dried bean from the flap. "Just these confinement cells."

"Well get ready for a parallel universe," said Delilah. "This place is crazy. Or it was before all the quarantines. No telling how it'll look by the time you get out. That's like . . . late January?"

"Ugh, don't remind me."

"It'll go quickly," she said. "Just don't count the days. Keep looking forward to the next shower, the next meal, the next mail call . . . and before you know it, they'll be telling you to roll it up. When I get out, you'll be halfway through. If your friends can't figure out how to get you stuff back here, I'll send you some coffee and soap."

"Thanks." Miranda watched the orderly stack trays on a cart downstairs. "But I don't drink coffee. I just need to get to the law library."

The woman downstairs in 2108 was waving frantically. Her t-shirt was tied around her head like a turban. The orderly looked toward the officers' station, reached beneath her mask, and extracted something shiny with saliva and plastic wrap. She dropped it on the floor and nonchalantly kicked it under her cell door. The turban vanished from the window.

". . . My girlfriend was working in the library before all this Covid stuff," said Delilah. "General library though. Magazine rack. She thinks the law is boring."

Miranda wondered what the orderly kicked under the door. *A note? A cigarette? A Suboxone strip?*

"Well anyway," Delilah's voice wafted down the empty tier, "what I wanted to ask you was . . . have you heard anything about the election?"

The election! Miranda leaned against the door, ran her fingers through her hair. With everything collapsing around her, she had forgotten all about the presidential election. "What day is it?"

"It's Wednesday," said Delilah. "The polls closed last night. But none of these guards seem to know anything about it. I've been asking every time they walk through."

"Let me guess." Miranda massaged her temples. "You want to make America great again . . . again."

"Hell no!" Her neighbor's door rumbled. "I'm going home in a few years. I'd like the world to still be around when I get there."

Dixie cracked her knuckles, rolled over, and broke wind.

"I'm with you," said Miranda, but not with her normal polemic fire. Her thoughts were elsewhere. Super Tuesday was November the third, which meant today was the fourth. When the guard walked through for midnight count, she would be twenty years old.

21

A presence hovered over her. She could sense it. Even in darkness, even in sleep. Her eyes fluttered open. Her cellmate's face pulled into focus, even more startling in the moonlight. She gasped awake, a scream stuck in her throat.

Dixie pivoted and spun back into the center of the cell, her white sock slicing up through the darkness, higher than her shadow. Her hands formed opposing letter Cs, as if holding an invisible orb. She rotated her hips, chambering it, then slowly pushed the orb forward, the Cs becoming a V, presenting it.

Miranda watched in silence as her terror slowly diminished. The only sound in the cell was the subtle rustle of air passing through the scar tissue of Dixie's nostrils. There was something calming in the fluidity of her movements. Ballet blended with yoga. Tai chi with precision and grace. Her hands brushed the floor as her foot extended behind her, almost sinking into a deep reverse lunge. Another pivot, another spin, and suddenly she was hovering over her again, eyes blank and straight ahead as the sequence began anew.

Miranda searched her window for signs of dawn but found only darkness on the horizon. A moth circled the perimeter light, its wings clapped chalky airborne particles into the yellow glow. She needed to pee, but it seemed like a bad time. Better to hold it than get kicked off the toilet by an errant roundhouse.

In the center of the cell, Dixie continued her lethal and graceful dance, only now every move was punctuated with power. Her uniform pants snapped with every kick. The invisible orb wasn't merely presented, it was thrust forward as if she was hurling a fireball. Her back foot no longer extended, it shot behind her with force.

A burst of staticky radio traffic erupted outside the door. A flashlight beam followed, streaking across the plexiglass, but the guard didn't bother to look in. Counts were perfunctory after lights out, especially in confinement units where the doors remained locked 24 hours a day.

The urge to use the toilet grew more and more insistent. Dixie began bouncing on the balls of her feet, transitioning from the spinning back kicks and liquid strikes of whatever martial arts style she was practicing, into the straight jabs, hooks, and punishing overhands of traditional boxing. Her blurred fists whistled through the dark, hammering some imaginary opponent. Although her body was heavy with rippling muscle, her feet were as light as linen. Her head bobbed and weaved as if slipping unseen punches, then she returned fire with another blistering combination.

A droplet of sweat hit Miranda on the cheek. She wiped it way without comment. It did not occur to her to question why her Amazon cellmate was up before dawn practicing combat. Maybe it would have last November, but not now. Disciplinary confinement was a new experience—prison was a new experience—but she had been locked up for over a year, long enough to understand that people had different ways of dealing with inner pain and isolation. Some found Jesus, some found a girlfriend—*Some found Suboxone*—Dixie shadowboxed.

"Mind if I use the bathroom?" said Miranda when she could hold it no longer.

Her cellmate threw a couple more punches before signaling grudging acquiescence by walking over to the door. Her body heat steamed the window.

Miranda's bladder throbbed as if she was still forty weeks pregnant and Cameron was using it as a trampoline. There was no time to strategically place dainty strips of toilet paper over the seat. She yanked down her uniform pants and braved the frigid stool. The urgency of her pee hitting the bowl seemed to echo throughout the quad. The lights clicked on before she could finish.

Dixie's blue uniform top was dark with sweat and plastered against her broad back. Miranda watched her shoulders swell and plummet as her breathing leveled off. The cell was still warm from exertion. She quickly cleaned herself and flushed the toilet.

The awkward art of bathroom diplomacy was a delicate issue that varied from cellmate to cellmate, especially when the bathroom in question was just a steel toilet in the back of a cell. Tussie Jones didn't care. The old lifer would drop her pants mid conversation with a guard standing at the door. Amity was similarly shameless. Miranda's first interaction with her occurred in the clutches of violent diarrhea from opiate withdrawals which set the tone for the ensuing ten months. Dixie was different. Her size alone made her intimidating, but coupled with the grafted flesh of her face, her violent reputation and her stoic silence, it was almost like living in close quarters with a large, strange man.

The unit door popped. Downstairs, she could hear the squeaky wheels of the food cart bringing in the breakfast trays. Her cellmate grunted.

"Male on the wing!" shouted a deep masculine voice.

Miranda washed her hands and sat on her bunk to wait. The sky outside her window was finally pinkening with the first light of dawn.

"Y'all need to be up and in your Class A uniform if you're eating!" the voice commanded, his footfalls heavy on the metal stairs.

She picked at the raised flesh of a slow-to-heal chemical burn on her forearm, the skin discolored and chapped but no longer painful. Compared to the marbled scars that extended from Dixie's forehead to her neck, it was nothing. A trail of ant bites.

"Good morning, Adams." The voice paused outside her cell. "How's it going in there?"

She grunted. Her massive frame eclipsed the entirety of the plexiglass.

"Do me a favor and step aside so I can get a visual on your cellmate. Just need to make sure everybody's alive."

Dixie leaned to her left. Miranda glanced at the door: white shirt, biceps, his cologne seeped through the flap. Clearly he was expecting misery, if not blood. It felt

important to smile. "Good morning, Lieutenant." Disap-
pointment snuffed the cocky light in his eyes like water
splashed on a flame. He was gone before she could read
the name embroidered on his uniform.

22

"Hey Delilah?" She had to shout over the other women
talking from cell to cell. She looked over her shoulder at
Dixie, trying to gauge whether her cellmate was irritated
by the noise. "Come to the flap."

"Are you talking to me?" Her neighbor's voice came
back down the tier. "I told you my name is Erin . . . Erin
Maynard."

"Oh, sorry," said Miranda. "I keep doing that."

"Eh, it's okay. It's actually sorta sexy. Very retro."

"What?" Miranda pressed her ear to the flap.

"I said it's sexy," she enunciated. "Retro . . . in an Old
Testament kinda way. Please tell me you've heard something about Pennsylvania or Arizona. Trump's probably
going to win Georgia but if Biden can just hold
Pennsylvania . . ."

"I haven't heard anything," Miranda shouted over the
thirty ongoing conversations in Tango two. "You're the
only person I talk to about politics. You're the only person I talk to *period.*"

"Yeah. Your cellmate is not known for her chattiness. Hey, isn't this Daniels' shift? I thought I saw him downstairs before lunch. He's the only one who will tell me anything. Wouldn't it be crazy if the election went all the way to the Supreme Court and that woman Trump picked to take RBG's place cast the deciding vote in his favor?"

"I don't know about crazy." Miranda leaned against the door. "Depressing maybe."

"I'm just surprised it's come down to this. A handful of states still counting votes five days after the election? I figured it would be a blowout . . ."

The noise level gradually compounded until it drowned out her voice completely. Miranda stared through the flap at the faces across the wing. It seemed like every woman was on her door; yelling for the orderly, signing through the window, fishing from one cell to the next with unraveled thread tied around bars of soap.

"Hey next door! Did you hear me?"

"It's so loud in here," Miranda shouted. "Say that again."

"I said I thought it was going to be a blowout," she shouted back. "Between all the inner circle indictments and unpaid taxes and Covid and bleachgate and quid pro quo and that embarrassment of a debate last month . . ."

Wow, her inner narrator broke in, *she sounds exactly like you. I wonder if she's a Scorpio. Or a redhead. Her name is Erin. Doesn't get much more Irish than that.*

". . . and let's not forget Stormy freakin' Daniels! Can you imagine how the GOP would've reacted if Obama paid $150,000 in hush money to a stripper?"

The wing had fallen quiet during her diatribe. A toilet flushed. Someone coughed.

"Hey upstairs!" A woman called. "What's the GOP stand for anyway? I hear them say that on the news all the time."

"Grand Old Party," Miranda and Delilah answered in tandem, their voices echoed from the cinderblocks.

"Grand Old Party?" said a woman downstairs. "For real? That shit *sounds* racist."

"Right?" Delilah laughed. "Like a cross between the Grand Dragon and the Grand Ole Opry."

"Hey, what's wrong with the Opry?" drawled the orderly as she mopped past Miranda's cell. "I grew up on classic country. It's a lot more wholesome than the shit that passes for music nowadays."

The noise level quickly ratcheted back to thunderous as conflicting opinions were hurled like grenades from every flap in the unit. Miranda declined to participate. She wasn't passionate about music. She was barely passionate about politics anymore. Washington D.C. felt worlds away from Tango 2212. Life on lockdown would be the same no matter who was in the oval office. No president could give her baby back or get her dad off a ventilator or get her out of disciplinary confinement and back into a courtroom.

"Hey Erin!" Miranda shouted into the chaos.

"Call me Delilah."

Miranda smiled. "What's the lieutenant's name who walked around at breakfast this morning?"

Downstairs, a cigar stub of a woman with frosted hair and polished boots was going door to door slamming flaps.

"What?"

"The lieutenant from breakfast! What's his name?"

"I didn't get up for breakfast," she said. "Describe him."

Miranda glanced back at Dixie. She was staring at the ceiling of the cell, her arms folded over her chest. Thick veins spiraled up her forearms like vines.

"Um . . . thirtyish, average height, shirt sleeves hemmed to show off his arms, cruel . . . He presided over my DR hearing."

"No idea," she shouted back. "But his name should be on your paperwork."

The guard took the stairs two at a time.

"I flushed my paperwork," said Miranda.

The metal banged in her face like a gunshot. She flinched and screamed. Dixie shot her an agitated look. She slid down the door and landed hard on the concrete as the rest of the flaps on the tier were slammed in rapid, rhythmic succession.

The dead zone between lunch and dinner had officially begun, the longest part of the day. She was learning that it was not the isolation that made disciplinary confinement so brutal, nor was it the three weekly showers, the occasional hunger pangs, or the suspension of privileges. The most deceptively cruel element of life on lockdown was the relentless, soul-sucking, day-to-day boredom. She found herself craving a fat Russian novel worse than a Suboxone strip.

Something beneath her cellmate's bunk caught her eye, something she hadn't noticed before. Pressed tight against the wall was a stack of manila envelopes, water stained and timeworn, as intriguing and mysterious as Tussie's photo albums. They made her think of stolen birth certificates and infant sons lost to the foster care system. A shot of pain rippled outward from the epicenter of her heart.

Dixie noticed her looking, rolled onto her side, and stared defiantly into her eyes. The scar tissue that twisted around her mouth pulled back over sharp feral teeth, and a raspy voice said, "Grantham."

23

Miranda's eyes widened. "You speak?"

Dixie shrugged. "When I have something to say."

"N-n-nice to meet you," she stammered. "I'm Miranda."

"No shit." Dixie nodded at her inmate ID. "You don't have to wear that in here, you know. It's not like you're going anywhere."

At least not for the next 79 days, said her inner narrator.

Miranda pulled the tag from her shirt. "Who's Grantham?"

"Lieutenant Grantham?" Dixie swung her tree trunk legs over the side of the bunk. Her bare feet slapped the concrete. Even her toes appeared to have muscles. "He's the white shirt who walked this morning. The one you were just asking your snowflake buddy about before the guard slammed the flap."

Her voice was familiar, a cross between her dad's *Godfather* movies and her perpetually hoarse high school history teacher, Mr. Nicolas. When she stood, Miranda had to tilt her head back to maintain eye contact from her spot on the floor. Her biceps were the size of cantaloupes, her triceps steel horseshoes. Far more impressive than Lieutenant Grantham's. Her shoulders rolled beneath her collar as she strode across the cell. Her head swiveled and cracked on the thick fulcrum of her neck. When she bent over the sink to slurp water from the nozzle, her glutes flexed. Solid muscle.

"Are you transgender?"

She turned and glared at Miranda. "What did you just say to me?"

Good job, Snowbunny Red, her inner narrator applauded. *Ask her what she's in prison for while you're at it. Better yet, ask what happened to her face.*

"I'm going to pretend that you didn't just disrespect me, and restrain myself from putting you through that flap . . . this time."

Miranda wanted to tell her that putting her through the flap would be physically impossible because its dimensions were six by twelve inches, plus it was locked, but she didn't want to come off as a know-it-all and she definitely didn't want her to try.

"Sorry," said Miranda. "You're just so . . ."

Do not say manly.

". . . big."

She walked back to her bunk and sat down. Her baleful eyes locked on Miranda. It felt rude to call another woman hideous, even in the privacy of her mind, but it was difficult to find a more fitting adjective. Her face was a patchwork of mottled scar tissue.

"Grantham moved you into this cell to get hurt," she rasped. "They know I don't get along with people."

"I heard about the last woman." Miranda stared at her hands.

"Three," she said. "It was the last three women they tried to put in here."

"Why don't you get along with people?"

"That's my business. My issues. We're not going to have that discussion." She cracked her knuckles. "But I'm not going to hurt you."

"Thank you," said Miranda. "Why not?"

A hint of amusement touched her eyes and hardened into ice. "Because I don't work for prison guards."

Images of her predawn routine bubbled to the surface of Miranda's mind. Memories of spinning back kicks and lightning jabs and violent sequences of elbows and knees so fast that they defied the laws of physics. Miranda felt bad for the three unfortunate women that came before her. "Was that karate you were doing this morning?"

"No," she said. "Any more questions?"

Miranda glanced under her bunk. "What's that stack of papers and manila envelopes down there?"

"My legal work."

"Can I read it?"

Awkward silence. Breath, stillness, the subtle hum of existence.

"The reason I'm asking," Miranda scrambled to explain, "is because I'm trying to learn the law."

The reason you're asking, her inner narrator clarified, *is because you're bored out of your mind.*

"Let me get this straight." Dixie stared at her. "You want to read my court transcripts."

Miranda nodded, smiled.

"All the juicy details," her eyes twinkled from a cage of flesh, "so you can gossip about me to your little friends."

"I wouldn't do that."

"Sure you wouldn't," she rasped. "You in for murder?"

Miranda shook her head. "Armed trafficking."

"Mmm, drug dealer," said Dixie. "I hate drug dealers. Almost as much as I hate liberals."

This is going well, said her inner narrator.

"What makes you think reading a capital murder case will help you?"

"I don't know. I guess I just thought . . ." The words evaporated before reaching her lips. What *did* she think? Whatever it was, it was gone now.

Dixie leaned forward, elbows on knees, hands clasped. Her terrible face hovered inches from Miranda's. Close enough to smell the soy patty from lunch on her breath.

"I'm not here to do Grantham's dirty work. I should've guessed what they were up to when they moved the last girl in here." She paused, her eyes bottomless pools of pain. "But understand me on this . . . If I catch you going through my shit while I'm sleeping, I will beat you until your pretty little face looks just like mine."

24

Delilah sent her a King James Bible. Not exactly *Anna Karenina* but it was something to read. The doughy-faced orderly in the sweat-soaked mask pushed it through the flap as she was going cell to cell with the broom and mop for cleanup.

For some reason Miranda was fascinated by the tattoo beneath her eye, the broken heart. She kept thinking about it as she plowed through the Book of Genesis.

Why would she permanently mark her face like that? her inner narrator wondered.

Because she was already marked . . . The answer came in the clarion voice of tragically gifted Ellen Miller. Ripped straight from the pages of *Like Being Killed*, the last novel Miranda was reading as a free woman. *Marked from birth. She's just showing the world what she's known inside all along.*

Something like that. Such a brilliant book, such a talented writer. The internet rumor mill said she was found unresponsive in a New York bodega. Gone before she could write another novel. Miranda wished she could read it again. Maybe the prison library had a copy. If not, she'd go with Donna Tartt's *The Goldfinch*, or Anthony Doerr's *All The Light We Cannot See*, or anything by David Mitchell.

She ached for literary input. Miranda craved books the way most prisoners on lockdown craved food.

Silver needles of rain pattered soundlessly against the window. The distorted taillights of a car on Perimeter Road glowed red over the slick black asphalt. Dixie rose from her bunk and pointed at the toilet. Miranda immediately rolled over and faced the wall. The movement and bubbles in the paint were familiar territory at this point. The same constellations emerged from the latex, forming the same profiles. Here was a confederate monument, here was Stephen Hawking, here was Woody from *Toy Story*.

"The Holy Bible, huh?" Dixie rasped over a powerful stream of urine. "Are you a Christian?"

"Not really." Miranda touched the wall. "My father is Irish Catholic, but it's been years since we went to church."

The toilet flushed. Water trickled from the sink. Dixie grunted.

She rolled back over. "What about you? Are you a Christian?"

A derisive snort. "You don't get a face like mine from turning the other cheek."

She wants to talk! "What happened to you?"

Dixie ignored the question. "Christianity has made the world soft with its message of meekness and kindness. It goes against the most fundamental law of nature: the strong survive. Do you think a lion cares about your kindness? Do you think a rapist gives a fuck about your humility?"

Miranda blinked.

Everything about her cellmate was harsh. An electromagnetic field of pain and resistance seemed to crackle in the air around her.

"Liberalism is the bastard child of Christianity," she continued. "The powerful are silenced by guilt and shame while the weak are coddled. *Feed the hungry, take care of the sick, visit the prisoner* . . . Where else is that happening in nature?"

"What other species imprisons each other?"

"Save it." She rested a foot on the toilet seat and crossed her arms. "Or go whine about it under the door to your liberal friend."

"You know," Miranda opened the Bible, searched for her page, "most Christians are actually conservatives. The evangelical right is a pretty powerful movement."

"Sheep," Dixie scoffed. "All of them. The right and the left. That's why Trump is such a badass. He called them all out—anthem kneelers, protesters, Congress, Wall Street, China, Amazon. He's not ashamed of his strength and wealth and power. He beats his chest and says, *I run this shit!*"

"He's an international embarrassment." Miranda lay the Bible on her bunk. She knew she was playing with fire but couldn't help herself. "Our allies no longer trust us, our enemies laugh at us, our cities are burning, we lead the world in Covid deaths, and your strongman president can't even find the courage to debunk a conspiracy theory like QAnon or disavow the hate groups that have been flocking to him like a messiah over the last four years. Why? Simple. Votes. Drain the swamp? Yeah, right. He's backstroking in it."

"That's another thing I hate about the left." Her jaw flexed beneath the scar tissue. "They think they know everything. You watch way too much news. The liberal media has obviously brainwashed you."

"Every story that doesn't paint Donald Trump in a favorable light is suddenly the product of a liberal media agenda?" Miranda rolled her eyes. "If the president had his way, the first amendment would probably be repealed and there would be no more free press. Just Fox News. Do you know who George Stephanopoulos is?"

Dixie mimicked her voice. "Do you know who Rush Limbaugh is?"

"Sure," said Miranda. "He invented the term *feminazi* and got booted off *Monday Night Football* for making racist comments. Trump gave him the Medal of Freedom in January."

"Figures, you would only know those things." She shook her head. "He's done a whole lot more than that in his life. You should pull your head out of your ass and listen to him sometime."

25

Commotion on the wing. Miranda tore herself from the Book of Ruth, set her Bible on her stomach, and listened. She was beginning to recognize the various sounds and corresponding energy of day-to-day life in the box. Some noises warranted a trip to the door to see what was happening, others were so predictable that she barely looked up.

The thump and howl of a cell extraction differed from the wounded wail of a psych emergency. An actual psych emergency vibrated on a different frequency than a woman faking it to get moved into a S.H.O.S. cell in Tango one. Rolling doors on shower nights rumbled with less urgency than random shakedowns. Twelve on the wing, orderly on the wing, nurse on the wing, inspection team on the wing, chow, legal mail, property . . . Each carried its own energy, its own sonic signature.

"Twelve!" shouted the girl in 2201.

Miranda knew her high pitched voice by now. Her cell overlooked the quad door and she was the de facto lookout for the rest of the confinement unit. Any time a guard entered the wing she announced their presence by squawking the number twelve.

In another life, Miranda remembered certain heroin dealers referring to the police by the same name.

"Come on Gucci, you know I don't fuck with twelve."

A shiver of disgust rippled through her at the memory of her ex. Was he even an ex? She still struggled with what to call him. *Baby's daddy* was so Maury and *sperm donor* was such a cliché.

What about asshole, loser, traitor, coward? her inner narrator suggested.

"Hey Dixie, why do they call guards *twelve?*"

Her cellmate glowered at the wall, clearly not in a talkative mood.

She sighed and sank back into the story of Ruth. The relationship between the young Moabite widow and her Israelite mother-in-law was beautiful and touching. A feminine desert flower sprung from the pages of endless war and strife.

Movement in the plexiglass. She looked over the top of the Bible. A silver-haired woman with sergeant stripes was checking the number stenciled above her door. "McGuire?"

"070419" said Miranda. It was almost second nature after two months of master roster counts. "Ma'am."

"You've got mail." The sergeant smiled and slid an envelope beneath the steel.

She sat up in her bunk and stared at the white rectangle lying on the concrete. Someone had written her a letter! Aside from the *Return to Sender* stunt her dad pulled in the county jail and the birth certificate copy that the midwife sent her, she never received mail. She slipped on her crocs and approached it tentatively, reverently, as if it were some small bird that might scurry back under the door and fly away.

Hostility seethed in the periphery. She could feel Dixie's eyes on her as she knelt to pick it up. Her cellmate never received any mail either. She almost felt guilty. Almost.

The handwriting was neat and precise, four even lines in the center of the envelope.

Miranda McGuire #070419 T-2212
Lowell Correctional Institution - Annex
11120 NW Gainesville Road
Ocala, FL 34482

The return address was three baby blocks containing the letters FFN and a P.O. Box in Pensacola.

Cameron!

Her hands were trembling as she tore the tape from the back of the envelope. The letter had already been opened, to check for contraband she presumed. The postage stamp had also been ripped off for some reason. None of this mattered. When she unfolded the paper, three pictures of her son were staring back at her. Not merely staring . . . *smiling*.

Her heart broke and soared simultaneously. Tears streamed down her face. She had read something, long ago, that no big smiles during the first six months of life represented a high probability that the child would register somewhere on the autism spectrum.

I think we can check that worry off the list, said her inner narrator.

Miranda absently touched a dimple. He was perfect. She could smell the crown of his head through the paper, hear his baby babble, feel the softness of his skin.

In one of the photos, he was lying on his stomach in a onesie, resting his upper body on his forearms like a yogi mid-sun salutation. In another, his brow was furrowed in single-minded focus as he reached for a purple dinosaur. In the last, he was sitting—*sitting!*—on a carpeted floor surrounded by stuffed animals and toys and couch cushions. A pudgy middle-aged arm with a smattering of freckles kept him upright.

She lifted the paper closer to her face. It seemed like a trustworthy arm, an arm that might be good for hugging and rocking. One not likely to rear back in anger.

God, she hoped not. Never had she viewed an append-age with so much envy and gratitude and suspicion.

Reluctantly, she turned the page. A folded piece of yellow stationary fluttered down on her bunk. She could see the sprawling cursive before she straightened it out on her leg and began to read the short note.

Hello Ms. McGuire,

Hope this letter finds you doing well, all things considered. These reports are supposed to be mailed quarterly, but Covid has everything in our office backed up right now. The enclosed information is current as of 11/2/2021. Cameron is a happy baby with no major health issues to date. His foster mother has been keeping meticulous notes for you. Please let me know if your situation changes. Until then, rest assured that your child is in good hands.

Best wishes,
Karen Tate

She read it twice, her eyes drinking every word, filling her dehydrated heart. Then, vowing that her situation would most definitely change, Miranda tucked the paper back into the envelope and turned her attention to the report.

Child Case History and Status Update

Name: <u>McGuire, Cameron Patrick</u> Case No.: <u>21-248-ESC</u>

Date of Birth: <u>June 2, 2020</u> Date of Custody: <u>June 3, 2020</u>

Eyes: <u>Blue</u> Hair: <u>None</u> Sex: <u>Male</u> Race: <u>White</u>

Measurements

Age	Length	Weight
At birth	20 ¾ inches	8 lbs, 4 oz
2 weeks	22 ¼"	8 lbs, 9 oz
1 month	23 ½"	10 lbs, 15oz
2 months	24"	13 lbs, 4 oz
3 months	24 ¾"	14 lbs, 15oz
4 months	26"	15 lbs, 6 oz
5 months	27 ¼"	17 lbs, 13 oz
6 months	_____	_____

Vaccinations

Vaccine	1st dose	2nd dose	3rd dose	4th dose	5th dose
HepB	X	X	____	n/a	n/a
DTap	X	X	____	____	____
Hib	X	X	____	n/a	n/a
PCV13	X	X	____	____	n/a
IPV	X	X	____	____	n/a

Allergies

None known

Notes

First smile – 5 weeks, First laugh – 3 months,

First lifted head – 2 weeks, First reach and grab – 4 months,

First sat up alone – 5 months, First tooth (front left upper) – 5 months

She was barely aware of her cellmate trudging across the room, grabbing the toilet paper, and setting it next to her.

She didn't bother wiping away the tears. They spilled over her cheeks and fell from her chin, battering the report like rain drops on a tin roof.

Cameron was safe. That was the silver lining. But every day that passed was another inch, another tooth, another word, another missed memory.

She ran her fingers through her hair and glanced over at the Bible lying face down on her pillow. She could already recount from memory the genealogy from Adam to David as well as most of the 613 statutes and ordinances from the Torah. But Levitical Law was not getting her any closer to her son. What she needed was a *Florida Rules of Court.*

26

A key rapped against the plexiglass. Miranda's eyes snapped awake. The short guard with frosted hair was standing at the door. Dixie was doing pushups on her knuckles. The flap unlocked and fell open.

"Adams?" Her voice sounded like 50 years of nicotine and black coffee.

Dixie grunted but kept pumping. Miranda shrugged and smiled.

"Inmate Adams," the guard repeated.

Delilah's voice murmured something unintelligible from next door. Miranda could guess what it was.

"Damn it Maynard!" the guard turned and yelled down the tier. "What did I tell you about asking me about that stupid ass election! Biden won but they got evidence of fraud and the president ain't conceding. Now quit bugging me about it every time I walk through here. Next time I'm gonna write you up."

The muted sound of Delilah's voice again . . .

"I don't know. I'll think of something." The guard turned back to Dixie who was washing her hands. "Adams, you going to rec or what? I ain't got all day."

Her neighbor pounded three times on the wall in celebration of the news. *Biden won!* Miranda responded with three consecutive elbows.

Dixie shot her a withering look.

She held up her hands. "Sorry."

"Now Adams," the guard clicked her cuffs, "you know I can't let you out of this cell without your mask on."

Dixie exhaled a breath of disgust and stormed over to her bunk to retrieve the mask from beneath her mat. Then she walked back across the cell and shoved her clenched fists through the flap.

Metal clicked and locked. The guard drew her radio from its holster with a flourish, spinning it like a gunfighter in the wild west. "Tango, roll 2212."

"Can I go too?" said Miranda.

"Maybe next time, Red." The guard held up a folded printout with a list of names. "You've got to be in here for 30 days before you're eligible."

The door popped. Dixie stepped out on the tier. Miranda felt her hand raise to wave goodbye as the door slammed shut, a totally impulsive and reflexive act. Muscle memory. She caught herself on the way up and tried to pull back at the last second, but this only added to the awkwardness. Dixie scowled at her through the plexiglass, then she was gone.

Miranda stretched, yawned, and looked around the cell. At least she would have an hour or so of privacy. She had been holding her poop for a couple of days. She walked over to the door and watched the women downstairs cuff up and emerge from their cells, smiling behind their masks, shouting greetings to friends and lovers. They were escorted two at a time through a side door and locked inside the cages below her back window.

She dampened a square of toilet paper and wiped off the seat before wiggling out of her uniform pants, praying she wouldn't catch staph. She'd been lucky so far. Dixie's back was covered with zits and there was no reason to believe that conditions were any better south of her waistline.

One thing she did not miss about opiates was the constipation. It was nice to let nature do its thing without all the straining and sweating. She lifted her shirt to inspect her stretch marks. There were a few on her stomach and a couple more on her thighs. Not bad for zero cocoa butter, hard jail water, and a vitamin-deficient diet.

Battle scars, said her inner narrator.

As she finished up, her eyes came to rest on the stack of legal envelopes beneath her cellmate's bunk.

Don't you dare. Don't even think about it.

The rec yard for confinement was really just a spit of concrete with chain-link covering the top and sides, divided into sections—what many referred to as *dog runs*. She pressed her face against the cool glass and looked for Dixie. Her cellmate had a cage all to herself. She continued doing pushups on her knuckles as other women rolled up their sleeves and pants legs and attempted to wring the sun from the November sky.

Delilah pounded the wall again.

Miranda glanced back at the flap. It was closed.

More pounding.

She looked down at the rec cages once more then walked over to the door.

"Are you there?" Her neighbor's muffled voice barely registered through the steel.

Miranda buried her face in the crack. "Yes."

"Lay on the floor," Delilah instructed. "I can't hear you."

She sank to all fours, then her stomach. "I'm here."

"Your bunkie is extremely dangerous," said Delilah. "I wanted to tell you before, but I didn't want to enrage her by talking about her on the flap while she was in the cell."

"So I've heard." Miranda blew a dust bunny under the door. "What happened to her?"

"I heard she was in the military. Afghanistan. They say an I.E.D. blew up in her face."

"Wow. That's terrible."

"Yeah, but listen. She's not right in the head. Very violent woman. You should not be in there with her. My bunkie goes back to the compound on Tuesday. I'm gonna see if I can get you moved into my cell . . ."

Miranda was silent.

"I mean if you want," Delilah added.

"It's not what *I* want," said Miranda. "It's what Lieutenant Grantham wants. And he apparently wants my cellmate to rip me into little pieces and flush me down the toilet."

"Grantham? Is that who you were talking about the other day? He *just* made lieutenant." She laughed. "He can't override Captain McCauley. I was his security orderly for all of 2019. Trust me, he'll move you if I ask him to."

Again, Miranda stared at the mysterious stack of manila envelopes beneath Dixie's bunk.

Remember what she said? her inner narrator tugged at the hem of her consciousness. *She said she would make your face look just like hers if she caught you digging through her stuff. I believe her.*

"So Biden won!" Delilah shifted gears. "Finally, some good news, right?"

"Mm hmm, finally." Miranda continued to stare. "Listen, I'm going to get off this floor for a little while."

"Okay, but think about what I said. You're not sup-posed to be in that cell anyway."

She leapt to her feet with surprising agility. Between opiates and pregnancy and postpartum, it felt like ages since she was active. She attempted a couple of Dixie punches on the way to the back window.

Don't kid yourself, her inner narrator smirked.

The cages were packed with women. A few were stretching, most were talking, masks slung low like chin straps. The guard propped her chair against the build-ing, her short legs swinging in the shade. In a nearby cage, two middle-aged women wrapped skeletal fingers around the chain-link and hung on her every word. Against the silence of the cell, their exaggerated laughter was even more pronounced, more pitiful. Buttery teeth and tomato gums flashed from pale malnourished faces. A few feet away, Dixie stalked. A caged lioness. When her granite glare turned up toward the window, Miranda took a step back.

She wondered how long rec lasted. Delilah would know, but calling her back to the door meant another conversation about the election and Miranda had other things on her mind.

This is not about learning law, said her inner narrator. *This is about you being nosy. This is about you invading your cellmate's privacy. She's in prison for murder! That should tell you everything you need to know. Let's read the Bible some more. See what David's up to. Come on.*

Miranda crawled beneath her bunk and carefully grabbed the stack of envelopes and documents, dragging them out into the center of the cell. After another quick check of the window, she grabbed the first thick packet, sat cross-legged on the floor, and opened Dixie's trial transcripts.

It was mostly dry reading, but through tedious questioning of the medical examiner, a forensic psychologist, a DNA expert, and the Miccosukee airboat pilot who found the bloated corpse of a South Miami drug dealer in the sawgrass, a story began to emerge.

Dixie was arrested in 2007 for the brutal murder of a man named Rudy Rodriguez. She might have gotten away with it were it not for the hair of a dog. After an estimated month decomposing in the Everglades sun, neither the rain nor the humidity nor scavenging animals could completely compromise the crime scene. The victim's tattered clothing contained traces of something called Presa Canario, better known as Canary Island Mastiff. A trip to the home of a local breeder led detectives straight to Dixie, whose altered face matched the description of a person of interest whom the victim's Coconut Grove neighbor referred to as *el feo*, Spanish for *the ugly man.* She attempted to escape into the mangroves but was slowed by the taser of the arresting officer. A pat search located the murder weapon on her person, something called a karambit knife (Exhibit F). Although no traces of DNA remained, the hooked blade and serrated edge were consistent with the victim's numerous lacerations and puncture wounds, the most gruesome of which was to the scrotum. Mr. Rodriguez's testicles were never found.

The trial lasted three days. The defense called a paltry number of witnesses: an aunt, a medical practitioner, a mental health counselor. Dixie did not take the stand. In a matter of hours, the jury returned a guilty verdict and the judge sentenced her to life without parole.

Deservedly so, said her inner narrator.

The next manila envelope contained a notice of appeal followed by something called an *Anders* brief, which was basically the public defender's office for the Third District Court of Appeal saying they found scant appealable issues in her case. The next document was from the clerk of court notifying her that her judgment and sentence had been *per curiam affirmed*. Miranda stared at the paper and tried to make sense of the Latin. The word *affirmed* generally carried positive connotations, but something told her it was exactly the opposite in the inverted world of the legal system. The final document erased any doubt. A single sheet of paper with the word *Mandate* in bold font at the top. Her life sentence was official.

She reached for the next item in the stack, a bloated packet of single-sided pages held together by a rusty staple. The heading caused her pulse to quicken. *Motion to vacate, set aside, or correct.* This was what Tussie was referring to in quarantine, a 3.850 motion, the proper vehicle to challenge the ineffectiveness of her attorney, Colton Tipton.

Comes now, it began—

The door rumbled slightly. Her head whipped to the right, her heart thumping in her ears. Close-set eyes narrowed over a black FDC mask.

"What are you doing?" said Lieutenant Grantham.

"Reading," she swallowed and held up the motion, grateful that it was not Dixie returning from rec.

"You're not supposed to have any property in disciplinary confinement," he sneered.

"It's just legal work," she said, praying he would not press the issue.

He glared at her for another few seconds, possibly surveying her skin for signs of violence, then he sauntered off. She jumped up and went to the door in time to see him going down the stairs. The wing was otherwise mausoleum silent. She checked the back window once more. Dixie was still pacing. The orderly was passing out Styrofoam cups of water from a bright yellow cooler. Miranda sat back down on the floor in front of the stack of envelopes and continued reading the 3.850.

The writing was horrible. Clunky and meandering sentences, kindergarten punctuation, disfigured words. She was fairly certain that *pro se* meant that Dixie had authored the motion herself. No self-respecting law school graduate would dare file such drivel in a court of law. Still, there was a discernible format that she could follow in the anatomy of the brief—the case statement, the standard of review *(Strickland v. Washington),* each ground in bold below a roman numeral followed by sub-paragraphs of (a) background facts, (b) deficient performance, and (c) prejudice.

In ham-handed and unartistic prose, Dixie attempted to lay out her public defender's ineffectiveness, citing four separate issues that appeared to be copied from a book: counsel's failure to file a motion to suppress evidence, failure to conduct adequate pretrial investigation, failure to object to hearsay, failure to file a sufficient judgment of acquittal.

The language and legibility devolved from there.

A door slammed. She barely noticed. She was too busy imagining her own 3.850. What issues would she cite for deficient performance? If what Tipton promised her about gain time was untrue, then she had at least one legitimate claim. But there was also the fact that she accepted her plea agreement in a dense postpartum fog. She wondered if that was grounds for relief. And then there was the search and seizure itself.

So much to investigate, so much to learn. If she could only get to the law library . . . She sighed as she reached for the largest envelope. Someone else's name was blacked out with a marker and Dixie's DC number was written below it. Rolls of masking tape had been used to offset erosion and fortify against tearing. She reached inside and tugged on the contents. Some type of booklet. It appeared to be homemade—a mustard-yellow folder wrapped around a thick sheaf of paper, swollen with time and Florida humidity, bound with rubber bands. She flipped it over and read the peeling cover.

The Prisoner's Guide to Post-Conviction Relief by Tussie Jones.

Goosebumps rippled down her arms. She gawked at the title. But just as she began to remove the rubber bands, she heard laughter and shouting out on the wing. Still clutching the folder, she jumped up and hurried over to the door.

Dixie was halfway up the stairs. Her diminutive escort was gripping her massive elbow, more hanging on for dear life than providing stability and balance.

Miranda quickly gathered the spread of documents and did her best to arrange them in the order she found them, then she pushed the stack back under the bunk. Fear and excitement coursed through her bloodstream like atoms in a particle accelerator. *Tussie Jones!* She could not believe that Dixie had a typed manual authored by her old cellmate stashed in her legal work. What were the chances? Her dad would call it a glitch in the matrix. Professor Bonilla would label it a statistical anomaly. Amity would say it was a breadcrumb from the universe.

She could hear keys jingling on the tier. "Damn it Maynard! Can I just walk past your cell *one time* without you asking me some political question? I don't know who won the Georgia Senate seats and I don't give a damn, okay?"

Miranda smiled and glanced over at the stack of envelopes a final time. *Destiny?* To her horror, there was a clear dragline swerving through the dust beneath Dixie's bunk.

With alarm bells clanging in her head, she sprang into action, snatching a maxi-pad from beneath her mat and diving for the incriminating evidence. One rainbow swipe erased her tracks. Two more, and she was raking a blanket of dust into the center of the cell.

Hair and dead skin cells, announced her inner narrator as she turned to her own bunk.

She could feel Dixie's massive presence appear in the plexiglass, but she kept cleaning. "Gosh, this place is filthy."

"Tango, roll 2212," rasped the guard.

The door popped open. Her cellmate stepped inside. Miranda busied herself wiping down the toilet as Dixie's handcuffs were removed. Once the flap slammed and they were alone, Dixie stood over the mound of dust in the center of the cell.

"What is this?"

"Huh?" Miranda looked up, vigorously scouring the sink. "Oh, I'll get that. It's just dust. When was the last time you cleaned in here?"

Dixie crossed her arms. "If you fucked with any of my shit, I'm going to kill you."

27

She arranged the envelopes on her bunk, removed the contents of each, and methodically thumbed through the pages, scowling as she searched for signs of malfeasance.

"So, am I going to live?" said Miranda with forced flippancy. "Or should I prepare to meet my maker?"

Dixie muttered something under her breath.

"Because, I'll be totally honest . . . I'm a little nervous." She patted her Bible. "So far, He doesn't seem like a very tolerant guy."

"You talk too much," Dixie growled.

"I'm sorry about what happened to you. The roadside bomb? That must have been so painful . . . and terrifying." Miranda searched the wreckage of her face. "Thank you for serving."

"Shut up."

Cell doors and flaps continued to slam down the wing as more women returned from rec.

"Fine." Miranda grabbed the letter from under her pillow. "I'll be over here reading my own legal mail if you need me."

Cameron's smile burst forth from the envelope when she opened it. A line from the Book of Psalms came back to her as she traced his cherubic face. Something about God "knitting together a child in the mother's womb."

That was her baby—perfect, flawless, God-knit. She had to get home.

Satisfied, Dixie began to stack the transcripts and documents that were spread out over her wool blanket. "Who's he staying with? Your momma?"

Miranda looked up. "He's in a foster home. I told you that the other night."

"The other night? I couldn't make out a word you said. All that damn blubbering."

She returned to the pictures. He wore a blue little onesie with a sailboat on it. His expression was curious, similar to the night of his birth. *Do I know you?* Out of the corner of her eye, she noticed Dixie shaking her head. She carefully refolded the pictures and slid them back into the envelope.

"What is it?"

"Huh?"

"Why are you shaking your head?"

Dixie knelt beside her bunk and pushed the stack of legal work all the way back against the wall. Then she stood and clapped the dust from her hands. "Have you ever been in foster care?"

"No," said Miranda. "Have you?"

"I got lucky." Her gravelly voice filled the cell. "I had an aunt take me in."

Miranda scooted toward the end of her bunk. "What happened to your mom and dad?"

She deflected the question with a scowl. "That's irrelevant. But I worked inside grounds with a girl, maybe ten years ago. She had a kid in foster care. The cops raided the house on a tip from a neighbor and found her son locked in the closet, eating drywall. Thirteen years old and he weighed less than 40 pounds."

"That's . . . that's horrible."

Dixie nodded. "The guardian wasn't missing any meals though. I saw her mugshot in the paper. She probably had forty pounds in neck fat alone. Those DCF checks can really fill up a refrigerator."

"Well, my son is in a good home," said Miranda. "And anyway, he won't be there long. I just need to get to the library and get this motion filed."

You're just going to breeze in and file a motion, are you? her inner narrator smirked. *You might need to actually learn the law first, Mensa.*

"What motion is that?" Dixie rasped.

"A 3.850."

"Good luck," she scoffed. "Ten percent of the people who file those things might get a hearing. Maybe two percent get relief."

Miranda wondered if she got her statistics from Tussie's homemade manual. "Why are you so negative?"

"I'm just a realist." She leaned back in her bunk, crossed her massive arms.

The hum of recycled air filled the cell. Miranda picked at her blanket. She kept finding metal shavings embedded in the wool, lighter than Brillo. *Tinsel?*

"The president says a person needs three things to be happy: someone to love, something to do, and something to look forward to."

Dixie looked mildly surprised. "Really? Trump said that?"

Miranda shook her head. "Biden."

"He's not the president yet. You heard the guard say they were recounting."

"True," said Miranda, not wanting to argue. "But politics aside, what Biden said makes sense. I love my son and my dad. That one's easy. My *something to do* is to commit every ounce of brainpower I can generate into learning the law. And I'm looking forward to getting out of here. Those things keep me going."

"Good for you," Dixie muttered.

"What about you?" Miranda pressed. "I know you like to work out and practice martial arts. What about the other stuff? Who do you love? What are you looking forward to?"

"Love?" Dixie chuckled. "Get real. Look at my face. Do I look loveable to you?"

Miranda tried to hold her gaze but was unsuccessful.

"What am I looking forward to? You shutting the fuck up would be a nice start." A half-smile flickered and dimmed on the scar tissue of her lips. "Especially all that liberal nonsense you spew under the door. Do you really think 80-year-old Joe Biden is going to come galloping in on his white horse and save America?"

"He's 78," said Miranda.

"Same shit."

"I think he'll lower the national temperature. Just like he promised. That's a start."

She pushed exasperated air through the thin flesh of her lips. "That's the difference between us. You see the government as the solution. I see them as the problem."

"What about Trump?" Miranda couldn't resist. "Do you see him as the problem?"

"Damn right," said Dixie. "He's a problem for radical Islam and illegal immigrants and Pelosi and the globalists and the swamp. He's the best thing that ever happened to this country."

Of course, Miranda saw it differently. The world had gotten meaner over the last four years. And dangerous. America felt less like a bellwether for freedom and democracy and more like a punchline for dysfunction. The needle of truth was buried in a haystack of fake news and alternate facts. Two hundred forty years of precedence and norms had been swatted aside by a spoiled billionaire, bloated with ego and power. Meanwhile emboldened copycat authoritarians were popping up all over the globe, hate groups were on the rise, scientists were receiving death threats, and Planet Earth was sputtering around the sun like a rickety ride at the Pensacola Interstate Fair.

They're still searching for her victim's testicles, her inner narrator pointed out. *That's pretty much a universal red flag. You've already rifled through her legal work. Do you really want to argue with her about the damaging effects of Trumpism?*

She cleared her throat, selected her words. "Biden will be inheriting an unparalleled mess—"

"Unparalleled." Dixie shook her head. "Typical elitist word. And Biden has to actually *win* the election to inherit anything."

"Right," said Miranda, "but if things continue to move in that direction, he'll have his hands full from day one. Between the global pandemic, the economic collapse, the racial unrest, and this deeply divided country—"

"Blah, blah, blah. You sound like ABC News. Have you ever had an original thought? Or do you just walk around parroting other people's opinions all day?"

Miranda closed her eyes. "I just want the world to be boring and predictable again. No matter what party is in power. I'm sick of the evening news being must-see TV. I used to be the only person I knew who cared about politics. Now it's all anybody talks about. Look at us, two prisoners on lockdown. We should be talking about cliché prison stuff—freedom and mean girls and gossip and drugs—"

"I hate drugs."

"—but instead we're in here talking politics. Just like everyone else in America. Look, Biden promised to lower the national temperature. That's all I care about at this point. A safer, less volatile world. For my baby's sake."

"Security is a myth. It doesn't exist in nature."

"Thank you, Dixie. That's very encouraging."

"I told you I'm a realist." She shrugged. "You want liberal coddling, go yell under the door to your little friend."

Miranda curled up in her bunk and slid the envelope beneath her pillow. "I think I'd rather take a nap."

28

A procession of days staggered by. Tuesday was the mirror image of Monday, and Wednesday and Thursday were identical. Dixie shadowboxed before dawn and did pushups before lunch. Miranda read the Bible after dinner. The orderly swept and mopped, the guards walked every hour. Only the meals changed and even those were predictable after a while.

Fat drops of rain began pelting the window on Friday night. By Saturday morning the rec cages were flooded, and lightning pulsed in the sky. Miranda normally craved this kind of weather—she could press her head against the plexiglass and watch it come down for hours. There was something so relaxing about thunderstorms. But on this particular weekend she was impatient for the sun to break free from the smoldering black clouds and shine its warm radiant light down on the prison. Especially the chain-link cages on the back side of Tango dorm.

Inclement weather meant no rec, and if recreation was cancelled, then it could be another week before she had the opportunity to sneak a peek at Tussie's post-conviction manual.

As if reading her intentions, an inverted Dixie glared at her from a handstand pushup position in the corner of the cell. Her face looked even more grotesque upside down and purple with strain.

"Adams! What in the hale are yew doing?" A round face with massive jowls and deep creases in his forehead fogged the window with breath. "Is that some type of yo-gurt?"

Dixie pushed her rigid body up the cinder blocks, held the position, then lowered herself back down.

A second chin swung in his mask like a hammock as he shook his head in wonder. "Well, would you looka there. Ain't too many cadets at the academy that could pull that off. I sure as hale can't. Not now, not twenty years ago."

Sweat dripped into the concrete beneath her as Dixie grunted and elevated yet again, ignoring him. Miranda noted the captain's bars on the collar of his white shirt.

He dug a finger in his ear. "McGuire?"

"Yes sir."

He inspected his nail, frowned at the findings, and wiped them on the door. "Pack up. You're moving."

Dixie paused, mid rep.

"Moving?" said Miranda. "Where to?"

"Next door." He jerked his head in the direction of Delilah's cell. "With Maynard."

Slowly, with incredible control and core strength, Dixie lowered her bare feet to the floor. Then she stood, rolling her thick neck as she grabbed the towel from the end of her bunk.

Miranda watched her stride across the cell. "Can I refuse?"

His face twitched with impatience. "Why in the hale would yew wanna refuse?"

I can answer that, said her inner narrator. *Because you want to rifle through your cellmate's personal belongings.*

But it wasn't just the mysterious manual tucked away in her legal work that caused Miranda to hesitate; it was the fact that Dixie was fascinating—the scorched terrain of her face, her physical mastery, her shadowy military past, her allegiance to Trump . . . If she were to move next door, what would the conversations be like? A vanilla political roundtable with no firebrand conservative to pound the podium and defend the indefensible. *Boring.* Plus leaving her felt like a betrayal. How many people had abandoned Dixie in her life? She said an aunt saved her from foster care, but she never received any mail and was obviously friendless. Amity weighed heavy enough on her conscience and on her heart. She could not allow coldness to become a pattern.

"I think I'm comfortable right here."

"Aw, looka there," drawled the captain, "the little red heifer is comfortable. Well, this ain't about yer comfort level, darlin'. It's about compatibility."

Did he just call you a little red heifer?

She glanced at Dixie. "We're compatible, right?"

Her cellmate's face was as impassive as ever. She swung the towel around her thick neck and gripped both ends.

"Naw, y'all ain't compatible. Adams is a close custody inmate serving a life sentence. Yew are a medium three. Now pack yer shit and cuff up. I ain't got all night."

Miranda was suddenly furious with Delilah or Maynard or whatever her name was. Nobody asked her to orchestrate this little power move in the first place. "So let me get this straight—our *compatibility* wasn't an issue for the last few weeks that I've been living in this cell, but for some reason today you just decided that it was an intolerable situation that could no longer persist."

He looked at his watch. "Something like that."

"It's okay," Dixie rasped. "Just let her stay. You know as well as I do that plenty of the girls back here aren't compatible. We get along all right. She's not in danger."

"Yew forget who was O.I.C. the last time we had to come down and pull yer poor cellmate out of there . . . on a stretcher!"

Dixie shrugged. "She wouldn't stop singing."

Note to self . . . said her inner narrator.

"I never sing," said Miranda. "I'm tone deaf and I have no rhythm. I don't even whistle."

He shook his head. "Sorry ladies. Policy."

"What if I told you that there was gonna be a problem if you moved me next door?"

He squinted through the plexiglass. "Are yew making threats?"

She could feel Dixie staring at her. "No, I'm just making you aware of the fact that there's an issue with the woman next door. I'm already stuck back here for assaulting one inmate. I would prefer to do my time in peace. Right here." She glanced at Dixie. "In this cell."

A burst of activity erupted from his radio. He adjusted the volume and glared at her. The standoff persisted for what felt like a full minute. Seconds fell like dominoes. Finally, he looked away, expelling a defeated huff of air. "Yew know what? Fine. Yew wanna stay in here, knock yerself out. But if something happens to yew, it's yer own damned fault."

He turned and lumbered down the tier. "I tried," she heard him say as he passed Delilah's cell.

"Yesss!" Miranda clapped and went for a celebratory high-five with her cellmate.

Dixie frowned at her hand.

29

"Twelve!" shouted the girl in 2201. "Yard closed!"

The door slammed. Keys rattled. A squeaky wheel shrieked.

"Bitch that ain't twelve! That's Daniels!"

"Hey sugar. Who you got with you?"

Miranda felt the tightening surge of oncoming cramps as she swung her legs over the side of the bunk. Her period would be coming soon. She walked to the door in her socks.

"Where you been, Daniels? Vacay?" a woman downstairs yelled under the door.

"I heard you was out with corona," yelled another. "You okay, baby?"

The inmate walking with the lanky guard looked vaguely familiar, but between the uniforms and masks it was difficult to tell anyone apart. Her crisp blues were tapered at the ankle like skinny jeans with razor sharp creases, her mahogany skin glistened beneath the fluorescent lighting. Her wavy black hair was faded on the sides like a mohawk. She pushed the noisy cart to the foot of the stairs and grabbed a bulky file from the metal basket. Daniels laughed at something she said on the way up the steps. They appeared to be familiar with one another.

"Hey law clerk! You got anything for me on that cart? Earlene Reeves? I wrote y'all last week!"

Miranda whirled from the window. "Law clerks come back here?"

Dixie stared up at the ceiling, fingers interlocked behind her shaved head. "Sometimes."

When she spun back around, they were standing outside the door. Duval winked at her and pressed a finger against her masked lips as Daniels unlocked the flap.

Miranda's eyes widened. "What are you doing back here?"

Duval set the folder on the flap and checked her name off the top of the confinement visit list. "I've still got my certification from my last time in prison. My homegirl got me back in the library. Rookie clerks always get the bullshit jobs. It was either argue with bitches about their time on the computers or make confinement rounds." Her eyes crinkled at the corners. "And I suck at arguing."

Miranda felt like crying. "I didn't know you were a law clerk!"

Duval nodded. "Law clerk, teacher's aide, impaired assistant . . . I've got every certificate they offer. I even got HVAC certified here back in 2014. Didn't do me any good when I got out though. Most air conditioning companies pass on black lesbian ex-convicts for some reason."

Miranda smiled. "How's Throkkie?"

"Messy as ever. We're in the dorm together. She tried to get me to play *Dungeons and Dragons* with her and some skinny little white girl with big teeth." She glanced over at Daniels. "Hey, let me holla at her for a minute."

The guard shook his head. "I can't leave you unsupervised. You know we're on camera."

Duval sucked her teeth. "I ain't asking you to leave. Just see what the girl next door wants. She was calling you when we walked by anyway."

"She wants to know how many people died from Covid so far." Daniels rolled his eyes. "I don't pay attention to that stuff."

"250,000," said Duval. "I saw it on Good Morning America yesterday. Now go."

Daniels hesitated.

"Go on," she urged. "I need to holla at my girl in private."

Pouting, he stomped over to Delilah's door and unlocked the flap.

"Is that accurate?" said Miranda. "250,000 people?"

Duval nodded, opened the folder, and knelt at the flap. "Yeah, it's bad out there. Bad on the compound too. But check this out, I've got some shit for you." She pushed a stack of paperwork forward. "Here's the caselaw you requested."

"I didn't request any caselaw." Miranda frowned. "Wait, I can request caselaw?"

"Girl, quit acting like you just got off the damn county van!" she hissed. "Of course, you can request caselaw."

Miranda thumbed through the pages. "None of this applies to my charges. It's all armed robbery . . . racketeering . . . sexual battery?"

Duval glanced toward the ceiling and shook her head. "I swear, you're as green as Rocky sometimes."

Miranda smiled at the mispronunciation. It was good to see her friend.

"Just make sure you read Maddox versus Florida thoroughly. Okay?"

Miranda nodded.

Duval looked her in the eye and reiterated for emphasis. "Maddox, thoroughly."

"Got it," said Miranda.

"You know you owe me, right?"

Miranda remembered the bag of canteen that was stolen along with Cameron's birth certificate. "I don't have any money Duval. I'm sorry."

She pushed more paper through the flap. "You do now."

Miranda scanned the top page. "A 1040 Form? You're not wanting me to commit tax fraud, are you? I'm already in so much trouble and I'm trying to get home to my baby before—"

"Girl hush! Ain't nobody telling you to commit fraud. A new ruling just came out in the Northern District of California. Scholl versus Mnuchin, however you say that shit. That stimulus check that Trump cut earlier this year? Prisoners get it too!"

Miranda turned the form over. The last time she filed a tax return was for her dad in 2019.

"Long as I've been doing time, I've never seen no shit like this. Twelve hundred dollars for every prisoner in America? I hate to see Trump go. I know you can't stand him but . . . Obama never sent me an *economic impact payment*." She pushed an example form through the flap. "*E.I.P.* You put those letters right at the top, see? Fill it out just like this."

Officer Daniels returned. "We need to wrap it up. I still have to feed and get laundry passed out before shift change."

"Almost done," said Duval. "I brought you some extra stamped envelopes to send in the form and also to write your people. I'm sure they're worried about you. Give one to your bunkie too." She looked behind Miranda and into the cell for the first time. "What the fuck! Girl, who they got you in there with? A damn monster?"

"A friend." She glanced over her shoulder at Dixie. "A good friend."

"Oh." Duval swallowed, visibly shaken. Then her eyes widened. *"Ohhh . . ."*

"Not like that." Miranda changed the subject. "Hey, can you send me information on how to file a 3.850?"

"Just send a request to the law library for whatever you need. Statutes, caselaw, whatever. I'll send you the whole law clerk training manual if you want."

"Please," Miranda breathed.

"You got any request forms in there?"

She shook her head.

Duval slapped a stack on the flap. "Here."

Officer Daniels removed his keys from his belt. "All right. We gotta go."

"One more thing." Duval carefully removed another small stack of paper from the folder and pushed it through the slot. "I made you a few copies, just in case."

Cameron's birth certificate. "When . . . how did you?"

"I had it the whole time," said Duval. "I put your property under the bench with mine that morning."

Relief washed over her as she stared at his little footprints. "Why?"

"My canteen was in your pillowcase. Remember? I didn't want nobody to steal it."

"Why didn't you stop me?"

"Wasn't no stopping you," said Duval. "You were on a mission! Before I could even get a word out, you were choking the shit outta that girl." She laughed and shook her head. "I didn't know you had it in you."

Daniels reached around her and gently shut the flap before she could say anything else. Duval smiled and shot her the peace sign. "Maddox. Don't forget."

Miranda nodded and made a heart with her thumbs and fingers. "Tell Throkkie I said hi."

She pressed her face against the glass and watched them vanish down the tier. Then she walked back to her bunk, smiling at her baby's footprints.

You should be ashamed of yourself, her inner narrator scolded. *That poor girl.*

She sat down and separated the certificates from the 1040s and request forms and caselaw, sorting them into piles. The sample tax return form was stapled to a letter from a prisoner advocacy group with detailed instructions and a mailing address for the Department of the Treasury.

Twelve hundred dollars. She wondered if she could send hers to Cameron.

Raucous laughter exploded from the next bunk, filling the cell. She dropped the instructions and stared at the back of Dixie's convulsing head. Dixie the grouch. Dixie the lifer. Dixie the detesticalizer. Dixie, who rarely spoke and never smiled . . . laughing her ass off.

"What's so funny?" said Miranda.

It took her a moment to answer. She gathered herself, wiped tears on her sleeve. "You beat that chick's ass for absolutely nothing. I keep picturing you blowing a gasket . . . taking her down." Another outburst. She fell back in the bunk, holding her side. "Classic."

30

Dinner was a pile of suspicious-smelling gray meatballs on a bed of cold spaghetti. Miranda nibbled a slice of bread and gave the rest of her tray to Dixie.

For the first time since she moved into the cell, her bunkie hesitated. "You sure? You're going to waste away in here if you don't eat something."

Miranda waved her off, pulled her hair into a bun, and got down to business.

Most of the cases were from one of Florida's five district courts of appeal. There was also a United States Supreme Court decision that dealt with juvenile life sentences and a Federal 2255 out of the Northern District of Ohio. None of them applied to Miranda's charges, nor did they have much to do with one another. They seemed to have been printed randomly with no rhyme or reason. She spread them out over her bunk and scanned the bold print.

Alien phrases and impenetrable legalese leapt up at her from every page, esoteric terms like *stare decisis* and *fatal variance* and *manifest injustice*.

Fruit from a poisonous tree? What the hell is that supposed to mean?

The words taunted her. Doubt began to seep in. What did she think she was doing? People went to college for an additional three years to grasp the intricacies of jurisprudence. She was out of her league.

I know, right? said her inner narrator. *That Colton Tipton was a real scholar.*

The dimpled chin and gelled, cowlicked coiffure of her frat boy public defender swam to the surface of her memory.

She chewed her lip and stared at the rambling case citations. *348 So. 2d 1119; 2005 . . .* The foreign sequences were a language all their own. They read like thorny polynomial expressions. She was a stranger in a strange land, a tourist with no dictionary and no road map.

It's a puzzle, Andy. Her dad took a drag from his cigarette and blew smoke across the kitchen table of time. *You love puzzles. Just relax and focus. You'll get it.*

She reached for *Maddox v. Florida* and leaned back against the wall that bordered her bunk.

"Hey Dixie Adams," a voice thundered. "Bring your big Xena Warrior self to the door!"

Miranda looked up from the case summary. Surprisingly, Dixie rolled straight out of her bunk. There might have even been a smile on her face. It was difficult to tell with her. "Who's there?"

"Ooohh, your voice is so raspy. You sound like Vin Diesel . . . making me horny."

Her cellmate glanced back at her with a sheepish expression, her scar tissue reddening with embarrassment. "What do you want, Tasha?"

"You know damn well what I want. Revenge! You still got your board in there?"

Dixie crossed her arms, spoke to the door. "You can't win."

"That's a lie and you know it. I beat you plenty of times when we were on close management. Remember quad four during the hurricane? Yeah, now you got amnesia. I even beat you last time I was downstairs in 2112. I bet somebody in here remembers that. It was right before I got moved to the psych cell."

"Which time?"

"Oh you got jokes, like your big musclebound bipolar ass ain't never went psych. You know I know better." Her laughter filled the wing. "Hey, this white girl in the cell with me is talking shit about Trump. Want me to punch her in the face for you?"

Dixie turned and shot Miranda a look. "Maybe just slap her around a little."

"Stop it!" she mouthed. Delilah was still not speaking to her.

"You serious?" said Tasha.

"No!" Miranda yelled. "She's not."

"Is that your bunkie? She know about you?"

"Do you want to play or what?" Dixie rasped.

"Set the damn board up."

She avoided eye contact as she knelt beside her bunk and pulled out her legal work.

"Who is that?" said Miranda.

"An old enemy," she muttered.

Miranda sat up straighter when she noticed the thick, taped manila envelope that Dixie selected from the stack. She watched with rapt attention as the manual was removed and the constraining rubber bands pulled from the folder.

The Prisoner's Guide to Post-Conviction Relief by Tussie Jones.

Dixie dropped it on her bunk, flipped through the typewritten pages until she found an envelope. Then she walked back to the door and sat down in front of it.

Miranda craned her neck to read the open page.

When determining claims of ineffective assistance of trial counsel, the court must evaluate the defendant's claim under the two-prong analysis set forth in Strickland v. Washington . . .

Dixie pulled two folded gain time sheets from the rumpled number ten envelope and smoothed them out on the concrete. When she turned them over and placed them side by side, a perfect grid of 64 black and white squares appeared beneath the fluorescent.

Miranda tossed the Maddox case aside and walked over to the door, lingering briefly at Dixie's bunk to absorb more of Tussie's legal writing.

Defense counsel's failure to _____
was deficient performance that prejudiced defendant because _____. *Consequently, defendant was denied effective assistance and due process under the State and U.S. Constitutions . . .*

Dixie overturned the envelope. Small squares of paper rained down like confetti. Some were shaded in pen; some were left white. Each had a letter in the center, etched in bold.

"Is that a checkerboard?"

"Something like that," Dixie rasped.

"What do the letters mean?"

She looked annoyed. "Have you ever played chess?"

"Sure," said Miranda, "on my phone."

Dixie reached for a white piece of paper emblazoned with a capital *Q*. "This is the Queen." She positioned it on its home square, then began arranging the others. "*R* for Rooks, *B* for Bishops and *P* for the Pawns. I use *N* for the Knights since the King gets the *K*."

"Naturally," said Miranda as she surveyed the makeshift board. She thought back to the summer of 2019. Before Covid, before Cameron, before the bottom fell out of her old life. She remembered playing the *Checkmate* app in the lobby of the financial aid office at school. Never in a million years did she imagine that by age 20, she would be a spectator at a confinement unit chess match inside the nation's largest women's prison complex.

When Dixie placed the final black Pawn on its proper square across the board, she yelled under the door. "I'm white."

"Why do you always get to be white?" Tasha protested.

"Is that a trick question?" Dixie rasped. "I'll take the high road and just say it's because I kicked your ass the last time we played."

"I don't see why white should get to go first every time anyway," complained Tasha. "That is some racist ass, white privilege shit."

"Whenever you're done whining . . ." said Dixie.

"Hang on! I had to make some more Pawns."

Miranda frowned at the board. "How do you know where each other moves?"

Dixie cracked her knuckles. "The vertical columns are called *files*. They run *A* through *H*. The horizontal rows are called *ranks*, numbered *1* through *8*." She picked up her Queen's Knight. "This was on *B1*." She dropped it in front of the Pawn on the third column. "Now it's on *C3*. Knight to *C3*."

"Is that your move?" yelled Tasha.

"No, radar ears." Dixie returned the Knight to its home square. "It's not."

"Well, tighten up then," said Tasha. "I ain't got all night!"

"Yeah? You going somewhere?" Dixie pushed her King's Pawn to the center of the board. "Pawn, *E4*."

Tasha immediately countered with "Pawn, *C6*."

Miranda watched in fascination as Dixie reached across the board and slid the black Pawn forward to reflect her opponent's move. The ensuing rapid-fire sequence was so thrilling that, for a moment, she forgot the open manual on Dixie's bunk.

"Okay," Dixie rasped, "since you're giving me the center . . . Pawn, *D4*."

"Pawn, *D5*."

"Knight to *C3*."

"Pawn takes *E4*."

"My Knight takes your *E4* Pawn."

"I'm bringin' my Knight to *F6*."

"Queen, *D3*."

"That's a good move," said Tasha. "I remember I used to play like that. King's Pawn to *E5*. Let's dance."

"I'll take it," said Dixie. "*D4* takes *E5*."

"Oh you wanna trade Queens? Hell nah. Queen to *A5*. Check."

"That's a rec yard move," said Dixie. "Bishop, *D2*."

"Good, I'll take this Pawn. Queen, *D5*."

Dixie safely moved her King two squares to the left and brought her Rook to his right flank. "Castle."

"Why you runnin', Xena?" Tasha laughed. "Let's get some Knight-on-Knight violence in this bitch! *E6* all over *E4*." She let loose a passable horse whinny. "I believe that puts me up a piece."

Dixie studied the board.

Miranda studied Dixie.

After an ice age of silent contemplation, she picked up her Queen and dropped it on the *D8* square right next to Tasha's King, effectively sacrificing her most powerful piece.

"Why?" Miranda gasped.

Dixie looked back over the mountain range of her shoulder and said, "Queen, *D8*."

"Have you lost your damn mind?" said Tasha. She paused for a moment, then said, "You know I gotta take it. King, *D8*."

Dixie removed the white Queen from the board then slid her dark-squared Bishop diagonally up from *D2* to *G5*. "Bishop, *G5*. Check."

"Let's see, what do I wanna take this with? My Knight or my Queen?"

"Neither," Dixie rasped. "You're in double check. Look at the Rook. You have to move your King."

"Yeah, yeah. I see it now," Tasha grumbled. "King to *C7*."

"Check Mate," said Dixie. "Bishop to *D8*."

Miranda stared at the board, marveling at what she just witnessed transpire: Grandmaster-level chess shouted under a confinement unit door. She was the one with the alleged Mensa-level IQ, she was the one who spent two semesters of her junior year in the Washington High School Chess Club, yet it was obvious that either Dixie or Tasha would carve her to pieces on a chess board.

"I can't believe you sacrificed your Queen," said Tasha.

"I can't believe your game has gotten so predictable," Dixie taunted. "I should've taken my Queen off to begin with. It would've made it more interesting."

"Run that shit back!" Tasha's voice thundered beneath the door. "And this time I'm white."

She spun the board and began rearranging the pieces. Miranda clasped her hands behind her back, eased over to Dixie's bunk, and took a longer look at Tussie's handiwork. She wondered how long ago it was written.

"Hey, can I see this legal manual thing on your bed?"

"No," Dixie answered without looking up.

"Come on. Why are you being so mean? You know I'm trying to learn the law."

"So read the caselaw your friend brought you," Dixie growled.

"I will." She glanced at the Maddox case splayed out on her bunk. "I am. But I need to know the rules before I start researching cases. This post-conviction manual seems like it can teach me things that caselaw can't. Please."

"Pawn to *E4!*" shouted Tasha.

Dixie ignored her and glared across the cell at Miranda. "Quit begging. You're worse than Deuce."

"Who's Deuce?"

"My dog," she rasped.

"Can I get a move, please?" yelled Tasha.

"Don't be in such a rush to get your ass kicked!" Dixie barked at the door before turning back to Miranda. "Take the damned manual. Don't touch anything else."

"Thank you, thank you!" She hopped up and down.

With a look of disgust, Dixie turned her attention back to the makeshift chessboard. "Pawn, *E5*."

"Bout time," said Tasha. "Let's dance."

31

Lunch, Thanksgiving Day. The trays the orderly pushed through the flap were noticeably heavier. And for the first time since Miranda had been in confinement, the food smelled delicious. Her stomach rumbled as she surveyed the five slots: sliced turkey over mashed potatoes and gravy, a mound of stuffing with cranberry sauce, fresh salad, sauteed green beans, dinner rolls and pumpkin pie.

"Hell yeah!" Tasha shouted from next door. "Them girls in the kitchen did their thing on this one! Hey Dixie? Why don't you lead us in prayer?"

"Shut the fuck up." Her cellmate stuck a roll in her mouth.

"Amen and amen," Tasha laughed.

Miranda ate while she read.

Aside from the occasional misspelling, the maddening semicolons that seemed to sprout like weeds every three sentences, and her overuse of the word *hence*, Tussie's manual was concise and informative. After two readings she felt like she had a handle on the post-conviction process—time limits, frequently raised claims and controlling caselaw, even the history of the statutes. Now, as she sporked stuffing and cranberry sauce into her mouth, she drilled herself on what she had retained.

What is a 3.850 motion?

A secondary attack that challenges factual allegations not on the record and moves for post-conviction relief.

What's the difference between a 3.800 and a 3.850?

A 3.800 attacks only the sentence; a 3.850 attacks the judgment.

Name the five most common grounds for post-conviction relief as well as respective controlling cases.

Number one—the ineffective assistance of counsel, *Strickland versus Washington*. Number two—prosecution's failure to disclose materially exculpatory evidence, *Brady versus Maryland*. Three—prosecution's failure to disclose *possibly* exculpatory evidence, *Youngblood versus Arizona*. Four—prosecution's knowing use of perjured testimony, *Giglio versus United States*. Five—constructive denial of counsel, *United States versus Cronic*.

Many of the answers appeared in her mind just as they appeared in the manual: black typeface on quarter-century-old paper, the hook of the lowercase *r* consistently faded at the bend. Like a photocopy.

When she was a third grader, she used to think it was cheating. She felt guilty for doing it and hoped her dad never found out. But the rote memory technique that Ms. Sullivan inflicted upon her classroom seemed to drone on for hours. *"4 x 1 = 4, 4 x 2 = 8, 4 x 3 = 12 . . ."* Her mind would wander. The information didn't stick. When she was jarred from a daydream and forced to answer a question, she would panic and pull up a mental screenshot of the multiplication table. It was like reading the answer from the textbook.

Dixie ogled her tray from across the cell. "Anything you don't want . . ." she said through a mouthful of food.

Miranda took a bite of mashed potatoes and continued to go over Tussie's advice and analysis. Seeing the words in her head was one thing, and reciting them at will was useful, but she was not looking for topographical knowledge. She didn't merely want to repeat what she read, she wanted to grasp it. She wanted to know the soul of the law as it applied to her case, and she would keep drilling herself until it was a second language. This way, when the scanned documents in her mind began to dim and fade, as they always did, the knowledge would remain.

What are the two prongs of Strickland versus Washington?

"In order to prevail in accordance with the Strickland standard," she mumbled to herself, "defendant must show that counsel's performance was deficient, *and* that the deficiency prejudiced the defendant." She dipped a roll in gravy and took a bite. "Florida has applied this standard by requiring the defendant to demonstrate that the deficient performance had a reasonable probability of leading to a different outcome at trial."

"Are you talking to yourself?" asked Dixie.

Miranda shook her head and held out her tray. "Here, the turkey is yours."

"Seriously?" Dixie walked over and snapped up the two pieces of processed white meat. "You a vegan or something?"

"Sometimes," said Miranda. "Hey, you've read this manual a few times, right?"

"A few," Dixie grunted.

"Do you believe what she says about *Gideon versus Wainwright,* the 1963 Supreme Court decision that guarantees indigent defendants counsel under the Sixth Amendment?"

Dixie chewed her turkey. "What about it?"

"She says the motion was written on a piece of toilet paper by an inmate at Florida State Prison."

"Folklore." Dixie waived a dismissive hand.

"Yeah probably," said Miranda, "but still fascinating. I can't believe that up to that point, people who couldn't afford an attorney were just screwed."

She scoffed. "They're still screwed."

"What do you mean?" Miranda nibbled a bit of pumpkin pie as her cellmate carried her own empty tray to the flap.

"My public defender had 40 other people on his caseload," said Dixie. "He didn't even recognize me at jury selection, and I've got a pretty memorable face. He kept dozing off during my trial."

Miranda thought of Colton Tipton. "Mine wasn't as bad as yours, but . . . I see what you're saying."

"Are you gonna eat those green beans?"

She took another bite of pie and held out her tray. "Here."

Dixie licked the scar tissue of her lips. "Are you done?"

Miranda nodded. A half-eaten Thanksgiving tray was the least she could do for allowing her unrestricted access to Tussie's self-help legal manual.

Dixie sopped up the remaining mashed potatoes and gravy with a half-eaten roll then went to work on the green beans. She motioned toward the open manual. "You know that's old, don't you?"

Miranda flipped through the coffee-stained pages. "Mm hmm."

She held the tray to her mouth and slurped the bean juice, draining every available calorie. "Some of it's bad law."

"What do you mean?"

"New rulings have come out since she wrote that." Dixie wiped her mouth on her sleeve.

Miranda closed the manual and settled back on her bunk. "Do you know Tussie?"

She shook her head. "I know she's floating around the system somewhere if she hasn't died from Covid. When I got here, she was next door at the main unit. Already banned from the law library by that time."

"For what?"

"They said she was hustling but it probably had more to do with all the women she was getting back into court," Dixie rasped. "I found that book in an empty locker my first time on close management."

"Tussie was my cellmate in quarantine at the reception center," said Miranda. "She told me that she used to be a law clerk but I didn't realize she was like . . . a legend. She seemed more into her recipes than anything."

Dixie walked over to the flap and set Miranda's empty tray on top of hers. When she returned, she sat on the toilet next to Miranda's bunk. "Have you read that case yet?"

Miranda stared at her. "What case is that? Gideon?"

"Uh uh." Subtle shake of the head. "The one your friend made you promise to read."

"Oh, Maddox." She patted the stapled packet of papers lying face down next to her. "I'm only on page three so far. I put it down when you gave me Tussie's manual. I don't know why she wants me to read it anyway. It's so long, and it has nothing to do with my case. None of what she brought does."

"How long have you been in prison again?" It was always difficult to tell when Dixie was smiling.

"Since September, so . . . two months?"

She shook her head. "Let me see that case."

Miranda handed it over. "But I was in the county jail for almost a year."

Dixie flipped through the packet once, twice, then she stopped a third of the way through, isolating one page from the rest.

"What are you doing?" said Miranda.

"This." She tore into the back of the page which was actually two pages glued together. Then she turned it around and held up her findings.

Miranda leaned forward, eyes wide. "What is it?"

32

The plastic wrap was taped to the paper. She gently pulled it loose then began unraveling it.

Look at you, said her inner narrator. *Are your palms sweating? Pitiful . . .*

"Please don't start," Miranda mumbled.

"Start what?" said Dixie.

She looked up. Her cellmate was staring at her. "Oh, I wasn't talking to you." She unwound the Saran and placed the coiled tassel on her knee. "I was talking to myself."

Dixie walked over to her bunk and sat down, her tense jaw working beneath the stretched and scarred flesh of her face.

The orderly appeared at the door, dirty blond hair tucked behind her ears, broken heart tattoo shiny with sweat, humming as she worked.

"Hang on," said Miranda when she grabbed the trays. "I need that spoon."

The dope was sunburst orange with a hint of rose, about the size of a postage stamp. She pulled the staple from the Maddox case and straightened it on the sink. Then, gently, tenderly, she carved off a sliver.

"Want a piece?" she asked Dixie.

Her cellmate was usually difficult to read. Not this time. Disgust poured off her like steam from a kettle.

"I'll take that as a no," said Miranda.

Like you wanted to share anyway, her inner narrator smirked.

She snapped the tines off the plastic spork and ran the water until it heated up. She only needed a few drops. Then she set the utensil on the sink, pressed her finger against the strip, and airlifted it to the waiting warmth of the liquid where it would soon disintegrate.

"Hey Xena!" Tasha's voice rang out. "Wanna run a game while they've got these flaps open?"

Dixie ignored her.

"Oh, I see what's up," she shouted. "You got some food in that belly and now you wanna lay your big musclebound ass down! I bet you ate your cellmate's tray too."

Dixie glowered at the cinderblocks across the cell.

"That's okay. Go ahead and play sleep. You'll be back on this door sooner or later. *Hey Tasha,*" her voice deepened in a wheezing, passable impression. "*I'm bored. Come to the door and play chess with me* . . . And when you line that shit up, I'ma snatch your assbone out."

Miranda grinned as she swirled the fragmented Sub into the water with the staple.

"That was a joke," said Tasha.

Dixie worked her jaw.

"Cuz you're so big."

Crickets.

"Okay, well, I guess I'm gonna teach Hillary Clinton over here how to play then . . . Happy Thanksgiving girl."

Without the tines, the spork was more like a small square shovel. She carefully pinched the sides, raised it to her right nostril, tilted her head back and snorted. Then she licked the remaining residue from the white plastic. Unlike a Roxy or a Dilaudid, there was no post-nasal burn or bitter crushed-pill aftertaste. There was also no immediate soothing warmth. It came on slow, like a quiet storm.

"Why are you being so mean to her?" said Miranda.

Dixie folded her powerful arms over her hard chest, body language Miranda had come to recognize. It reminded her of Trump before the press on the White House lawn. All she needed was a red tie, an oversized blazer, and the signature orange combover. Just when she thought her cellmate was descending into her internal military bunker, Dixie cleared her throat. "A wise woman speaks because she has something to say . . . a fool, because she has to say something."

Imminent warmth approached, comfort at a cellular level. "You think Tasha is a fool?"

"I think you're both fools."

Miranda scratched her nose. "I have an IQ of 135."

"Congratulations."

She began rewrapping the Suboxone in the Saran. "What makes you think I'm a fool?"

Dixie shifted her focus from the cinderblocks to Miranda. "Well, besides the obvious," she scowled at the dope, "there's the fact that you seem driven by the need to fill every precious silence with a bunch of words . . . just like Tasha."

"I don't talk that much." Miranda flattened the plastic-wrapped square and stuck it in her Bible. "And I'm only using this stuff to quiet my emotions and focus while I learn the law. Once I file my 3.850, I'm done."

"Tell yourself whatever you need to."

"You're being judgmental," said Miranda.

"I'm not judging anyone." She leaned back in her bunk and shoved her hands behind her stubbly head. "I just don't want to hear any more high and mighty, liberal elitist bullshit out of you. Not while you're in here with a spoon stuck up your nose."

Nausea bloomed in her abdomen like toxic algae. It was difficult to tell whether it was a byproduct of the dope or Dixie's careless words.

Maybe the truth makes you nauseated, said her inner narrator.

"And I'd find a better place to hide that if I was you," Dixie spoke to the ceiling. "They shake down the cells every time we go to the shower. That's one of the first places they look."

33

The Antiterrorism and Effective Death Penalty Act, known to most prisoners by its acronym—the AEDPA—did not sound like it applied to Miranda, so it was understandable that she flipped past it in her first few readings of Tussie's post-conviction guide.

She was not a terrorist and was not sentenced to death, therefore the chapter represented an unnecessary detour on her road to accelerated learning.

But the following Sunday morning, constipated from Suboxone and seeking mindless reading to distract her bowels into submission, she lay toilet paper over the unforgiving steel and opened the tattered manual to page 4.

Important Information Regarding
A.E.D.P.A. Time Limits

A 2254 is a habeas corpus petition which is filed in United States District Court. Under normal circumstances you will only file a single motion under rules 3.800, 3.850, and 9.141 (ineffective assistance of

appellate counsel). Once those proceedings
have run their course and you have lost all
your attempts to obtain relief at the state
level, you will have the opportunity to lay
claim to any constitutional issues you may
have in the form of a 2254. Make sure when
filing your initial motion for post-
conviction relief that you "federalize"
each claim. This simply means that you cite
which constitutional violation occurred.
The most common are your 4th Amendment right
against unreasonable search and seizure,
your 5th Amendment right to due process,
your 6th Amendment right to effective assistance of counsel, and your 8th Amendment
protection against cruel and unusual pun-
ishment.

She read those four amendments twice, cementing them in her mind. Even with her limited knowledge of the law she felt like she had a valid argument that each of these rights had been violated in her case.

Dixie stretched, yawned, and glanced back at Miranda on the toilet. "Aw shit." She rolled back over and pulled the blanket over her head.

Miranda was too consumed by what she was reading to be embarrassed. The AEDPA *did* apply to her after all. It applied to every prisoner, and it contained critical in-formation regarding time limits. To think she almost skipped over it. *Lesson learned: read everything.*

"Hey Dixie."

"Don't talk to me while you're shitting," her muffled voice came through the blanket.

"I'm not," said Miranda. "I haven't in days. You know that. One question though."

"What?"

"Did you file a 2254 motion in federal court?"

"Yeah. Denied."

"I don't understand about this AEDPA one year time limit. How can you have two years to file a 3.850 but only one year to file a 2254 when the 2254 is supposed to come *after* the 3.850, and the time for *both* starts running thirty days after sentencing?"

No answer.

"Dixie?"

"You said one question."

A key rapped against the plexiglass. Miranda flinched and covered her privates with the manual.

Frown lines. Frosted hair. "Adams." The guard stared at her list. "You going to rec this morning?"

Dixie exploded from her blanket and slipped on her size 12 crocs. "Let's go."

"Don't forget your mask." The guard looked over at Miranda. "What about you, McGuire?"

Fresh air, vitamin D, a break from the same four walls for the first time in over a month. "I'm coming." Miranda pulled up her uniform pants.

"I hope you've got that stuff put up good," Dixie mumbled covertly as she tied on her mask. "They're gonna shake down the cell if we're both gone."

Miranda's eyes flashed to her bunk, where the plastic-wrapped package was still sitting on her blanket. She had just snorted a strip after breakfast. Her schedule was *every other morning*. It required discipline but stretched her supply from fifteen days to thirty while simultaneously preventing withdrawals.

The guard clicked her cuffs. "Same for you McGuire. Get your mask on."

"Yes ma'am." Miranda covered the Suboxone with one trembling hand while reaching below her mat with the other. When Dixie approached the door, she popped the dope inside her mouth and pulled the mask over her face.

Look at you, said her inner narrator, *Miss Professional Prisoner.*

They filed out of the side door downstairs, two by two, like animals boarding the Ark. Once outside, the animal theme continued as she was locked in one of the chain-link cages. Miranda's foremost concern was that her saliva would penetrate the Saran and ruin her stash. As soon as her cuffs were removed, she pretended to stretch and transferred the package from mouth to sock.

"Wind's got a little slap to it this morning, don't it?" A fiftyish woman with sores on her face and stringy, urine-colored hair almost knocked her over.

She arose from her stretch and was formulating a response when the woman answered herself. "You're always complaining about something or other. That's one thing I hate about you . . ."

Miranda watched her pace the interior perimeter of the cage, arguing with her invisible adversary as she stepped around a woman who was meditating.

Talking to herself, her inner narrator scoffed. *Unbelievable.*

She glanced over at Dixie doing burpees in her own private cage. Apparently she was too dangerous to share a recreation space with anyone, even her own cellmate who shared a much smaller living space with her 24 hours a day.

Here comes Crazy Train again, said her inner narrator.

". . . so I told her I ain't working A.M. dishroom." She kicked a pebble and sent it skidding across the concrete. "Hang on, I think this bitch is trying to hear what we're saying."

Miranda nodded at her as she walked by, but the woman quickly looked away.

"Dixie Apollonia Adams," yelled a woman in corn-rows from the next cage. "You think you're just gonna come out here and exercise the whole damn rec and not talk to me? That's out!"

Miranda recognized the voice instantly. "Is her middle name really Apollonia?"

"Nah." Tasha smiled. "I just like fuckin' with her. I don't even know if she has a middle name. She don't volunteer that type of information."

Miranda watched her cellmate pace back and forth, her face covered in the cross-hatched shadow of the fencing.

"Your name's Miranda, ain't it?"

She turned back to Tasha. "Mm hmm."

"My old bunkie had a lot to say about you before she left."

"She got out?"

"Yesterday," said Tasha. "But I'm not surprised she didn't stop by your flap to say goodbye."

Miranda shrugged. "I think she was mad at me because I didn't want to move into her cell."

"I think she had a thing for you."

"Gross."

Tasha laughed. "Where are you from, girl?"

"Pensacola."

"Shut the fuck up!" Tasha screamed.

The napping guard opened her eyes. "Hey Pitts. Watch your mouth. Unless you want to go back to your cell."

"My bad." She held up her hands. Then, low enough for only Miranda to hear, "I forgot we're in preschool."

Crazy Train passed again, mumbling to herself. It occurred to Miranda that the only difference between her own inner narrator and the rambling dialogue of the woman with sores on her face was the fact that she confined those conversations to her head and called it *thinking*. Crazy Train either lacked the ability or the desire to do the same.

"What side of town are you from?" said Tasha.

"Ferry Pass." Miranda scratched her nose. "Olive Road."

"I'm from Ensley!" She slapped the fence. "Born and raised. Tasha *Prime Time* Pitts? You ain't ever heard of me?"

"Should I?" said Miranda.

"How old are you?"

"I just turned twenty last month."

"Twenty? Shit, I got a son older than you."

"I have a son too," Miranda said quietly.

"Well, way back in 2001, two years after I had Cedric, I heard on the radio that they were holding tryouts for an all-women's football team. The Pensacola Power. Remember that?"

Miranda shook her head. "Flag football?"

"Hell nah! We were hittin' out there. Shoulder pads, helmets, cleats. Just like on TV."

"I've never heard of it. The Pensacola Power?"

"Yeah, they're called the Riptide now, or some shit like that, but back when I was playing, it was the Power. And we ran shit. Our first season, we went to the championship after going undefeated. Thousands of people were showing up at our games. Dan Shugart was talkin' about us on Channel 3 News. I can't believe you don't remember."

"My dad might," said Miranda.

If he's still alive, said her inner narrator.

"I was only a baby in 2001."

"Well, we were kickin' ass all the way up to 2008, the year I came to prison. We didn't even lose a regular season game until 2006. We just couldn't win the big one, couldn't get past Detroit. They beat us once in the semis and twice in the championship. Those were some tough bitches. I gotta give it to them. Mean as hell too. Every single one of them looked like Dixie." She looked beyond Miranda and shouted, "Yeah, I'm talking about your big ass! You're lucky we ain't got a chessboard out here."

"That's strike two, Pitts," said the guard.

"What'd I say? Ass?" Tasha was incredulous. "Ass ain't no bad word. It's in the Bible."

"Keep on."

Tasha rolled her eyes. "Anyway, I was starting left cornerback for all those teams. I had 37 interceptions in my career, 9 returned for touchdowns. Most in the NWFA. Those records probably still stand."

For some reason she thought of Nebraska Jackson, her fellow news junkie from the county jail who peed standing up. She would have made a good football player. "What's the NWFA? Northwest Florida . . ."

"Ain't no Northwest Florida," Tasha quickly corrected. "*National . . .* National Women's Football Association."

"Impressive," said Miranda.

"Yeah, I was pretty good." Her eyes went middle distance, somewhere over the razor wire. "But my son, Cedric? That boy is next level. Strong enough to jam wide receivers at the line, can flip his hips and bail as quick as any corner in college football, ball hawk instincts, perfect technique, and unlike his momma, he can hit. I was a lazy tackler. Ced has been layin' wood since he played for the Salvation Army on Q Street. As a junior at Auburn, PFW's draft guide ranked him as the number two corner in the nation. Mel Kiper called him a generational talent."

"I have no idea what you just said."

Tasha blinked, grinned, came back. "Huh? Oh, my bad. I always get carried away when I talk about my son."

"I know how you feel." Miranda thought of Cameron. She wondered what potential was waiting to be maximized in her little boy. *The oak sleeps in the acorn.* "And you should be proud. Auburn University. That's a massive accomplishment."

"Yeah, well, he's fuckin' up now. Back-to-back dirty urines for weed, then he punched a teammate in the face on the sideline during the spring game. Got kicked off the team. Now they talkin' about cancelling the rest of the season because of Covid."

"I'm sorry," said Miranda.

She looked up at the white sky. "He'll be all right. Ced's a survivor. His agent said he could still go as high as the third round in next year's draft. But he was gonna be a top twenty pick. Maybe top ten. His knucklehead decisions are costing us millions of dollars. The plan was for him to use his signing bonus to get me a real attorney."

"You've got a lot of time?"

"Life." Her face hardened. "For killing his no-good daddy. It should have been a *stand your ground* case. I got railroaded."

It was strange how these conversations were now commonplace in her world. A year ago the idea of meeting a murderer would have been terrifying, but at this point every cellmate she had and most of the friends she made were lifers. She thought of Nebraska again, and the stories about her mother being abused.

"Do you know Nebraska Jackson?"

The smooth skin of her brow knotted as she searched Miranda's face. "Yeah, I know Brass. Everybody in Pensacola knows that bull dagger. Poisonous ass."

"Poisonous? What do you mean?"

"She's jumping on all those people's cases in the county. Bianca Bradshaw, Kim Robinson. Now they're saying she's gonna testify against that little girl on the sixth floor who killed her baby. What's her name? She's always in the newspaper. Amity something."

"Davenport," Miranda said softly.

"Yeah, that's it." Tasha shook her head in disgust. "Amity Davenport."

34

"Good morning!" a voice trilled from down the tier. "How's your mental health today?"

Miranda rolled over and opened her eyes. Dixie was shadowboxing in the corner, her powerful body feinting, striking, weaving on a trapezoid of sunlight across the cell floor.

"Good morning, Ms. Suarez!" The voice neared. "How's *your* mental health today?"

She stared at the ceiling and thought of Amity.

That girl loved her some mental health counselors, said her inner narrator.

Miranda smiled. The way Amity talked about *Ms. Amber* in the county jail was like a kindergartner talking about her teacher. She attached to staff the way she did everyone who drifted into her orbit. Everyone except for Nebraska Jackson. She never liked Nebraska. Interesting to examine her aversion in light of what Tasha said at rec. It was probably just intuition, but Amity *was* the granddaughter of traveling fortune tellers. Maybe she sensed something all along.

"Good morning, Ms. Pitts." The voice had reached Tasha's door. "And how is your mental health today?"

". . ."

It was difficult to make out her response over Dixie's ragged breath and rumbling feet. She closed her eyes. Christmas was coming, Cameron's first. She imagined holding him in front of the blinking lights of a tree. She could see the wonderment on his little face as he pointed at snowflakes and other sparkly decorations.

"The psych lady's next door," Dixie muttered.

"I heard her," said Miranda.

She wiped the sweat from her face with her t-shirt, revealing rows of muscles that protruded from the taut skin of her abdomen like six small fists.

"Are you going to talk to her?"

"About what?" said Miranda.

Dixie gulped water from the sink, belched. "Didn't you say you were going to use postpartum depression to try to get back to court?"

"I didn't say I was going to *use* it. I just don't see how a plea could be knowingly and intelligently made under those conditions. I need to write the library to see if there's any caselaw on it."

"What you need to do," said Dixie, "is tell this psych lady that you're depressed and get on single dose."

"Medication? I don't want to be on any medication."

Dixie smirked. "Oh, that's just sink water I hear you snorting from a spoon every other morning."

Checkmate, said her inner narrator.

Miranda stared down at her hands.

"You just had a baby five months ago. It's logical that you would be depressed."

"Six." Miranda chewed her lip. "Six months, five days. June 2, 2020."

"Whatever. You just had a baby. No one is going to deny you if you say you need meds."

"But I'm okay now. I made it through."

"So lie," said Dixie. "Exaggerate. You're a liberal. It should come natural."

"For what?" said Miranda.

Dixie hooked her thumbs in the elastic of her pants. "If you're going to say that your plea was not voluntary because it was made under the heavy influence of post-partum depression, it seems like a doctor's diagnosis and prescription would be a helpful exhibit in an evidentiary hearing."

Miranda stared into the mine shafts of her eyes as she processed her words. Then, slowly, she shook her head in wonder.

"What?" said Dixie. "You think you're the only one in this cell who's read Tussie Jones' post-conviction manual?"

A smile bubbled over from her heart, touching her eyes, playing on her lips, stretching them in unfamiliar directions.

"Put that away!" Dixie hissed. "You're supposed to be sad."

"Good morning, Ms. Adams!" The counselor appeared in the plexiglass. "How is your mental health today?"

"I'm good," said Dixie. "But I'm a little concerned about my cellmate here. I think she's depressed."

35

INMATE REQUEST	**STATE OF FLORIDA** **DEPARTMENT OF CORRECTIONS**	Mail Number: _____ Team Number: _____ Institution: _____

TO: (Check One)	☐ Warden ☐ Asst. Warden	☐ Classification ☐ Security	☐ Medical ☐ Mental Health	☒ Dental Other LAW LIBRARY

FROM:	Inmate Name McGUIRE, MIRANDA	DC Number 070419	Quarters T-2212	Job Assignment CONF.	Date 12/11/20

REQUEST   Check here if this is an informal grievance ☐

PLEASE SEND ME TERRY V. OHIO, STRICKLAND V.
WASHINGTON, AND CALDWELL V. STATE (FL 2010),
ANYTHING YOU MAY HAVE ON POSTPARTUM
DEPRESSION AFFECTING THE VOLUNTARY
NATURE OF A PLEA AGREEMENT, AND THE
LAWS PERTAINING TO THE USE OF TESTIMONY
BY JAIL INFORMANTS.

                    THANK YOU

All requests will be handled in one of the following ways: 1) Written Information or 2) Personal Interview. All informal grievances will be responded to in writing.

--- **DO NOT WRITE BELOW THIS LINE** ---

RESPONSE   **DATE RECEIVED:** _____

attached

[The following pertains to informal grievances only:

Based on the above information, your grievance is _____, (Returned, Denied, or Approved). If your informal grievance is denied, you have the right to submit a formal grievance in accordance with Chapter 33-103.006, F.A.C.]

Official (Signature):	Date:	12-14-2020

Original: Inmate (plus one copy)
CC: Retained by official responding or if the response is to an informal grievance then forward to be placed in inmate's file

This form is also used to file informal grievances in accordance with Rule 33-103.005, Florida Administrative Code.

Informal Grievances and Inmate Requests will be responded to within 10 days, following receipt by the appropriate person.
You may obtain further administrative review of your complaint by obtaining form DC1-303, Request for Administrative Remedy or Appeal, completing the form as required by Rule 33-103.006, F.A.C., attaching a copy of your informal grievance and response, and forwarding your complaint to the warden or assistant warden no later than 15 days after the grievance is responded to. If the 15th day falls on a weekend or holiday, the due date shall be the next regular work day.

DC6-236 (Effective 6/12)

Incorporated by Reference in Rule 33-103.005, F.A.C.

36

"McGuire!" A red-faced goliath of a guard unlocked the flap and slammed it down. "Now or never."

She rolled out of her bunk, grabbed the thimble-sized white cup from the sink, and filled it with water. "Coming."

The guard leaned against the railing as a petite nurse in a Florida Gators mask stepped forward and emptied a small envelope into her hand.

Miranda popped the pill in her mouth without looking, securing it between the gumline and her cheek, then she opened wide for inspection.

The guard shined his flashlight.

"That's not necessary," said the nurse.

"Just trying to help." He slammed the flap.

Their voices faded down the tier.

She stepped in a puddle on the way back to her bunk; whether spilled water or Dixie's sweat, she couldn't tell. She spit the pill into the toilet and used a maxi-pad to wipe her toes.

A violent sunrise exploded against the black horizon, ember red and marigold. She reached behind her mat and found the well-worn square of Saran. It wasn't her day. It was an *even* day, and she only indulged on odds. But it was also Christmas Eve, and she deserved a present.

She was down to her final two strips, maybe three if she cut them small. She carefully unfolded the plastic and squinted at the microscopic remnants. *Definitely two.* The staple was in the corner of her bunk. She dug it out with a fingernail and made her incision. Then she grabbed her spork and went to the sink to run the hot water.

It sounded loud against the backdrop of the quiet cell. Incriminating. Dixie rolled over and grumbled. "What the fuck? *Every* morning now?"

"It's Christmas," Miranda dropped the strip into the pool of warm water. "I made an exception."

"It's just another day in prison," said Dixie, "and you made an excuse."

"I prefer the term *mitigating circumstances.*"

"You've been reading too much caselaw." Dixie flung her blanket aside and stretched like a lioness. "I need to piss."

Carefully, Miranda carried the plastic utensil to the front of the cell and stirred its fragmenting contents while she surveyed the quiet wing. Empty plexiglass windows on bolted steel doors seemed to stretch out into eternity like some mind-bending M.C. Escher print. She lifted the spork to her nose and vacuumed every drop of the medicinal liquid.

"Pathetic," Dixie rasped, flushing the toilet. There was no convincing her cellmate. It didn't matter to Dixie that Suboxone was not an opioid, but an opiate *blocker* that actually helped people kick heroin. Didn't matter to her that it was really a synthetic drug that plugged into receptors in the brain to replicate the opioid high. She didn't care that it was legal and safe and prescribed by doctors all over the world. She just saw it as a drug, and Dixie hated drugs. She was similar to Amity in that respect.

Amity. Miranda fluffed her hopeless pillow and climbed back into her unforgiving bunk. *Why would the prosecutor even allow Nebraska to testify? Why would they need her testimony?* She closed her eyes. Warmth washed over her like the Gulf tide. The answer was out there somewhere, in the watercolor beyond. Where the emerald sea met the cobalt sky. A distant ship, a lonely cloud. She attempted to focus but was nodding before the blurry white specks could sharpen into finite objects.

Hours passed. Her cell light stammered into fluorescence. A galaxy away, Dixie pounded out her morning pushups, her life force pulsing from across the room like a secluded star. Lunch came and went. She drifted along. It was time to get up and study caselaw, time to delve into chapters six through ten of the inmate law clerk training matrix that Duval had stapled to her most recent request. So far, all she had done was scan each page while she searched unsuccessfully for another hidden package.

Just a few more minutes.

It occurred to her again that Suboxone was a slightly different animal than the various opiates that had enslaved her since her junior year of high school. If she closed her eyes, she could nod like she snorted a Roxy; if she sat up, she could zero in on a given task with hydrocodone efficiency. The quintessential bliss and single-minded focus were two sides of the same coin, each enacted by will. But whether slumped or engaged, nodding or studying, there was perpetual presence riding shotgun in the seat of her soul—a yearning unbound by the will, something she could not shake, a dangerous hitchhiker who only knew one word: more.

"Twelve!" the girl in 2201 shouted. "Daniels coming in!"

The door buzzed open and banged shut. She could hear the usual suspects yelling the usual things. Dixie walked over to the door and watched through the plexiglass, her back muscles expanding and contracting with her breath. A woman screamed, then another. Suddenly the entire unit was erupting in cheers. Dixie shook her head.

"What is it?" said Miranda.

She cleared her throat. "Apparently the gestapo is releasing some of the sheep back to the compound for Christmas."

Miranda sat up in her bunk.

"Don't get too excited," said Dixie. "We've both got assault DRs. They like to keep us animals in cages. How many days do you have left anyway?"

"Thirty." Miranda scratched her nose.

"Yeah, I've got about the same thing," said Dixie. "But I've got a life sentence. I don't give a fuck where I serve it. Here, the compound, it's all the same to me."

She could hear the stairs rumbling as Officer Daniels made his way up. The unit was in full celebratory mode. Women were shouting to other women across the wing.

Doors rattled. "Merry Christmas, bitches!" yelled a woman downstairs.

"Pitts," Daniels lisped over the noise. Then, "Y'all shut up so I can get this done! Pitts!"

Dixie turned and raised a scar-tissue eyebrow. "Tasha's out of here."

"Pack up," said Daniels. "You're going to the compound."

Miranda was happy for her Pensacola neighbor. She needed to get to a phone to talk to her football player son. But she was also a little sad for Dixie. Although always gruff and occasionally downright mean, there was a noticeable uptick in Dixie's mood since she had been playing chess with Tasha.

Daniels stopped in front of their door and looked up at the paint-stenciled number, then looked down at his clipboard. Dixie scowled and walked over to her bunk.

"Adams, McGuire." He read their names off a list. "Pack up. Everything but your pillows and mats."

Miranda glanced at Dixie, eyes wide. "Where are we going?"

"To the compound." He checked the clipboard again, as if he couldn't believe it either. "Per the warden. Everybody under thirty days." His eyes softened. "Merry Christmas."

PART THREE
The Pound

37

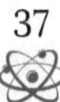

Daniels held the door. One by one they filed into the hallway, twenty-seven women in rumpled blue with matching masks. Dixie's legal work was slung over her shoulder. Many of the others carried pillowcases stuffed with clothing and accumulated mail. Miranda hugged a stack of caselaw and her Cameron envelope to her chest.

"Girl, look how ashy I got back there!" Tasha held up a skinny arm, inspecting both sides. "You don't really notice in them cells."

"What's ashy?" asked Miranda.

She appeared to be on the verge of an explanation when she frowned and reached for Miranda's face. "What's ashy?" She rubbed a spot on her eyebrow, flakes of dandruff rained down on her mask. "Your damn eyebrows girl. That's what's ashy."

Dixie towered over them, surveying the chattering crowd, two thirds of her face concealed in pleated blue polyester. "I just hope they don't put me in an open bay dorm."

"I hope they put us all in the same dorm," said Miranda.

The front door buzzed.

Tasha patted her hair and smiled at her reflection in the window. "We're about to find out."

The crisp December night air filled her lungs as she stepped inside the painted yellow line on the concrete. Dixie fell in behind her. High above the prison, planets and planes and satellites flickered in the starlit sky. The cathedral ceiling of the universe was as breathtaking as it was vast.

The line began to move. She took a step forward, then another. Her head touched the nape of her neck as she located familiar constellations. Somewhere in time, a little redhead in pigtails lay next to her dad in the backyard, looking up at the stars. Aching to give her son a similar tour of the Milky Way, she wondered if the foster mother ever took him outside at night. *"Twinkle, twinkle little—"*

She was still stargazing when she walked straight into the soft tissue of Tasha's backside.

"Aw hell nah!" her friend laughed. "You *definitely* owe me a soup for that. Nobody touches this for free."

Miranda felt her face flush. "Sorry."

The spotlight from the tower tracked their movement. She glanced up at the windows of Siesta dormitory as they left Tango behind. Women stared back from their cells. The fenced and quartered yards that made up the interior of the annex were cleared for the evening. Wind blew through abandoned pavilions, moonlight shone on an empty basketball court.

The gate popped.

"Shit," Dixie muttered behind her.

"What's wrong?" said Miranda.

"We're going the wrong way. Mike dorm is over there. Nothing but open bay dorms on this side of the compound. I can't live in open bays."

"Hold up right there," said Officer Daniels.

The line staggered to a halt in front of R dorm; a two-sided, one-story building that looked exactly like the orientation unit at the reception center.

"When I call your name, step out." Daniels removed a folded *movement sheet* from his back pocket. "Adams . . ."

"Fuck," said Dixie.

"Barrientos, Davis, Jernigan, McGuire, Page, Pitts, Savage, Williams . . . all of you are moving into side one. Everyone else is going to Quebec dorm." He pulled the radio from his belt. "*Security seventeen to Romeo, pop side one please.*"

A burst of static, a metallic click, Tasha held the door. Dixie was the last one in, grumbling every step of the way. "Fucking open bay dorm . . . I can't live like this. They can put me back in the box now."

"Aw, come on Xena." Tasha let the door slam. "We ain't ever lived on the pound together. Not in the same dorm. It'll be fun. We can play chess on a real board, work out together, you can do my hair."

"Shut up," said Dixie.

A seventy-year-old guard with twenty-year-old boobs was waiting at the officers' station window. On the other side of the glass, a crowd of women were gathering in the day room, smiling, waving, watching. The confinement releasees formed a line and held up their IDs to be assigned bunks. Miranda, Dixie and Tasha were the last three.

"Let me see here," the voluptuous elderly guard went down her alpha roster with a chewed pen. "McGuire, you're in eleven low, Adams, you're in eight upper—"

"A top bunk?" Dixie muttered. "You gotta be shitting me."

"—and Ms. Pitts . . ."

Tasha batted her eyelashes. "Hey, Ms. Gillespie."

"1137 single." The guard smiled. "Are you planning on staying with us longer than a week this time?"

"Depends on how many messy bitches you've got on the other side of that door."

"Messy?" said Miranda as they were walking away. "Why? Is it real dirty in there?"

"Not messy as in dirty." Tasha shook her head. "Messy as in *all up in my business.* Like you are right now. Touch your nose."

Miranda reluctantly obeyed even though it was concealed by her mask. "Why?"

Tasha erupted in laughter. "Dixie, this girl is green as grass. I thought you was schooling her over there."

"She's one of those liberal know-it-alls," said Dixie. "You can't tell her shit."

"I think she likes you." Tasha squeezed her arm as they walked through the door.

Miranda scanned the layout of her new home—eighty-six steel beds slathered in dark blue paint, bolted to the floor and situated in rows beneath bright fluorescent lights. The bunk beds lined the walls while the single racks filled the middle.

This is what activists mean when they talk about human warehouses.

A water fountain stood sentry outside a steam filled bathroom just over her left shoulder, a television blared from the dayroom to her immediate right. It was as if she was back in Echo dorm at the North Florida Women's Reception Center and the last couple of months were all a dream.

"Hey Red," a familiar voice called from a nearby bunk. "You get that stimulus check yet?

It wasn't difficult to locate Duval. A gold chain swung outside her clean white tank top, her pants were creased and tapered. A pouty-lipped blonde stood behind her, massaging her neck and shoulders.

First thought: *I wonder if she has any Suboxone.*

Second thought: *Am I a bad person because my first thought was "I wonder if she has any Suboxone?"*

Duval turned and murmured something into the ear of her masseuse who then nodded and sashayed into the dayroom.

"Damn," said Tasha as she walked by.

"If it wasn't for this global pandemic," Miranda smiled at her friend, "I would hug you so hard right now. Thank you so much . . . for everything."

"Don't thank me, pay me," said Duval. "We're at a hundred right now. I'll give you two more for fifty apiece.

Friends and family discount. That'll put us at an even two."

Miranda chewed her lip. "Two hundred dollars?"

"Nah, two hundred soups." Duval rolled her eyes. "Yeah, two hundred dollars. You can stand it. Trump just signed another stimulus bill. Six hundred more. We get all that. Did you send in the 1040 I brought you?"

She nodded. "Last month."

"You might already have it then. A few girls bingo'd in the canteen line yesterday. Right on time for Christmas." She glanced at the officers' station before opening her drawer. It was packed with food and hygiene items. She removed a baby powder container, popped the lid, and shook out two plastic-encased Suboxone strips. "Here you go."

Miranda's fingers closed around the precious merchandise without hesitation.

"I see you brought your bunkie with you." Duval raised her chin in acknowledgement. "Does she get down?"

Miranda glanced behind her. Dixie was still standing there, arms crossed, defiantly looking over the dormitory. Many of the women in the surrounding bunks seemed to be deliberately avoiding eye contact.

"What do you mean, does she get down?"

Duval jiggled the baby powder container and raised an eyebrow.

"Oh, no." Miranda shook her head. "She detests drugs."

It's not a drug, it's an opiate blocker.

Arms suddenly wrapped around her, body heat enveloped her. A sloppy wet kiss was planted on the side of her mask. "Miranda!"

She looked down at the bifocaled face and freckled nose of Daphne Throckmorton. "Throkkie! Where is your mask? You're going to catch Covid."

"Same old Miranda. You're such a mom. My mask is in my locker somewhere. I've already had Covid. Pretty much everyone in here has." She stopped talking abruptly. Her mouth fell open. When she spoke again, her voice was laced with awe. "Who is that?"

Miranda answered without looking. "My friend, Dixie."

"Dixie," Throkkie whispered. "What happened to her?"

"Roadside bomb," said Miranda. "Afghanistan, I think."

"So she's a warrior?"

Miranda considered the question. "Absolutely."

Throkkie swallowed. "You'll have to introduce us."

38

Someone had taped a shirtless picture of Ryan Gosling to the bottom side of 1111 upper, right above her head. His abs glistened in the California sun as he emerged from the ocean. It appeared to have been ripped from the pages of some celebrity gossip magazine. She imagined him quoting caselaw to her as she laid in her bunk on Christmas morning.

Before granting or denying the defendants claims for post-conviction relief, Florida courts must evaluate each claim to determine whether an evidentiary hearing is necessary for a ruling. The courts should grant a hearing unless (a) the files and records in the case conclusively show that the prisoner is entitled to no relief or (b) the motion or particular claim is legally insufficient.

Throkkie plopped down on her bunk and pushed her glasses up on her nose. "Merry Christmas. I brought you a present."

Miranda sat up and looked out over the sleeping dormitory. "What time is it?"

"Eight," said Throkkie as she handed her a Chapstick cap.

Miranda looked down and saw a massive piece of Suboxone submerged in the water, three times the size of what she was doing every other morning in confinement. "I can't accept this," she said. "I already have some."

"Me too." Throkkie smiled. "Plenty. It's your Christmas present. Take it."

"Do you have something to—"

Throkkie passed her a pen cap. "Way ahead of you."

She stirred the pinkish strip until it disintegrated then held it to her right nostril and vacuumed it up.

"I saw your friend doing Karate in the dayroom this morning before breakfast. She's so powerful and muscular and ... huge." Needle-point pupils stared through thick, black-framed bifocals. "Is she, like, a trannie?"

"A what?" Miranda handed the cap back.

"Transgender," said Throkkie. "She's very masculine."

"You know I asked her that same question when we were cellmates."

"Really?" Throkkie cleaned the cap with her tongue. "What'd she say?"

"She said she would put me through the flap if I ever asked her that again."

"Good to know," said Throkkie. "What's a flap?"

"The little rectangular thingy on the doors where they push the trays through."

"Oh. Wow, that's small."

Miranda nodded. "Yeah."

"Do you think she plays D&D?"

"Doubtful." Miranda smiled. "But possible. I know she plays chess."

Throkkie leaned back on her elbows and frowned. "Is that Ryan Gosling?"

Miranda looked up. "Mm hmm. Some previous occupant taped him up there. He's been staring at me over the top of those sunglasses all night. I haven't been to sleep yet. I think it's the transition from two months in that little cell to being surrounded by all this."

"Yeah. A lot goes on in here after dark. Especially when Ms. G is working." She grinned a crooked-toothed grin. "You'll see . . . But I love Ryan Gosling. Especially in the movie *Crazy Stupid Love.*"

"What about *La La Land*?" said Miranda. "That sound-track has been playing in my head since master roster count."

"I tried to watch that on Kim's tablet last weekend. Couldn't do it. Too jazzy. You know I'm a metalhead."

"Who's Kim?"

She crossed her ankles revealing white shoelaces in scuffed black brogans. "Duval's girlfriend. One of them. You probably noticed her hanging around last night. Blond chick with selfie lips."

Miranda smiled. "Where did you get the boots?"

"I'm assigned to maintenance. My boss hardly ever pulls me out to work though. Life in the Covid era. Plus, he thinks I steal from the shop."

"Do you?"

She shrugged. "Sometimes."

"Hey Rock!" Someone called from the dayroom. "On you!"

She stood, stretched. "I'll be back. It's my turn on the kiosk."

The kiosk! "Who's after you?"

"There's a line," said Throkkie. "But I'll say I forgot you were next." She skipped down the aisle and called back over her shoulder, "That's what everyone does to me anyway. Bout time I got some revenge."

39

Tasha and Dixie were straddling the back bench, looking over the chess board that sat between them.

"Good morning," said Miranda, already feeling a little nauseated.

Tasha nodded. Dixie grunted. Neither looked up.

A handful of women sipped coffee on the first two rows, staring up at the television that was mounted to the wall. An actress on Good Morning America was plugging her new Netflix docudrama while quarantined to her Manhattan apartment. She compared it to prison.

"What a joke," said Throkkie as she banged away on the metal keyboard of the kiosk.

The bottom line reduced the daily news into bite-sized sentences and dragged them across the screen in a ribbon of blue. *Covid death toll nears 320,000 · A New York City nurse becomes the first American to be vaccinated · The Electoral College formally certifies Joe Biden as 46th President of United States · Trump defiantly maintains election was stolen, poll shows 77 percent of Republicans agree . . .*

"Hey Miranda."

She turned and walked over to the kiosk. Throkkie was talking to an older woman with sad brown eyes and a tightly knotted mask.

"Ms. Donna is after you in line, okay?"

Miranda nodded and sat down in front of the screen. The cursor blinked. The Suboxone and sleep deprivation were simultaneously making their presences felt. She reached in her shirt pocket for her pin number.

"Ms. Donna is Erica's mom," said Throkkie.

"Erica?" Her mind was suddenly gauzy.

"The girl you jumped on when we were being transferred."

"Ohhh." Miranda struggled to key in her DC number. "Wait, her *mother* is here?"

"Not her real mother," said Throkkie. "Her prison mom. Her grandma is probably running around here somewhere too. Not to mention a bunch of sisters and aunts. It's weird. Male prisoners join gangs, women organize themselves into families."

"Do you have a prison mom?"

"Nah. Just an uncle. Uncle Duval . . . and I just got my sister back." She smiled and touched Miranda's shoulder. "Here, let me type that in for you. You're gonna be here all day."

A spinning blue circle appeared on the screen. Her head lolled as she unconsciously followed its rotation.

"You haven't ordered a tablet yet, have you?

"Not yet," she slurred.

"We'll do that in a sec. Let's check your messages first." Throkkie gave her a little shake. "Stay with me."

She aimed the cursor at the inbox and clicked. The most recent emails were from JPay notifying her of free stamps for the holidays, reduced price videograms, and $4.99 movies. There was also an inspirational message from the Secretary of the Florida Department of

Corrections, then a stern message from the Colonel about wearing masks in the dormitories *("Your usual cooperation is expected in this matter.")*, then more JPay notifications.

"Buncha spam," she scrolled down and clicked on older messages. "You need to go get in your bunk after this. The wrong guard sees you like that and you're going straight back to the box."

Miranda focused her one open eye on the blurry screen.

"Hey, here's one," said Throkkie. "Who's Patrick McGuire?"

It was as if someone splashed cold water in her face. She sat ramrod straight and clenched the sides of the kiosk with white knuckles. "Dad?"

Throkkie clicked on the message.

Hey Andy! Bet you didn't expect to hear from me so soon. I got 5 years probation. My public defender said it was a good deal so I signed. Anything to get out of that godforsaken Castle Grayskull. The guys in my pod thought the state attorney felt sorry for me because I was on a ventilator for 67 days. Whatever it takes. I'm just grateful I lived to smoke another Marlboro :) Although the only thing I've been smoking lately is cheap rolling tobacco. I'm living in Hollis T, Williams Park. It's a homeless encampment beneath the I-10 overpass. The woman in the next tent just got out after serving 7 years at the Lowell Main Unit. She told me all about JPay. I put some money on your books and sent you 10 stamps. I'll

*send more when I get my stimulus check. I wish I could
take care of my grandson until you come home but I can
barely take care of myself. This Covid stuff is lingering
and I'm still too weak to work. You probably wouldn't
want him living under a bridge anyway. I pray he's safe,
wherever he is. I thought of you on election night. Hope
Biden lives up to your expectations. It kills me that you're
in there Miranda. You deserve so much better. Can't wait
to be a family again. Stay safe. Write back when you can.
Love Dad.*

40

A heavy weight crashed against her stomach. She opened
her eyes. Ryan Gosling coolly appraised her from a beach
2,000 miles away. She blinked and glanced down at the
dense green object occupying her abdomen. A book.
Florida Criminal Practice and Procedure.

Duval pushed her legs aside and sat down on her
bunk. "Ufferman. It's the 2019 edition but we have two
copies of the 2020 in the library. I figured nobody would
notice if I cuffed it."

Miranda reached behind her pillow, grabbed the roll
of toilet tissue, and blew her nose on the abrasive paper.

"You still studying, right? Still fighting your case?"

Her nod was imperceptive.

"Don't tell me I was wasting my time sending you all that caselaw back there, risking my ass making copies of the law clerk training manual and sneaking them to you. I hope you ain't one of these bitches that gets all inspired about fighting her case in confinement, then hits the compound and never steps foot in the library."

"I'm not," she said quietly.

"Good. Cuz I've been sweatin' my boss to hire you as a trainee. We're down a clerk as it is, and even though I'm certified, I've got too much going on to be helping these illiterate bitches write their motions. The only reason you ain't hired already is because you jumped on Erica Ward and called that guard a nigga."

She bolted upright in her bunk. "Duval, you know me. I would never say that word!"

"I thought that might get you up." Her friend laughed. "They assign you a job yet?"

"Dormworker." Miranda exhaled heavily and looked up at Gosling. "I clean the water fountain."

Duval followed her eyes. "Who's this cracker?"

"Ryan Gosling. He's an actor."

"You in his fan club or something?"

She shook her head. "He was there when I moved in."

Duval considered the picture a moment longer then turned her attention back to Miranda. "So why have you been moping around the dorm with your head down, not going to chow, not bathing? I've barely seen you out of this bunk. I know you've been going hard on Subs, but still . . . that ain't like you."

Miranda thumbed the pages of the book with a gnawed nail. "Don't pretend like Throkkie didn't tell you."

"Maybe she did." Duval's chiseled features hardened. "I still wanna hear it from you."

"You already know my son is in foster care. Some stranger is rocking him, feeding him, he's probably calling her *mama* by now." She paused, tucked her bangs behind her ears. "Then the other day, I got a JPay message from my dad. He caught Covid in the county and was on a ventilator for two months, still not 100 percent. He can't work, he lost the house while he was in jail, now he's living in a tent beneath the interstate. All because of me."

"All because of you?"

"Yes. If I don't get arrested, none of this happens."

"That's why you've been over here crying under your blanket?"

She chewed her lip. "I haven't been crying."

Duval stroked her chin. "Hmm . . . I told you my nana is an amputee?"

Miranda shook her head.

"Diabetes," said Duval. "She's a big woman. My mama takes care of her. I got them out of the projects and into a house on the north side when I was out there hustling. Kept the power on, groceries in the fridge, all that. Then one night I get in a fight with my girlfriend, she calls the cops, and they pull me over with two ounces and my fire in the car."

"Armed trafficking?" said Miranda. "We have the same charge."

"Yeah, but I had only been out of prison eight months at the time. They hit me with the PRR. Life sentence. Game over. Now the women who raised me are on the verge of losing everything and being out on the street. All because of *me*. But do you think I'm gonna just lay down and let that happen?"

Miranda shook her head. "No."

"Fuck no," said Duval. "Not on my watch. I'm gonna pump these Subs and flip this money and hustle and grind my ass off to keep a roof over they head and food on they table. Just like they did for me when I was a shorty."

Her eyes burned with such intensity that Miranda was forced to look away. But Duval wouldn't let up. She grabbed her chin and pulled it back so that they were face to face. "What about you?" she said. "You gonna lay down? You gonna give up? Or are you gonna fight for the people you love?"

Miranda met her eyes. "I'm going to fight."

"Yeah?"

She nodded. "Yes."

"That's what I'm talkin' about." Duval flashed a rare smile. "Now get your ass up, go catch that shower. And shave these prickly white legs while you're at it. I'll get Kim to come over and do your makeup later. It's New Year's Eve! We're gonna hang out tonight. We got Ms. G in the booth, your homegirl Tasha is supposed to score two gallons of wine from her friend in the kitchen, Rocky's gonna hook up the stinger so we can cook . . . We're gonna bring in 2021 right! Then tomorrow we'll get to work. Sound like a plan?"

Before Miranda could respond, she was wrapped in her friend's powerful embrace. Warm, sinewy arms held her steady.

"Damn, you smell like shit," said Duval.

She broke away and playfully slapped her on the arm. "I do not."

It was then that she noticed Kim watching from across the dorm. Her pouty lip curled into a malevolent snarl.

41

The cord was a foot long and it appeared to be cut from some appliance. Positive and negative wires were separated and threaded through two small, flat pieces of metal and wrapped tightly with Saran, a half inch apart.

Throkkie emptied a few salt packets into the bucket of water.

"Fascinating," said Miranda. "Conductivity, right? To enhance electrolysis?"

"Seriously." Throkkie dropped the plastic-wrapped prongs and wire into the water and glanced at the officers' station. "I consider myself a nerd and I have no idea what you're talking about. But if you mean salt makes it boil quicker, you nailed it. Do me a favor and pull that trash can over here. Just to block. Ms. G doesn't care but we still need to respect her."

"You're going to electrocute yourself," said Miranda as she moved the stinky can to the wall.

"No I'm not." Throkkie fearlessly pushed the plug into the socket. "I made this myself."

A wisp of steam rose from the bucket. Miranda was intrigued. "How did you learn?"

"An old lifer on my maintenance crew sells them. She calls them stingers. I watched her cut the cord off a dusty television in the education building and followed her around until I figured out what she was doing." Throkkie held out her hand, Miranda helped her up. "Let's go get this food."

Dixie was crushing up ramen noodle soups and Shebang chips when they arrived. Tasha was then emptying them into a contraband Ziplock bag already loaded with refried beans and string cheese.

"Hello Dixie." Throkkie smiled and pushed her glasses up the bridge of her freckled nose.

She was acknowledged with a growl.

"Don't take it personal," said Miranda. "She does that to everyone."

Dixie growled again.

"See what I mean?" She turned to Tasha. "Nice to see you guys getting along.

"We always get along. Teamwork makes the dream work, right Xena?" She reached over and patted Dixie's bulging quadricep. "Hand me that soup."

"Don't touch me."

Tasha laughed. "She's getting drunk tonight."

"No, I'm not," said Dixie.

"Yes hell, you are. A bet is a bet. Hey Rock?" Tasha shook the bloated bag of food. "What kind of drunk do you think Dixie is? A belligerent drunk? Or a horny drunk?"

"Maybe a violent drunk," said Throkkie.

"Damn, I hope not." She handed over the bag. "She'll clear out this whole dorm if she gets pissed off."

"I'm not drinking," said Dixie.

"She hates drugs," Miranda attempted to bail her out.

"This is not a drug. This is alcohol."

"Same shit," Dixie rasped.

"No, it ain't the same shit. That's why they say drugs *and* alcohol. If it was the same, they would just say drugs. Now you said you'd drink a bottle if I beat you—"

"I took my Queen off the board."

"Nobody made you do that dumbass shit! Just like nobody made you bet. But you're gonna keep your word. All these years I've been knowing you, one thing is for sure—Dixie Adams always pays her debts."

"Like a Lannister," Throkkie blurted, wide eyed.

The three women turned and looked a collective question at her. "Like a what?" said Tasha.

"Nothing." Throkkie glanced across the dorm at her bucket. "Miranda, grab those chili packets and come on. Duval should be back from the library any minute."

The water was boiling by the time they got there.

"I'm impressed," said Miranda.

"Don't be impressed." She wiped the steam from her glasses. "Be efficient. Drop that chili in the bucket."

"You sound like Dixie."

"Really?" She stood up a little straighter. "Thank you."

42

It was dark in the dayroom. Images of an eerie windswept Times Square flickered across the television screen. The women in the front row swayed and sang along with a taped performance of a pop artist Miranda didn't recognize. A surreal finale to a surreal year.

Last New Year's Eve she was barely into her second trimester, a mysterious viral infection was brewing in Wuhan China, Amity was babbling in the top bunk, and she was still holding out hope that Nick might bond her out of jail.

"I'm stuffed," she announced to no one in particular.

"I'm drunk," said Dixie.

"Me too." Throkkie took a final gulp and slammed her bottle on the bench beside her.

"Are you gonna drink the rest of that?" Dixie rasped.

"Have at it," she said. "Between the chili and the wine and the Subs, I'm about to puke in my lap."

Dixie twisted off the cap, downed the contents, and grimaced. "Aghh, that's strong."

Tasha cackled. "Look at you. All social and shit. I bet I'd smash your drunk ass on the chessboard right now."

"Set it up!" Dixie slurred. Then, "Hey Tisha? Did I ever tell you how much your friendship means to me?"

"It's *Tasha*," she laughed, catching Miranda's eye and shaking her head. "And y'all are my witnesses. Last night of 2020. Dixie Adams finally said something sweet to me, after all these years."

"No, seriously." Dixie belched. "I know I'm ugly, or *unsightly* as the warden puts it, but . . . you never treated me that way."

"You're not ugly." Throkkie touched her hand. "You're awesome."

Duval took a swig of wine on the next bench, her arm around Kim, Kim's head on her shoulder. She looked back at Dixie. "You know, I thought you was a stud when you first moved in. I was gonna pull up on you and let you know that this is my dorm. I'm the alpha in here." Her hand fell to Kim's backside. "But what's understood doesn't need to be said. Plus I know Red fucks with you. That's good enough for me. What *are* you into anyway? Men or women or both?"

The dayroom fell silent. Dixie's jaw worked beneath the scar tissue. "None of the above," she said. "I'm into pain."

"No shit." Duval held her gaze. "We got something in common then."

"I doubt that."

The sudden tension was palpable. Electrons swirled and crackled in the stale dayroom air. Miranda could feel it despite the alcohol and Suboxone that were seeping through her bloodstream. She attempted to steer the conversation into safer waters. "Guys?" Her tongue felt thick and lethargic. "It's the last night of this weird year. We're . . ." She squinted at the clock. "Ten minutes from 2021. One year closer."

"Closer to what?" Duval took another drink. "Death?"

"Home!" said Miranda.

"I ain't going home. I told you I have a life sentence, remember?"

"It's okay bae." Kim wiggled closer to her and glared at Miranda. "We've got each other."

"Don't look at me," said Tasha. "I've got an elbow too. Second degree murder."

Dixie stared at her hands, shook her head.

Nice work, her inner narrator's muffled voice echoed down a dimly lit hallway in her mind.

"Okay." She pinched the bridge of her nose. "Maybe the *one year closer* thing was a poor choice of words."

"I'm one year closer," said Throkkie. "They gave me 25 years for aggravated assault with a deadly weapon and great bodily harm. I'll be 50 when I go home."

Miranda closed her eyes, exhaled a gust of wine. "I'm sorry. I didn't realize you had . . ." She groped for elusive words like a hand grasping at smoke. Finally she altered course. "Well, anyway, what I was going to ask you guys is—what was the most memorable event of 2020? For you.

Lots happened, right?" She hiccupped. "Covid, protests, elections . . . For me, it was June second, the day I gave birth to my son."

Tasha quickly picked up the thread. "Hmm . . . memorable event. Maybe when my Cedric ran back that 99-yard interception against South Alabama. I've got the newspaper clipping in my photo album."

"Who's Cedric?" Throkkie asked.

"My boy," said Tasha. "Don't worry, you'll see him playing on Sundays next year."

"What about you, Throkkie?"

She scratched her nose, shrugged. "I don't know. I guess coming to prison is a pretty memorable event. And, you know, the pandemic. But I think I'll go with the Secretary's message about RPGs as my most memorable moment of the year."

"What the fuck is an RPG?" said Duval.

"Role playing game." Throkkie blinked behind her glasses. *"Dungeons and Dragons* was actually banned in Florida prisons until this year. The Secretary decided to allow it last month. Now I just need a few people to join my campaign."

"Don't look at me," said Duval. "I already told you how I feel about that shit. We don't play them type of games in Duval County. Not in my hood at least."

Kim's eyes sparkled in the dark. She whipped her hair over her shoulder and turned to kiss Duval on the neck. "You are my most memorable event, bae. Not just of this year, but of this lifetime."

Throkkie smirked at Miranda and mimed sticking a finger down her throat. She had to agree, there was something about Kim that grated on her.

"What about you, Duval?"

The television splashed light against the chiseled features of her face as the ball began its annual descent. "Me? That's easy. When I pumped up to two grand on my cash app."

"Yay," said Kim, plastic smile intact.

Miranda looked over at Dixie. "And last but not least . . ."

The countdown began. The women under the television counted along with millions of Americans watching in their living rooms. "10 . . . 9 . . . 8 . . ."

Dixie mumbled something under her breath.

"What was that?" asked Tasha.

"I said . . ." Dixie jerked her head toward Throkkie. "When she gave me the rest of her bottle."

"That's your most memorable event of 2020?"

She nodded.

Tasha erupted in laughter just as the ball flashed *2021* over a confettiless Times Square. "Girl, you drunk!"

"I'm feeling all right. Better than I was when she gave me the rest of her bottle." She turned to Throkkie. "That was very thoughtful of you."

Tasha glanced at Miranda, eyebrows raised.

"It was no big deal." Throkkie swung her legs.

"It was to me. You gave me your last. I owe you for that." She leaned closer and whispered, "And a Lannister always pays her debts."

Throkkie's eyes widened, almost filling her bifocals.

Dixie winked. "I was behind the door for three years. You don't think I read any George R.R. Martin?"

The television clicked off. The dayroom lights flashed. For the first time in 2021, the women of Romeo dorm made their way to their bunks for the midnight count.

43

1:30 a.m. Miranda staggered down the aisle to the bathroom, her plastic confinement spork secured in the elastic waistband of her pants, a piece of Suboxone cuffed in her left hand.

It felt as if her brain was sloshing around in wine and limbic fluid with every uneven step. She paused at the water fountain and peered into the darkened officers' station. Ms. G was kicked back in her chair, talking on the phone.

The bathroom lights were also dimmed. She stumbled through the entrance and placed a palm on the Formica countertop while her eyes adjusted. To her right, a bank of sinks extended toward the far wall in front of an elongated mirror, directly across from six ceramic-tiled stalls. She turned on the hot water and let it run.

Since there were no cameras in the bathroom, the stalls made decent blind spots. The convenience store anti-shoplifting bubble mirror, high in the corner, was little more than a distorted decoration. It was difficult for an officer to obtain an unobstructed visual from the station. Not that Ms. G was trying to see anyway. There were guards who came to work to take their lives' frustrations and disappointments out on the inmate population, and those who were simply there for the check and state benefits. Officer Gillespie was clearly in Group B.

Miranda dropped the Sub in the warm liquid and waited for it to melt. She didn't need to do another piece; she could probably nod in her bunk till lunch from the strip she did with Throkkie earlier. But it was New Year's. Mitigating circumstances.

Faintly, she could hear her inner narrator sucking her teeth. She stared at herself in the mirror.

"Whatcha cookin' up in that spoon, Red?" Beyond her reflection, she could see a woman wiping herself in stall one. "I want some."

She cringed and looked away.

"Aw, come on sugar." The toilet flushed. "Don't be like that."

She needed privacy. Carefully, she lifted her spork and moved down the row in search of an empty stall.

Two was occupied. A woman was sitting on the filthy floor, head in hands, sobbing, while her friend attempted to comfort her.

She only caught a glimpse of stall three, but a glimpse was more than sufficient. Clothes were draped on the stall wall. A wild-haired woman was splayed on the toilet, naked except for her mask, touching herself vigorously, almost violently, to an image on her tablet.

Her shrieks of laughter followed Miranda to stall four, where two lovers looked up from a passionate embrace. A quick glance in five revealed a similar encounter.

Note to self, her inner narrator's voice cut through the fog. *Never enter the bathroom after midnight.*

A snow-white tennis shoe and ankle-high sock stretched beyond the wall in stall six. There was no reason to invade more privacy. She hurried past without looking and went to the last sink. She was considering ducking behind the shower wall when a silky voice beckoned.

"Hey Red. Check me out."

Duval. She should have recognized the shoe. She was sitting on the toilet seat. A rolled cigarette dangling from her lips. "Wanna hit this?"

"You know I don't smoke cigarettes."

She held a wire to the top of a battery until it turned red, then puffed until the pungent aroma of marijuana filled the bathroom. "This ain't no cigarette. This is loud. 180. Exclusive shit." She patted her knee. "Come here and sit down. You're drawing heat."

Miranda chewed her lip. Duval exhaled a mushroom cloud of smoke and made a *hurry up!* motion with her hand. "Come on."

She looked around and quickly ducked inside the stall. Then she tilted her head back and snorted the sub.

"Yeah." Duval extended the joint. "Now we partying. Happy New Year's."

Miranda took a tentative hit, remembering the last time she smoked—right before her arrest. Duval's hand was firm on her lower back. Her skin tingled. Shadows swam across the tiles.

"You barely hit it." She laughed and took another deep pull, followed by another torrential exhalation. "Want me to blow you a shotgun?"

Before Miranda could answer, Duval turned the stick around and pushed it into her mouth, ember first. Then she seductively slid her hand between Miranda's shoulder blades, all the way to her neck, pulling her close while blowing a powerful stream of smoke against her lips.

She closed her eyes and surrendered, allowing her lungs to expand as her friend's velvet mouth brushed against her own. Time slowed to a morphine drip, the universe condensed into a prison bathroom stall, the billions of cells that composed her body ignited at once. When she finally exhaled, it wasn't merely cannabis smoke and carbon dioxide; it was tension, longing, fear, guilt, shame . . .

Duval took another drag and studied her, the hard lines and angles of her face illuminated in the crackling glow of the cherry. "You good?"

She nodded solemnly. "I've just never kissed a girl before."

"I ain't no girl and that wasn't no kiss. I just gave you a shotgun." Duval laughed and nodded toward stall five. "Now *they're* kissing."

Miranda realized she was still clutching her spork. She glanced over the wall as she stuck it back in the elastic of her blues. They were doing much more than kissing next door. She quickly looked away.

Duval took a final pull from the joint, dropping it into the toilet with a hiss. "Do you want me to kiss you?"

She shook her head without conviction.

Duval smiled and leaned closer. Her eyes were hypnotic, her touch warm and sensual. "I read somewhere that a kiss . . ." She cradled Miranda's face in her hands. ". . . can either be a comma . . ." She kissed her softly on the corner of her mouth. "A question mark . . ." Her tongue darted between Miranda's open lips. "Or an exclamation point." She kissed her passionately, ravenously, overpowering her with will and desire, alternately crushing and nibbling her lips.

Miranda was breathless when she finally pulled away. Waves crashed within her. A strange fire burned in her belly. The bathroom pulsed and swayed. She wrapped a trembling hand around Duval's neck to steady herself. "I'm not . . . into women."

"Me neither." Duval held her hips, kissed her again. "I'm into energy. And I'm feelin' yours tonight."

The truth was that Miranda was feeling her energy too, along with the wine and the weed and the Subs. Although *feeling* was too weak of a verb—she was broadsided, storm-tossed . . . Prison was nothing like she imagined.

"Hey ladies." A hazy shape appeared at the entrance of the bathroom. "Don't kill the messenger, but Ms. Gillespie says y'all gotta clear out. Her relief is coming through the gate now."

The mass exodus was instantaneous. Toilets flushed. A crowd of women bolted from the stalls.

Duval smacked her butt. "Go! We'll pick up where we left off later."

Miranda stumbled into the fray. A raven-haired girl in tight shorts and sports bra bumped into her on the way out, knocking her into the counter. "Oh sorry." She smiled sweetly. "Hey, were you just in the back stall with Duval? Did she and Kim break up? I thought they were—"

"Mind your damn business bitch!" Duval's voice thundered from behind them. "You keep watching me, and you're gonna get exactly what you're looking for!"

She paused to check her hair in the mirror, shot Miranda a knowing glance, and was gone.

44

"Last call for chow!" announced a stern guard in a state trooper hat and sergeant stipes on his sleeves. "Masks on, shirts tucked in!" He stood at the window, hands on hips, surveying the throng as they packed into the hallway.

"You! Carrot top!" He singled Miranda out. "Shut that door."

"Hang on, one more!" Throkkie wove her way through the maze of single bunks, leaping the last one, and sprinting past the officers' station.

"Inmate Throckmorton." Bloodshot eyes peered out from a sun-cracked face. "Where's your mask?"

She frowned and touched her face, then searched her pockets. "Right here sir."

"ID card?"

She glanced down at her shirt. "Shit."

A couple of women behind Miranda snickered as Throkkie bolted for her bunk and returned ten seconds later, sliding past the officers' station, ID card in hand.

He shook his head. "Why are you always last, Throckmorton?"

"I've asked myself that very same question many times sir." She clipped the ID to her shirt. "It's actually my New Year's resolution to be more punctual."

"It is? Well, you get straight Fs so far."

Throkkie stared at her feet. "Yes sir."

"Go." He signaled Miranda to close the door. "And if you pull this again at dinner, you'll be going to bed hungry."

The front hall was little more than a cattle shoot, a claustrophobic nightmare of a foyer where 80 women packed in, shoulder to shoulder, three times a day for meals.

So much for social distancing.

The hum of conversation swelled all around her—bickering, chatting, singing, laughing—each voice competing to be heard, the collective volume rising incrementally.

Miranda leaned toward Throkkie and spoke through her mask. "You handled that well."

"I'm fluent in asshole." She shrugged. "My mom attracted them like Ringwraiths when I was little."

Miranda smiled at the *Lord of the Rings* reference. "You're such a little nerd."

She pushed her glasses up the bridge of her nose. "That means a lot coming from the highest IQ to ever pass through the North Florida Women's Reception Center."

"I can think of at least 20 things that I've done since then that are not indicative of a superior intellect."

"Are you counting last night?"

Miranda glanced sharply at her.

Intelligent blue eyes blinked behind thick lenses. "Look around. Do you think secrets can survive in this environment?"

She scanned the crowd as a barrage of sensory images and memories inundated her temporal lobes, the heavy aroma of smoke, her blurry reflection in the spinning stall, warm hands, soft lips, the seductive tone of Duval's voice.

"It's not a big deal," said Throkkie. "I've already burned through a couple girl crushes of my own since I've been in here. Even though I was never really into that when I was free. *Gay for the stay.*" She smiled. "I just thought you were focused on your case . . . and your baby."

"I am," Miranda protested.

"Plus, I don't know, *Duval?* She's my friend and everything but . . . she's kinda like a serial player."

The front door finally buzzed open, and the crowd pushed out into the brisk New Year's afternoon. Dixie and Tasha were waiting on the pavement.

"Single file, ladies," drawled an officer with a faded dip can ring on the back pocket of his pants. "Behind the yellow line."

She fell in with her friends as the line snaked past Q dorm. Generally referred to as *Quebec* in radio nomenclature, the Q at Lowell Annex would have been better by represented by the word *Quarantine.* There had been a biohazard sign taped to the door of side two since she was released from confinement.

"I call the leftovers on Miranda's tray." Tasha winked at her.

Dixie growled.

"Oh, now you wanna growl at me? Last night you was all sentimental and shit. 'I love you Tasha.' What's wrong, girl? You got a hangover?"

Dixie's jaw flexed.

"You're just mad cuz I called Miranda's scraps." She playfully squeezed the bulk of Dixie's back arm. "Just cuz y'all was cellmates don't mean that you have exclusive rights to her leftovers for the rest of your life."

"Don't touch me."

Throkkie looked up at Dixie as they walked through the gate. "You can have my chicken."

The library and education buildings were on the same end of the compound as the dining hall. Miranda had developed a habit of looking longingly through the windows at the rows of books as she passed. Except for verified legal deadlines and a handful of inmate clerks, the library remained closed due to Covid.

"Damn, they got Duval working on New Year's Day?" said Tasha. "Mr. Silva don't never take a day off."

Miranda spotted her just inside the front door, leaning against a counter and talking with a professorial type in a plaid mask and a thick mane of gray hair. A spark went through her as she made eye contact. Duval acknowledged her with a nonchalant tilt of the chin. She quickly looked away.

"His wife died of cancer," Throkkie explained. "That's how come he always works."

The line slowed as they neared the dining hall entrance. She could hear the same tired guards shouting the same tired commands through the open door.

"Less talking and more eating, ladies!"

"Three minutes!"

"Row two, pick up your trays. You're done!"

She glanced behind her. Seven or eight women lingered at the end of the line whispering intimately in one another's ears. Fingers discretely brushed and clasped, kisses were stolen in the shadows. Hungry eyes shined from flushed familiar faces. It dawned on her that the same group of women hung back the day before, and the day before that. The end of the line was apparently a hook up spot for lovers and lifers and the terminally lonely.

Her inner narrator sounded off, clear as Throkkie standing beside her, loud enough to make her flinch.

Is this the life you want?

She chewed her lip.

45

Unlike the yoga mat that doubled as Miranda's mattress, Duval's bunk was thick and luxurious, custom stuffed and lined with foam by the girls in laundry. It sank an inch when Miranda sat down.

"What's on your mind?" said Duval as she rummaged through her locker for deodorant and cocoa butter, her hair still glistening from the shower.

Miranda's nerves were fortified by another sizable strip of Suboxone. "I wanted to talk to you about last night."

"What about it?" Duval plopped down next to her. There was a gold herringbone dangling from her neck that had not been there the night before, probably a gift from some woman in another dorm. "Did you eat good?"

Miranda nodded. "More than I've eaten in the entire time I've been locked up."

"Did you drink good? Snort good?" Sidelong glance. "Smoke good?"

"It was a New Year's Eve I'll never forget."

"Damn right." Duval worked the lotion into her arms and shoulders. "So what's the issue?"

She hesitated. A woman was hovering within earshot, fortyish with an overbite and mousy brown hair. "Excuse me," said Miranda. "Do you need something?"

"Oh, I's just waiting to talk to the law clerk here." She flashed a nervous smile in Duval's direction and stepped forward. "Have you heard anything about the new laws Tallahassee's 'posed to be passing this session? Sixty-five percent gain time and no more minimum mandatories and—"

"Whoa." Duval threw up a lotion-slathered stop sign. "First of all, you're violating. I've been in the library since seven this morning. You think I wanna come home and talk about the law?"

The woman blinked. Uncertainty clouded the bland features of her face.

"Second, the legislative session doesn't even pop off until March this year. It's January the first."

"Well, Happy New Year," she said. "I just heard—"

"And last," Duval said forcefully, "we're talking. You can't see that? You're interrupting us. You got a legal question, write the damn law library."

The woman backed away in a series of contrite little bows, a lowly restaurant server berated by a rude and privileged patron. "I 'pologize ma'am. I'll go do that right now."

"Who the fuck you calling ma'am?" Duval rolled her eyes and turned back to Miranda. "You sure you wanna be a law clerk? You're gonna have to deal with ignorant bitches like that every day of your life."

She watched the woman hurry back to her bunk. "Maybe you'll be able to give her some good news in March."

"Please," said Duval." Tallahassee ain't got nothing for no prisoner. It's the same thing every year, a bunch of reform talk and no action. Every bill they pump in the newspaper ends up dying in the House without even being heard. We ain't going nowhere."

"Maybe now that Biden is president—"

"Don't start talking to me about Biden. I don't wanna hear that shit."

Miranda held up her hands. "Okay."

The scowl remained on Duval's face as she leaned back on her pillow. "So, what's on your mind?"

"Well . . ." Miranda swallowed. *How do you tell someone that you are not interested in having an intimate relationship with them?*

"Aw fuck," she muttered. "I ain't got time for this."

Enough was enough.

"You're being rude," said Miranda. "I'm sorry you've had a difficult day. I'm sorry you don't like your job. But that's no excuse to treat people so horribly. Especially not your friends. Now, this will only take a second."

"Not you." Duval touched her hand and nodded toward the bathroom entrance. "Look."

Miranda turned and saw Kim standing by the water fountain. Her makeup was smeared and strands of hair clung to her face with tears and snot. An older woman attempted to comfort her as she sobbed, but she pushed her hand away. Hatred flared in her eyes when she noticed Miranda. She wiped her mouth on the back of her hand and shouldered through a group of women standing nearby.

"Just be cool." Duval stood to meet her. "I've got this."

Kim was trembling when she arrived at the bunk. "How could you do this to me?"

"You're trippin' bae. You got high yet today?"

She jerked a polished thumb at Miranda. "And with *her?* That's disgusting. You really are a dog."

Miranda spotted Dixie across the dorm, wading between the single bunks.

"Come on now. Red's our friend. It ain't like that."

"Liar!"

"You're making a scene." Duval reached in her locker, grabbed her baby powder bottle, and twisted off the top. "Here, go get yourself together and come holla at me when you ain't so emotional."

Kim stared at the cellophaned Suboxone strip in her outstretched palm.

"Go ahead." She dropped the bottle on the bunk and it rolled next to Miranda. "You need to get your mind right. You're talking crazy."

"I'm not talking crazy." She snatched the dope from her hand. "Everybody in this dorm knows you're cheating on me!"

"Who told you that lie? I'll beat her ass."

She sniffled. "Are you gonna fight the whole dorm?"

"For you, I would. I'd fight this whole prison." She touched her face, pulled her close. "Come here."

Kim staggered into her embrace, her arms dangling at her sides. Fresh tears streamed down her cheeks as she allowed herself to be hugged.

"You know I'm fucked up 'bout you girl." Duval kissed her eyes, then her lips.

"Awww," cooed a woman on her way to the shower. "That is so sweet."

What occurred next happened so fast that Miranda's arms and hands were speckled with blood before her thalamus could relay the violent data from optic nerve to visual cortex.

Kim spun out of her grasp with surprising agility, a razor blade pinched between her thumb and index finger.

Duval blinked and rocked back on her heels, her eyes telegraphing confusion. The crimson-beaded incision that slanted from her left temple to the right side of her jawline held for a moment, then opened like the flap of an envelope, drenching her t-shirt in bright red. Her hands flew to her face as she crumpled to the floor in shock.

Women in nearby bunks gasped and screamed. The guard in the booth pounded the glass while shouting into his radio. Kim calmly walked over to the foot of the bunk and stood before Miranda.

"You guys are made for each other." She raised the blade. "So much in common. Now your faces will match too."

Run! her inner narrator urged.

The cushy mat was suddenly a straitjacket. She squeezed her eyes shut. Adrenalin and cortisol are commonly referred to as *fight or flight* hormones, yet as the razor slashed down toward her face, Miranda neither fought nor fled. Instead she did what she normally did in the face of danger: she froze.

Thwack!

Contact. An image of Cameron flashed in her mind as she awaited the pain. Even if her case were overturned, even if she was able to get him back, she would show up on his doorstep as a stranger . . . a stranger with a scary scar.

"Let me go you ugly freak!"

Miranda touched her face, opened her eyes. Between her fingers she saw Dixie clutching Kim's bony wrist, caught mid-slash.

"Drop it," her old cellmate growled.

"Fuck you!"

Dixie dug her giant thumb into a pressure point until the blade released, tumbling silently to the floor like a leaf in the forest, inches from where Duval lie groaning in a puddle.

The door buzzed. A cadre of masked guards burst into the dormitory.

"Jesus Christ. Someone get medical down here ASAP!"

"There's the razor, Sarge. Right there next to her."

"Everybody on their bunks! Now!"

Chaos. Dixie shoved Kim out of the way. Miranda stood and took an unsteady step. Two burly guards snapped on blue latex gloves and lifted Duval from the floor.

"Get her in the hallway," ordered the Sergeant.

She took another step and glanced back at the bunk. The baby powder bottle was laying on its side.

Don't even think about it, said her inner narrator.

"Let's go, ladies! On your bunks!"

She couldn't just leave it there for the guards to find. There were at least a hundred individually wrapped Suboxone strips in the bottle, maybe more. With a deep breath she turned back, scooped the baby powder from the mat, and made a beeline for eleven low.

46

She sat on her bunk and inspected her trembling, blood-flecked hands as women poured from the dayroom and bathroom into the living area, herded along like cattle by shouting guards.

Across the dorm, Duval's area was a crime scene. The sergeant stood sentry over where she had fallen, redirecting traffic around the ominous puddle.

She ran her fingers through her hair without thinking as the trauma replayed in her mind; from stiff embrace to rapid separation to her friend's face unzipping a few feet from where she lounged to Kim standing over her, razorblade poised.

A couple rows behind her, a pair of dirty New Balance tennis shoes dangled from the top bunk, patched and sewn. *Dixie*. Thank God for good friends. Were it not for her old cellmate, she'd be bleeding in the hallway next to poor Duval. Tussie Jones warned her to steer clear of these exact situations. No wonder she was so adamant.

"Psst!"

She looked around.

"Down here." A familiar bifocaled face blinked up at her from beneath her neighbor's bunk.

"Throkkie! What are you doing?"

"Shh!" she hissed. "Gimme that baby powder."

"What?" Miranda placed a protective hand over her drawer. "No way."

"Oh my God. Stop being a junkie for one second and listen to me!"

"I'm not being a—"

"Listen!" She glanced toward the officers' station. "There's not much time."

Miranda followed her eyes. A group of guards were gathered around the monitor, pointing, gaping, shaking their heads. She noticed the bulging biceps and white shirt immediately. "Is that . . . Grantham?"

"Among others," said Throkkie. "They're reviewing cameras to see what happened. Any minute they're gonna come and cuff Kim. Then they'll be over here."

"For what?" Miranda gnawed her pinky nail." I didn't do anything."

"You took a baby powder bottle stuffed with Suboxone off Duval's bunk. Right after she popped the top and handed a strip to her hysterical girlfriend . . . on camera." Her eyebrows shot above the thick frames of her glasses. "You don't think that might lead them over here to check your locker?"

Miranda glanced over her shoulder again. Grantham was at the officer's station door. The others were pulling on gloves. She could not go back to confinement. It had only been a week since she was released to the compound. She was still waiting on her first law library callout. "What should I do?"

Throkkie pulled an identical baby powder bottle from her pocket and rolled it between her crocs. "Trade me. We can figure out what to do with it later."

"Are you crazy?" Miranda looked at the camera high above her bunk.

"It can't see straight down," Throkkie explained. "Do you think I'd be laying on your floor if it could?"

The door buzzed.

"Hurry!" She urged.

The sergeant scanned the panorama. "Shut up! Or I'll have you in here for the rest of the night."

Every woman was now on her bunk—except Throkkie. Her neighbor stared straight ahead, indifferent to the legs that extended from beneath her house like the witch's in *The Wizard of Oz*.

Duval's stash was in the front of Miranda's partially open drawer, leaning against her soap dish. She grabbed it and tossed it to Throkkie who quickly belly-crawled away. Then she replaced it with the bottle between her feet.

The guards went straight to Kim. Eighty inmates watched as she stood and placed her hands behind her back. Handcuffs clicked. Someone on Miranda's row showed her support by telling her to *keep her head up* as she was escorted out.

"Zip it," said Lieutenant Grantham. "Unless you wanna be her cellmate. Where's the redhead anyway? McGuire. Where are you?"

She raised her hand.

"There she is." His breath caused his black FDC mask to flutter. "Just reviewed the camera. Why am I not surprised? You almost had your pretty little face slashed too, didn't you? Good thing Freddie Krueger over here saved the day." He tapped the steel of Dixie's bunk with his radio as he passed. "What were you doing sitting on inmate Griffin's bed anyway? I thought you didn't like dark meat."

Don't, her inner narrator cautioned. But the words were out before she could stop herself.

"I wonder what the Florida Administrative Code has to say about officers calling prisoners *dark meat* or *Freddie Krueger* or, in my case, *pretty.*" Her voice was firm and unwavering. "I mean, I'm flattered that you see me that way, but I'm guessing it's against the rules to comment on an inmate's appearance."

"Yeah?" he snarled. "Do you know what else is against the rules? Drug possession. Step aside, McGuire."

She squeezed by him and stood out in the aisle as he descended on her drawer, ripping it open. He seized the baby powder instantly, holding it up like a prized catch. The sergeant ambled over.

"Can you guess what this is, Sarge?" His eyes sparkled with arrogance.

"Uh, not what it looks like, I reckon."

"This is 60 days in confinement and 180 days loss of gain time for Inmate McGuire over there. Possession of unauthorized drugs. Watch this." He pulled off the lid and emptied the bottle's contents onto the vacant bunk above Miranda's. A small hill of baby powder formed on the steel.

The sergeant leaned forward for a better look as Grantham sifted through the talc with his finger.

"Unauthorized drugs?" Miranda frowned. "If you're implying that powder is actually cocaine, I'm going to have to insist that it be sent to a lab."

A vein appeared on his increasingly scarlet forehead. "Shake her down," he commanded the sergeant. "Give her the fine-toothed comb treatment. And if you find anything in her locker—altered clothing, an extra roll of toilet paper, an overdue library book—write her a disciplinary report and put her in administrative confinement."

Miranda moved out of his way as he stormed past, leaving a trail of cologne and testosterone and three menacing words.

"This ain't over."

47

She awoke before dawn. Shirtless Gosling looked a question at her over the top of his mirrored shades: *What are you gonna do?*

The first thing she was going to do was rip his stupid picture down. A paparazzi photo torn from an *In Touch* magazine did nothing to inspire her. She balled it up, saving only the tape, and replaced it with pictures of her baby.

Now she was motivated.

As she padded down the aisle to the trash can, she noticed water boiling in a small bucket against the wall beneath the electrical socket. Throkkic was already up. Dixie was too. She found them in the dayroom doing Tai Chi in the dark. The muted local news was like a strobe casting flickering light over their serene faces as they moved in tandem.

"Ready hands," Dixie growled as Throkkie echoed her movements. "Lion plays with ball, white crane spreads wings, brush grass . . ."

Miranda leaned against the kiosk, the trauma from the last 48 hours melting from her neck and shoulders as she watched the familiar sequence. She remembered waking to Dixie's routine back in November, during her first week in disciplinary confinement. It was pretty terrifying then—the kicks, the strikes, her hovering face in the moonlight—but now it had the opposite effect: she found it soothing.

Maybe that's because you snorted enough Suboxone to tran-quilize a rhinoceros.

"Miranda!" Throkkie noticed her and skipped over. "I've got the stinger going. We're gonna have hot cocoa after we stretch. Want some?"

She chewed her bottom lip. The violence was still so fresh in her own mind, not even a quarter strip in a plastic spoon could turn it off. How could her friend be so chirpy?

"There were 137 total in that bottle." Throkkie lowered her voice. "68 apiece. I'll sell the last one and get us some food. My bunkie will buy it for eighty off the card."

"What about Duval?"

"What about her?" Throkkie blinked. "She's not coming back on the compound. Not after that. Wait . . . are you in love with her?"

"No," said Miranda. "It's just *her* stuff. And I'm the one who took it off her bunk."

"And saved her from getting an outside charge," said Throkkie. "You did her a massive favor, Miranda. She would've went to close management as soon as she got her face stitched up if you left that bottle on her bunk. This way, she'll probably stay in protective custody for a month or two and then get shipped to Homestead C.I. or back to the reception center." She frowned. "I doubt she'll go next door. And I don't think she can go back to Gadsden . . ."

"Okay, but shouldn't we at least send her something?"

"How?" Throkkie pushed her glasses up on her nose.

"I don't know," said Miranda. "Maybe through the confinement orderly? I was supposed to pay her two hundred dollars when I got my stimulus check. The least I can do is give her some of her stuff back."

"You can do whatever you wanna do," said Throkkie, ". . . with your half. Lemme go get it." She held up a finger to Dixie and hurried off to her bunk.

Miranda stood there in stunned silence, digesting the conversation. How could Throkkie be so cold? Friends deserved better. Memories of their time together in orientation flashed and faded in her mind as the television spat artificial light on her trembling hands, hands that she had washed twenty times overnight. She knew they were clean yet she still imagined Duval's blood on them.

"I know what you're thinking," came a voice from the back corner.

She squinted into the shadows. "Tasha?"

"You're thinking your little friend is selfish, right? You're wondering how she's moving on so fast. Duval ain't even out of medical yet and Rocky's dividing up her shit and talking about her in the past tense."

"It crossed my mind." Miranda walked over and sat down next to her.

"Don't blame her." Tasha rocked in the dark. "Blame prison. This place makes you move on. Every day people going home, new buses coming in, women getting transferred, getting cut, *cutting themselves,* going to the box, going to CM . . . You get used to letting go." She looked over at Miranda. "And you get used to looking out for your own damn self."

Trump's face filled the television screen, along with the caption: *President urges Veep Pence "to do the right thing" and decertify election results.*

Dixie paused to watch, her eyes gleaming with reverence.

Miranda shook her head.

"She saved your ass, homegirl. You know that, right?"

"I know."

"Both of them did." Tasha leaned back on the bench. "One from Kim's blade and one from Grantham's handcuffs . . . Nice to have friends, ain't it?"

Throkkie appeared at the dayroom entrance just as the lights turned on. "Who wants hot cocoa?"

48

"McGuire!" the P.A. system boomed. "Eleven low. Report to the officers' station, Class A uniform."

She opened her eyes, scratched her nose. Cameron was smiling down at her. His fat little cheeks ignited a familiar ache in the depths of her being.

Dixie walked over and kicked her bunk. "That's you they're calling to the bubble."

"For what?" She stretched and sat up.

"Your guess is as good as mine," said Dixie. "Maybe a urinalysis."

She sat up straighter, banging her head on the bunk.

"Don't tell her that." Throkkie wandered over. "She's already a paranoid wreck as it is."

Miranda pulled on her uniform and fastened her inmate ID to the collar of her thin blue jacket.

"It's not a drug test." Throkkie touched her arm. "And even if it was, you'd be fine. They don't test for Suboxone."

What about those shotguns Duval was blowing you in the back stall the other night? Her inner narrator smirked. *Do they test for that? You better pray it's not a urinalysis . . .*

She slipped on her crocs and shot a nervous glance toward the officers' station.

Throkkie sighed. "Do you want me to hold down your stuff for you, just in case?"

Her *stuff* was currently residing in a hole slit in the waistband of her pants. "I'm okay."

The sergeant was awaiting her at the window, state trooper Stetson sitting high on his head, round bill as flat as a dinner plate. "Where is your mask?"

She dug it from her jacket pocket and tied it around the back of her head. "Sorry."

"And y'all wonder why you keep going under quarantine." He shook his head in disgust. "If you're off your bunk, I want your mask on. Are we clear?"

"Yes sir."

"Spread the word." He straightened his tie and admired his reflection in the glass. A five-second event that culminated in a curt nod. She half expected him to salute himself. "I don't want to start making examples but if I have to write some DRs to show that I mean business, I will."

Get a life, said her inner narrator.

"Yes sir," said Miranda.

He dropped a pass in the flap. "Mr. Silva is waiting for you."

"Yesss!" She beamed at the square piece of paper with her name scrawled across the top. *Destination: Library. Return to: Romeo.* Finally, some good fortune.

His steel gray mustache twitched with displeasure as he buzzed her through the door.

Icy needles of January rain greeted her as soon as she walked outside, intensifying with every step. By the time she passed the canteen she was thoroughly soaked.

Almost reflexively, she pulled her jacket over her head and took off running.

She recognized the folly of this impulsive decision instantly, though still a nanosecond too late; right around the time her cheap, treadless crocs hit the yellow, rain-slickened line, launching her cartoonishly into the cold and damp air.

"Ooph." The breath went out of her as she landed on her back.

The tower window opened and a bullhorn squawked the obvious. "That's why we don't run."

She arrived at the library shivering and sore with her hair plastered to her face and her socks soggy with rainwater.

A gaunt man in an oxford shirt opened the door. "McGuire?"

She held up the crumpled wet pass.

"Come in, come in." He stepped aside.

Mercifully, the library was heated. "It's freezing out there," she announced through chattering teeth.

"High of forty-five all week with rain and sleet for the next two days. Not exactly your stereotypical Florida weather, is it?" He closed the door. "So much for global warming."

Her Republican radar blipped. She ignored it and asked, "May I use the bathroom?"

"Sure. Right over there. It's unlocked."

She sloshed past rows of books, feeling better with every step. The smell of the library alone was comforting, worlds away from the overflowing trash cans and unflushed toilets of Romeo dorm. In the back, she could see a woman sitting in a cubicle with a stack of law books piled in front of her while another tapped away on a keyboard. A smile flickered beneath her waterlogged mask.

Inside the bathroom, she opened her jacket and checked the waistband of her pants—the only part of her that was dry. She removed the plastic-wrapped lump and held it up to the light. Not a single bubble of moisture. She breathed a sigh of relief as she pushed the dope back into the slit.

When she glanced in the mirror, her inner narrator was staring back. *Slave.* She looked quickly away, snatching off her socks and wringing them out over the toilet, then drying her hair with paper towels.

"Have a seat at one of the tables," Mr. Silva called from his office as she emerged. "Grab a magazine if you'd like."

She remembered Delilah telling her in confinement that her significant other worked the magazine desk in the library.

I wonder if she's here now, said her inner narrator as she scanned the covers. There were at least 30 different publications on the racks. *I bet Delilah had all kinds of nice things to say about you.*

Miranda glanced around at the empty desks and tables before returning to the magazines. She was on the verge of selecting a *National Geographic* when she noticed her hometown *Pensacola News Journal* at the bottom of a nearby shelf. The headline on the most recent edition made her heart shrivel and her stomach twist.

Jail informant testifies that Amity Davenport "bragged" about murder of infant.

There was a picture of Nebraska Jackson in a county jumpsuit raising her right hand below the caption. She grabbed the paper and sat down to read.

The article was short and the details sparse. Apparently on day two of the long-anticipated trial, the prosecutor used Nebraska's testimony in an attempt to cast doubt on the temporary insanity defense that Amity's public defender was expected to present later in the week.

"That lying snake," said Miranda.

"Excuse me?" The librarian pulled out a chair. Tired eyes assessed her through Ben Franklin spectacles.

"Oh, nothing." She straightened the paper. "Talking to myself. Sorry."

He drummed the table with his fingers; pinky, ring, middle, and index falling in sequential order, over and over as he studied her. Finally, he spoke. "So we have a law clerk trainee position open here at the library and it has come to my attention that you might be interested."

"*Might* be interested?" she blurted, "I would kill for this job."

"Careful with your words Ms. McGuire. Many of the women on this compound have killed for much less. The wrong one may hear that and view you as a kindred spirit . . . or worse, a threat."

"I understand," said Miranda.

"I do know, however, that you are not a part of that silent sorority and that your words are mere hyperbole." He raised a silver half-moon eyebrow. "Armed trafficking, is it?"

He spoke more like a college professor than a prison employee. It took a moment for his words to register.

"Yes sir," she said. "Armed trafficking. I'm innocent though."

"Your innocence or lack thereof is of little consequence to me. Competence . . . performance, that's what I'm interested in."

He ran his fingers through thinning gray hair. His wedding band glinted dull yellow beneath the naked fluorescent lighting. She remembered what Throkkie said about his wife dying.

"My most seasoned clerk is serving two life sentences for a crime she openly admits she would commit again if her husband and his mistress were brought back from the grave."

Is he trying to scare you? He must not know that you spent two months in a cell with Dixie Adams. Maybe you should tell him about the case of the missing testicles.

"My sole concern in this library is that our downtrodden—and many times illiterate—patrons receive quality assistance and are never denied legal access, an increasingly difficult task in the Covid era." He pulled down his mask and took a sip of coffee. "Which brings me to you."

Miranda sat up straight, fingers interlocked on the table in front of her, the universal posture of erudition and studiousness.

"I believe you're affiliated with one of my clerks. Actually, she's a former clerk at this point. Ernestine Griffin? You may know her as Duval."

"I do."

"Pity what happened to her." He shook his head. "But sadly an all too common occurrence in this place. Before tragedy struck, inmate Griffin was pestering me about hiring you as a trainee. The pandemic has decimated our little workforce and I'm woefully short on certified law clerks. This morning I received a DC-236 from her protective custody cell reminding me of what a fine employee you would make . . ."

His open-ended statement seemed to require a response. She cleared her throat. "I am confident that I would be an asset to this library."

"Oh, I have no doubt that you would be." He leaned back in his chair. "Your TABE scores are off the charts and there's a note in your file from a Dr. Avery remarking on your exceptionally high IQ. But the law clerk position requires more than mere academic prowess, it calls for patience and tolerance. Many of the women seeking assistance are . . . *unrefined*, to put it mildly."

"Patience and tolerance are what I do best."

"Is that so?" He cocked his head. "Your disciplinary history states otherwise."

She closed her eyes, exhaled, then met his gaze. "I thought a woman had stolen something very precious to me, my baby's birth certificate. At the time, I was dealing with the lingering effects of postpartum while trying to adjust to prison life. I've since been prescribed medication. It helps."

Helps what? her inner narrator scoffed. *Your aim, when you're spitting it into the toilet?*

It wasn't exactly a lie. Antidepressants did help lots of people. She just happened to prefer Suboxone.

"And is this postpartum depression also to blame for the racial epithet you used while addressing an FDC staff member?"

Ughh. There it is. The gift that keeps on giving. Based on the officer's statement.

"No," said Miranda. "That never happened. It was just something they tacked on after the fact. Apparently the sixty days in confinement for assault was not enough."

Again, the half-moon eyebrow went up.

Seconds passed. She quietly exhaled. "You've worked here a while. Don't tell me you've never witnessed a guard being untruthful."

A vitamin-deficient inmate in tight blues and tortoise shell frames appeared at the table. "Hey boss. Can you pull up the Seminole County Clerk of Court when you get a minute?" She smiled territorially at Miranda. "I need to see if an evidentiary hearing has been scheduled for Wiggins."

"We're wrapping up now, Ms. Hackett. I'll be with you in a moment."

"Is this the girl Duval has been trying to get hired? I hope to God so. I do *not* want to make confinement rounds."

He shot her an impatient look.

"Right," she said. "I'll just go wait outside your office."

He drummed the table again and glanced at his watch. "I'll be perfectly honest with you, McGuire. I'm not certain classification would sign off on giving you a job. ICT prefers for inmates to go at least a year without a disciplinary report before—"

"Please," said Miranda. "You have no idea how important this is to me."

"If not now, perhaps in October."

She had to restrain herself from grabbing him by the collar. "No! Look, I'll be the best clerk in this library. I'll help the difficult women, the ones no one wants to deal with." She nodded at Tortoise Shells. "She doesn't want to do the confinement rounds? I'll do them. I'll clean the bathroom with a toothbrush. Whatever you need me to do."

"You don't understand. It's not up to me."

"How long did it take your best clerk to get certified?"

He frowned and glanced over at Ms. Hackett. "What? Ten weeks?"

"Eight," she smiled.

"I'll do it in six," said Miranda. "And I'll ace every test. I've already memorized most of *Criminal Practice and*

Procedures and I'm about to start *Florida Rules of Court.* All that time in the box? I spent the majority reading a post-conviction manual and I have a working knowledge of most of the relevant caselaw. *Gideon versus Wainwright, Terry versus Ohio, Miranda versus Arizona, Strickland, Brady, Youngblood, Giglio* . . . I'm hungry for more."

He removed his glasses, breathed on the lenses, and cleaned them with his mask. "How old are you again?"

"I'll be twenty-one this year. I was a freshman at UWF when I was arrested. Now my mornings consist of *Maury* and my afternoons *Divorce Court* when I'm not perform-ing my job assignment—wiping down the water foun-tain."

Or snorting Suboxone in the back stall.

A hint of a smile touched his bleary eyes. "A college student?"

"English Lit."

"No promises." He replaced his glasses. "But I'll see what I can do."

49

Banners rippled above the throng like standards hoisted at a renaissance fair. *QAnon, Don't Tread on Me, Fuck Biden* . . . The sea of thousands swarmed the congres-sional steps. A girl danced on the railing as bearded, tattooed men in camo and animal skins urged the crowd onward. Police were beaten with *Trump 2020* flags and fire extinguishers. Walls were scaled, windows bashed, doors kicked in. Gallows were erected on the capitol lawn as onlookers shouted, "Hang Mike Pence!"

Miranda stared transfixed at the loop of live images being broadcast all over the world. *"If you don't fight like hell,"* the outgoing president urged, *"you're not going to have a country anymore."*

Tasha and Dixie were straddling a nearby bench, the toppled pieces of a forgotten chess game lay motionless on the board between them.

"If those were black folks they would've all been shot," said Tasha.

"If those were black folks," Dixie crossed her massive arms, "the media would be calling them freedom fighters."

More footage trickled in—of a police officer being crushed in a doorway, of the vice president being whisked to safety, of nervous congressional members stacking tables and chairs at chamber entry points—all while an orgastic news correspondent breathlessly ejaculated breaking details from a split screen.

Dixie chuckled.

Miranda frowned at her old cellmate. "You can't really be enjoying this."

"What?" Dixie growled. "You're not?"

"The implosion of our democratic system? Domestic terror?" Miranda shook her head. "No, I'm not enjoying it."

"Quit being so damn melodramatic." She pointed at the television. "You sound like that reporter up there. Last summer, when American cities burned in riots, the same liberal media was all *'violence is the language of the unheard.'* Well, you know what? Those people on those steps feel unheard too. Unheard and pissed off."

"They're attacking the capitol, Dixie! The very seat of our democracy. I can't believe a military veteran like yourself would applaud such an assault on the government . . . on the constitution itself."

"Everybody wants to talk about the constitution." She stared at the screen. "But they back down when it's time to do constitutional things. Not this time."

"Shit," said Tasha, "check out all that camo. It looks like the military is the ones doing the attacking. Except for the cracker in the horns and fur. Y'all think he killed that buffalo hisself?"

Someone tugged on her jacket sleeve. She turned to find Throkkie scratching her freckled nose. Her pupils were diminished to almost nothing. Even magnified by the powerful lenses of her glasses, they were barely dotted i's. Ultramicroscopic subatomic particles. She looked like she snorted an entire strip.

So judgy you are, said her inner narrator. *How much did you snort this morning?*

"Surreal, isn't it?" Miranda nodded at the violent images on the screen. "You'd expect this in some other country. Not in Washington, D.C."

Throkkie cut her eyes at Dixie and shrugged. "Well, they shouldn't have stolen the election."

"Wow," she sighed. "You too? Every single legal challenge thrown out, over forty and counting at this point. That includes the two Trump filed to the Supreme Court which, by the way, is stocked with his appointees . . ."

Dixie yawned. "You should be banned from the dayroom whenever the news is on."

"You do get a little crunk," said Tasha.

The volume on the television went up. *"Oh Nancy,"* a rioter's voice carried eerily down the capitol hallway. *"We're coming for you, Nancy."*

"Are we not watching the same footage?" Miranda was incredulous. "There's a hangman on the capitol lawn. Look at the confederate flags. And just a day after Georgia elects a black reverend and a 33-year-old Jew to the Senate."

"Typical liberal observation." Dixie rolled her eyes at Tasha. "They claim to be so anti-racism, yet they find the racial angle in everything."

"Hey Miranda." Throkkie pulled her sleeve again. "Ms. G just posted the callout on the bulletin board."

"She puts up the callout every day, Daphne."

"Daphne?" She put her hand on her hip. "Who are you, my mother? Why are you calling me by my government name?"

Miranda frowned. "Your what?"

"My government name." Throkkie pushed her glasses up the bridge of her nose and smiled. "That's what Duval used to say when I called her Ernestine. *Why you callin' me by my government name?*"

Miranda turned back to the television. A street vendor was hawking *Fuck Your Feelings* t-shirts to middle-aged suburbanites in Maga hats, a passerby with an American flag bandana tied around his head flipped off the camera, a group of young people appeared to be praying by a barricade.

"This is boring," said Throkkie. "I'm gonna lay down. I can't believe they cut into *Ellen* for this shit. Don't forget to check the callout," she said over her shoulder. "I'm pretty sure your name's on it... your government name."

Miranda watched her sidestep the woman at the kiosk and disappear around the corner into the bedding area. Curious, she glanced at the television once more, then she walked over to the bulletin board and stood on her tip toes to see over the small crowd.

The callout was eight pages long and consisted mostly of medical and classification appointments. Further down was dental, psych, chapel, property, and laundry. She found her name at the bottom of the final sheet under the heading, *Job Changes*. Her heart began to pound.

McGuire, Miranda #070419, From: Dormworker, To: Law Clerk Trainee

The crowd dispersed. She just stood there soaking it up, the electric blanket warmth of Suboxone multiplied by feel-good endorphins plugging into receptors. Her smile came on slowly. She could see it growing in the reflective plexiglass that encased the bulletin board. In that moment the rioters and reporters on the television were reduced to peripheral noise, Dixie's right-wing tough talk was forgotten, even the lingering trauma from New Year's Day subsided. After two months in the box and two weeks on the compound, a break had finally materialized. She was one step closer to freedom, one step closer to her baby.

It was time to get to work.

50

"Bienvenidos!" A bubbly Latina met her at the door. "You must be Miranda. I love your hair. Come in." She used her mask as a headband. Synthesized music blipped and ticked from her earbuds. Her heavily accented voice rose to compensate. "Vanessa is answering confinement requests right now. I'm supposed to show you around."

"Hold it down out there," Mr. Silva called from his office.

"I'm Yanisbel!" She introduced herself as she danced past the empty book checkout counter, her voluptuous body in motion beneath her tight blues. "But you can call me Yani, or Cubita, if that's easier to remember."

"Martinez!"

Miranda pointed at the windowed office where Mr. Silva sipped coffee in front of a computer screen.

"What's up boss?" She snatched out an earbud.

"If you insist on shouting over that disco, I'm going to insist that you leave your tablet in the dorm from now on."

"It's not *deesco*." She rolled her eyes, adjusted the volume. "It's freestyle." She smiled at Miranda. "You like Freestyle? Stevie B, Lil Suzi, Raquel, Shannon, Expose? This is my favorite playlist. Takes me back to Miami, 1988. The Bakery Center, Tropical Park, Skylight, Calle Ocho!"

"1988?" said Miranda. "How old are you?"

"Old enough." She leaned in close. "Old enough to know what teensy little pupils mean . . . Come on, I'll give you a tour."

Her warm hand clasped Miranda's and pulled her toward the book-lined shelves. Delicious titles leapt from spines like hooked fingers beckoning from misty alleyways, portals into different worlds, different lives.

"Although books are no true escape," her inner narrator mangled a David Mitchell quote, *"they will keep a mind from scratching itself raw."*

It occurred to her that Suboxone provided a similar service.

"So this is the general library," said Yani, pronouncing *this* like *these*. "Before corona, this place was packed. We had two girls working the checkout counter, one working the magazines, and all these tables were full. But we haven't had any general library callouts since last March."

Miranda pulled a random book from the shelf. *Sarah Maas, Throne of Glass.* Although she was unfamiliar with the author, there was something intriguing about the silver and violet cover, the sharp symmetrical font, the woman standing with two blades. She thumbed through the pages. So crisp. And the smell . . .

Her thoughts flashed to a naïve little redhead on her first day of college: English Lit major, Political Science minor, heart full of dreams and a purse full of pills. She was going to be a novelist! Then, after four years at UWF, maybe enroll in a prestigious MFA program. Those dreams felt like someone else's now.

"How do people check out books?" *Throne of Glass* seemed like something Throkkie would enjoy.

"Baby I can't hear you behind that mask," said Yani. "It's just us in here. You can take it off. Boss doesn't care."

Miranda reluctantly removed the thick material from her face.

"Look at you," the clerk gushed. "So *bonita.* How old are you?"

"Twenty," said Miranda.

"*Ai pobrecita.* What are you doing in prison?"

"It's a long story." She turned the book over in her hands. "But I plead no contest to armed trafficking of 28 grams of heroin."

"893.135 with a firearm enhancement," said Yani. "How much time did you get?"

"Ten years."

"*Tiene suerte.* You're lucky."

"I don't feel very lucky." Miranda stared at the coils of razor wire outside the window. "How did you know that statute off the top of your head like that?"

"Because I'm a certified law clerk," said Yani. "And because I'm serving a life sentence for the same charges."

Miranda impulsively touched her arm. "I'm sorry."

"They offered me twenty." Nonchalant shrug. "I went to trial instead."

The American Way, said her inner narrator. *Accept the plea bargain or pay the consequences.*

"Have you exhausted all your post-conviction remedies?"

"Listen to you." She smiled. "You haven't even taken the first test yet, *pero* you already sound like a little *abogada.*"

"Well, have you?"

She wrapped her headphones around her tablet and set them on the table. "I appealed to the 3rd DCA immediately after trial but when they affirmed my case, I gave up. Then, in 2005, I started coming to the law library and finding little things—pretrial motions my attorney didn't file, improper jury instructions, stuff like that. But it was too late at that point. Ten years had passed. I was time-barred. So I became a law clerk to make sure that doesn't happen to nobody else."

"Are you any good?"

"I'd say she's average." Vanessa Hackett strode over and dropped a stack of requests on the table. "For a minority clerk."

Stunned by her breezy rudeness, Miranda blinked.

"Had to teach her English first—"

"You did not."

"—she's come a long way though." Vanessa's pale brow furrowed in reflection. "Didn't you get someone an evidentiary hearing last year?"

"Actually, I got two people back to court."

"The 3800 doesn't count. Sentencing errors are gimme's." She turned to Miranda, sizing her up. "So you really think you're going to pass all nine of those tests in six weeks?"

Miranda nodded slowly, unsure what to make of her.

"It's possible, I guess." Her mouth smiled. "If you're a speed reader with a photographic memory."

Eidetic memory, her inner narrator shot back. *Bitch.*

"Like I said the other day, I did it in eight, but I had been researching and writing motions for a couple years before I got this job. How long did it take you to finish, Yani?"

"Nine months," said the Cubana.

"That's about the average." Another cold smile. "Especially for someone with no legal background. But good luck to you. We need another clerk. And if things don't work out, I'd be happy to do your 3.850. For a small fee, of course."

Yani rolled her eyes. *"Asquerosa."*

"What?" Vanessa feigned innocence. "I'm just offering my services."

"I would love some help either way," said Miranda. Some things were universal. Arrogant people and their fragile egos, for instance. Prison was no different than the classroom in this respect. No sense in offending the senior clerk on her first day in the library. "Unfortunately, I don't have any money."

"Nonsense," said Vanessa. "Have you filed a 1040?"

Miranda nodded. "In November. Duval brought me the form to fill out while I was in confinement."

"Among other things, I'm sure," she smirked. "Have you been to the canteen?"

"I didn't make it to the window. The women at the front of the line kept selling their spots."

"Typical." She turned and shouted toward the office.

"Hey boss! Can you check McGuire's account balance?"

Silence.

Vanessa stared at the ceiling and blinked theatrically. "Boss?"

"Okay, okay," Mr. Silva grumbled. "Number?"

She glanced at Miranda's inmate ID. "070419."

Tapping, clicking, waiting, then, "Eighteen hundred dollars."

"There you have it," said Vanessa. "Nice time to come to prison, isn't it? A free JPay tablet and two fat stimulus checks? Quite the little starter kit. We've come a long way since Julie Jones. Ten years ago we were eating chow hall TVP and worried about getting our bunks kicked by some horny inbred on the midnight shift."

Miranda was lost. *TVP and horny inbreds? Who was Julie Jones?* She glanced at Yani for clarification, but the Latina clerk only nodded sagely.

"So let me know if you want me to draft your 3.850." Vanessa lowered her voice and shot a quick look at Mr. Silva through the window of his office. "I normally charge five but I'll do yours for three since we'll be working together."

"Three dollars?" said Miranda.

Vanessa chuckled. "What did you say your IQ was again?"

"I don't see how my IQ has anything to do with—"

"Oh never mind." She looked at Yani and raised her plucked eyebrows. "Finish showing her around while I print the caselaw. I'll take her with me to do confinement rounds when they call. Might as well start training her early. Although I'm not convinced she'll pass the certification tests."

Miranda felt her face redden as the senior clerk walked back to her desk. "What a . . ."

"Puta?" Yani smiled. "Nah, she's just . . . how do you say? *Dura. Terca.* She's been in prison for a long time."

"That doesn't give her a pass to be so rude."

"You'll get used to it," said Yani. "She's not that bad. And she would probably do your motion for two *pedazitos* of Suboxone if you catch her when she's sick."

"I don't want her to do my motion." Miranda glared across the library at her back. *"I'm* doing my motion."

"Okay." Yani shrugged. "But she *is* good. That's why she charges what she does. I only charge a hundred."

Miranda frowned. "Do all the clerks charge?"

"Shh." She pressed a finger to her lips and glanced at Mr. Silva's open door. "We all hustle. Just like the *chicas* in laundry sell clothes and the ladies in the kitchen sell food. If someone doesn't have money, we still help. But everybody's got money right now because of the stimulus checks."

Including you, her inner narrator broke in, *1800 dollars! You can send money to Cameron. You can send money to Dad . . .*

"Ms. Hackett." The boss's chair squeaked. "Are you still taking the trainee with you to confinement?"

"Yes sir," said Vanessa.

"Officer Daniels just called from Tango dormitory. They're ready for you now."

Yani squeezed her hand and smiled. "*Buena suerte, Pelirroja.* I'll give you the grand tour when you come back."

51

The confinement cart was made of meshed steel and four wobbly wheels. A stack of folders gyrated in the top basket as she pushed it down the sidewalk toward center court.

An emaciated woman in a dirty sweatshirt spotted Vanessa from the pavilion near Oscar dorm and ran over to the fence. "Did you finish yet?" She asked with desperation in her eyes. A junkie begging her dealer for a hit.

"Working on it," Vanessa shouted over the clattering cart.

"Monday is the deadline." She jogged along beside them.

"I'm fully aware of your deadline, Janice. It'll be printed and copied and awaiting your signature by Friday."

The tower window slammed open. "Get off the fence!" a guard shouted through his bullhorn.

Janice raised her hands and veered into the grass, walking backwards. "Will I be on the callout?"

Vanessa pretended not to hear. "One thing about being a law clerk," she said to Miranda, "these women swear they're the center of the universe. They all expect you to push everything else aside and just focus on them . . . Especially if they're paying you."

Miranda nosed the cart up to the gate and waited to be buzzed through. After a few minutes, the guard looked down from the tower and acknowledged them. "Hackett, you know better than to talk through my fence."

Everything is theirs, said her inner narrator, *have you noticed that? Don't talk through my fence, don't pass food in my chow hall, walk inside my yellow line . . . We're the ones who live in this dump. It is more ours than theirs.*

"I wasn't talking sir," Vanessa lied. "I was just listening."

"Good answer." The gate popped. Mirrored shades assessed them from 100 feet above. "Who's the redhead?"

"The new law clerk trainee." Vanessa held the gate while she pushed the cart through. "I'm taking her with me to do confinement rounds."

"Oh, that's right. The other girl got her face carved up, didn't she? I hate it when that happens." His voice dripped with sarcasm. He was about to comment further when his radio erupted in a burst of chatter. He paused to listen.

"Come on," Vanessa said under her breath. Miranda followed with the rickety cart.

"Train her well!" the guard shouted behind them. "So she can help all those lost souls in confinement write their BS grievances on my fellow officers."

"See why I love going to the box so much?" Vanessa muttered as she smiled back at the tower. "And we haven't even made it to Tango dorm yet."

"Don't forget to teach her how to file PREA claims!"

"He could probably teach you a thing or two about that himself." Vanessa let the gate slam behind them. "I think he's had three since I've been here. That's why they won't let him out of the gun tower."

"What's a PREA claim?" Miranda spoke over the clatter.

"Prison Rape Elimination Act." Vanessa glanced at her. "You've got a lot to learn over the next six weeks."

They paused at the final gate. Miranda chewed her lip and studied the confinement unit through the fence. Her old home. Maybe she *was* in over her head. She had a passable grasp of the postconviction stuff but there was apparently more to certification than collateral attacks on criminal sentences, foreign things like civil law and the grievance procedure and PREA claims.

"Don't worry." Vanessa must have smelled her panic. "You're assigned to the library now. You're in. If it takes you a little longer to pass the tests, so what. Nobody will know."

Actually, a few people would know, said her inner narrator. *Including her . . . and she'd never let you forget it.*

Miranda knew the type—thin-skinned, average intelligence, and hyper competitive. There was one in every classroom dating back to the third grade.

"How long have you been a law clerk?" she asked.

"Almost ten years," said Vanessa. "But I've been getting women back into court for longer than that. Close to fifteen, probably. I just started off at the main unit and that snobby little clique over there did everything they could to keep me out of the library."

"Thank you for not doing that to me." She counted the window slats on the side of Sierra dorm through the chain-link. Her arm tingled from old chemical burns. "I need this job. You have no idea . . ."

"Well, Duval had been lobbying for you," said Vanessa. "So when she got her face slashed, it was the perfect fit."

Miranda shivered from the memory. "She was a good friend. I won't let her down."

"Just a friend?" Vanessa smiled knowingly. "My unconfirmed sources tell me otherwise."

The final gate buzzed. She pushed the cart through. "Whatever you heard is untrue. I'm not into that."

"If you say so." Vanessa reached out and slowed the cart. "No judgment zone, okay? But I also heard that she may have left some medication behind. If any of that is for sale . . ."

Miranda's hand moved protectively to the lump in her waistband. "I'll, um, I'll ask around."

They came upon Tango dorm quickly. A crow announced their arrival from its perch atop the death row recreation cage. Vanessa put her face to the plexiglass and peered through the door. "Aw shit. Seriously? This is why I hate doing confinement rounds."

"What is it?" said Miranda.

She stepped aside and motioned her to take a look. "Have you had the pleasure of crossing paths with this weapons-grade asshole yet?"

The door buzzed before she could maneuver around the cart. Vanessa sighed and pulled it open. Lieutenant Grantham was standing in the hallway.

He looked up from his flexed bicep and snarled through his mask. "What the fuck is this?"

"Law library sir." Vanessa tapped the stack of manila files in the cart. "We're here to do confinement rounds."

He didn't budge, just stood in the corridor blocking their passage, hands on hips like some low-level super-hero from the Marvel Universe. *Captain Asshole.*

After an ice age, he reached for his radio. "Station one to security seventeen, Officer Daniels. Did you call for law clerks?"

The radio crackled with static. "Ten-four sir."

Slowly, he slid it back into its holster and addressed Vanessa. "What is that clipped to your ID?"

She glanced down at her identification card and lifted it to reveal a green laminated badge that said, *Certified Law Clerk.*

He nodded and turned to Miranda. "Where's yours?"

"We have to make her one," said Vanessa. "She's the new trainee. Today is her first—"

"Shut up," he growled. "You think that little home-made badge makes you her attorney? She can speak for herself. As a matter of fact, take that cart and go wait for Officer Daniels by the quad one door."

"Yes sir." She avoided eye contact as she stepped behind the cart and pushed it down the hallway.

"You," he scowled at Miranda and reached for his keys, jamming the largest into a door on her right, "get in here."

The door opened into a small interview room. A dusty, faux wood desk piled with empty three-ring binders was pushed into the corner. A dated Department of Corrections *We Never Walk Alone* poster clinged to the wall with time-yellowed tape and grime. She glanced up at the hallway camera once more then crossed the threshold.

He followed and yanked his mask off. "That was a nice little stunt you pulled the other day."

His eyes bored into hers. She looked away, swallowed. "I have no idea what you're talking about."

"Don't fuck with me." His breath exploded in her face. Minty cruelty. "You humiliated me in front of my officers and all those inmates. I told you it wasn't over."

Her knees began to tremble. Her lip quivered.

Don't you dare cry, said her inner narrator.

"I know there was dope in that baby powder bottle," he growled. "I don't know how you hid it, or what you did with it, but I know it was there."

She could feel the plastic-wrapped bundle of Suboxone pulsating on her waistline, burning her hip like a lump of hot coal. "It was just . . . baby powder."

"You're a shitty liar, you know that? I bet if that camera over your bunk didn't have that little blind spot, we'd be having a different conversation right now." He dug a knuckle beneath her chin and forced her head back. She blinked up at the popcorn ceiling. "But there are blind spots all over this compound. And they can hurt you just as easy as they can help you."

Tears filled her eyes. She blinked them away.

"So what are you really doing back here, huh? And don't give me that inmate lawyer trainee shit. How many illiterate meth whores does it take to pass out DC-303 forms? You here to check on your lesbian lover?"

"No." Her voice trembled.

"You know what I think?" He leaned in closer. "I think you tagged along with your library buddy so you could drop off some contraband . . . maybe the dope that mysteriously disappeared from that baby powder, hmm? What do you have on you?" He hooked a finger in the vee of her collar and looked down her shirt. "You hiding something?"

She shook her head frantically.

"Then turn around and put your hands against the wall."

Toxic fear shrieked through her nervous system, impairing her ability to think, to speak, to move.

"Are you refusing a verbal order?" He shoved her against the wall and spun her around, kicking at her ankles to spread her feet.

Above her head, the poster of correctional officers in vintage D.O.C. brown looked on as she was being manhandled. *We never walk alone.* She stared up at the bygone catchphrase.

If only that were true, her inner narrator mused. *We need some witnesses.*

"You got anything on you I should know about?" His shadow fell over her, his beard stubble grazed her earlobe. "Knives, notes . . . Suboxone strips?"

It's over, declared her inner narrator. *As soon as he goes to your waist, he's going to feel that obvious lump and it'll be curtains for you. Another sixty days in confinement, fired from the law library on your first day. Grand opening, grand closing. Maybe Vanessa Hackett will do your 3.850 while you're in the box . . .*

"What are you shaking for?" He ran his hands beneath her armpits, then down her sides. "Are you scared?"

She was terrified, but there was no sense answering his rhetorical question. She closed her eyes and prepared for what was coming.

His breathing grew ragged as he squeezed her breasts. "You got anything in your bra?"

Her nipples were still sensitive from childbirth. It felt like a lifetime had passed since her baby came howling into the world, but it had only been six months. Come to think of it, she was overdue for a progress report from Karen Tate. Cameron was probably crawling by now. She shook her head, clenched her teeth.

His hands fell to her backside. "You've got a nice ass, McGuire. Anyone ever tell you that?" He gripped her roughly, causing her to whimper and stagger against the wall. "Careful now. You ain't gonna scream are you?"

"No," she managed to utter.

"Wouldn't do you any good anyway." He forced a hand between her legs and whispered, "I can smell your fear . . . It's making me hard."

So, the good news, her inner narrator pointed out, *is that he seems to have totally forgotten what he was searching for. I think we're safe there . . . The bad news, however, is that it appears you're about to get—*

The door buzzed and banged shut. Heels tick-tacked down the hallway. He spun her around so that her back was against the wall, then calmly walked across the room, yanking his mask up on the way.

". . . the choice is yours, McGuire." He sat on the corner of the desk, admired his biceps. "You can make the most of this law library opportunity, maybe actually help some people, or you can follow the crowd. Just be aware that the crowd usually ends up locked behind those doors back there."

A woman appeared in the doorway clutching a bottle of vitamin water and looking a question at the lieutenant. Miranda remembered her sunflower mask from a similar room in Sierra dorm.

"Ms. Brewer." He pushed off the desk and greeted her. "I was wondering where you were. You remember McGuire, don't you? She came in front of us for the assault and disrespect charges a few months ago . . ."

"Vaguely." The woman nodded at her.

He paused dramatically, cocked his head. "Did you . . . highlight your hair?"

Her cheeks flushed, a red sky over a field of sunflowers. She touched her bun. "Last week."

"Can't believe I missed that. It looks so good." His voice lowered, deepened. He glanced at Miranda. "That will be all, inmate McGuire. Go make your confinement rounds."

Her heart pounded with relief and outrage as she backed out of the room and hurried down the hall to find Vanessa.

"Put your mask on." His voice followed her.

52

"You okay?" Vanessa was waiting outside of quad one.

For a brief moment she considered unloading on the mercurial clerk, telling her everything: how he threatened her, how he pushed her against the wall, how he might have found the hidden lump of Suboxone strips on her waistline if he wasn't so busy assaulting her. But in the end, it was her inner narrator who held her back.

Why would you tell her anything? You don't trust her, don't particularly like her, and don't want her legal assistance. She already suspects you're holding Duval's stuff. Why confirm her suspicions? So she can harass you for a piece every day?

Miranda chewed her lip, stared at her coworker.

And if you tell her—or anyone—about Grantham, and it gets out, you will wind up behind one of those doors under protective custody or investigation. Either way, you'll lose your library job. This isn't about your feelings or your safety. It stopped being about you the second that baby was born. If you absolutely need to tell someone, tell Dixie . . . AFTER you've been certified and after your motion is in the court.

What she *absolutely needed* was her plastic spork, a little hot water, and five minutes alone. If only to drown out the annoying voice of her inner narrator.

And for God's sake, never, ever bring your dope to confinement . . .

"Are you talking to yourself?" Vanessa rearranged files in the cart.

She shook her head. "I was just replaying my conversation with the lieutenant."

"Yeah? Pretty one-sided conversation, I imagine. What did he have to say?"

Miranda glanced at her *Library Clerk* identification tag. "He was yelling at me for not having an ID like yours."

"What a dick." Vanessa rolled her eyes. "I'll get Yani to make you one this afternoon. That's who made mine. You don't *have* to have one. There's nothing in the inmate handbook or Chapter 33 that says you do. But if it'll keep him off your trail . . ."

Ha! her inner narrator scoffed. *Good luck with that.*

Officer Daniels smiled at her from the bubble on his way down the steps. "Well, look what the cat dragged in." He secured the officers' station door and continued to beam at her like a long lost relative. "Just couldn't stay away, could you?"

"Oh, you guys know each other?" said Vanessa. "Perfect. That'll save us time and spare us awkward introductions. I'm training her to do confinement rounds. With any luck she'll be coming back here by herself before the spring."

"Ten-four." Daniels spun his key ring on an elegant finger. "How many we got today?"

Vanessa pulled a printout from the top folder. "Twelve. But only three in quad one. Mendoza, Ross, and Griffin. The rest are in wing two."

He lifted his radio to his mask. "Seventeen to Tango, quad one please."

The door popped.

"Bring the cart," said Vanessa.

Quad one of Tango dorm was utilized almost exclusively for protective management cells, women being held under investigation, and S.H.O.S. inmates (Self-Harm Observation Status).

"The S.H.O.S. cells are basically psych cells," Vanessa explained as they headed for the stairs. "Most of these women are just *playing* crazy to get a cell change or get transferred or get on better meds. Although, it could be argued that if you smear feces all over your face and bark at the warden, whether you believe you're playing or not, you might have some issues."

Hollow eyes and malnourished faces filled the surrounding windows. Miranda remembered what it felt like to be on that side of the door.

"Leave the cart," Vanessa instructed at the foot of the stairs. She grabbed the top three files and opened the first. "See this request? Griffin is requesting assistance on her belated appeal. The other two are for copy service."

"Ernestine Griffin?" Miranda frowned at the familiar handwriting. "Isn't that . . ."

"Duval," Vanessa nodded. "She's one of the people we're here to see. They've got her in 1206. Notice how downstairs the cells run 1101, 1102, 1103 and upstairs they go 1201, 1202 and so on . . ."

Duval! She was in no way prepared for this. She surveyed the upstairs window slats with dread, resisting the urge to fake a medical emergency.

"Come on," Vanessa called over her shoulder.

She swallowed her fear and trudged up the stairs behind them.

Duval was waiting at her door. The puckered and stapled flesh of her scar glowed silver and pink beneath the fluorescent. She held Miranda's gaze as Officer Daniels unlocked the flap.

"Hey girl." Vanessa knelt by her door. "How are you holding up?"

"I'd be holding up a lot better if you sent me the money you owe me."

Vanessa smiled nervously at Daniels. "I was thinking I could help you with this belated appeal and—"

"I can do my own fucking legal work!" Duval slapped the plexiglass. "Don't try to hustle me like I'm some green little bitch fresh off the bus."

"I'm not," said Vanessa.

"Get that money to my cash app. Tonight."

"Okay." She stared down at the folder.

Daniels wagged a finger at the window. "Be nice."

"This *is* nice." Duval nodded at Miranda. "I need to talk to her . . . alone."

Miranda's heart began to pound.

"Why do you always do this?" Daniels glanced at the camera. "You know she can't be up here unsupervised. I could lose my job."

"Come on, Auntie." Duval smiled. Honey-colored plasma oozed from a staple above her lip. "I just need a couple minutes. You know they gonna ship me any day now. Let me holla at my girl."

"What'd I tell you about calling me that?" The guard's eyes narrowed over his mask. "I ain't nobody's auntie."

"Okay, my fault," said Duval. "Two minutes. Please?"

He looked back over the railing at the officers' station.

"I do have copies for Mendoza and Ross." Vanessa held up the files. "They're just a few doors down."

"Fine." He shook his head. "But if I get fired for this, you're gonna send me some of that cash app money you're always bragging about."

"I got you Auntie."

Miranda watched them make their way down the tier, glancing up at door numbers as women shouted Vanessa's name.

"You scared to look at my face?"

She swallowed, met her eyes. "No."

"I ain't as bad as that burn victim you hang out with."

The blunt force of her words made Miranda flinch. She looked past her, into the cell. A woman much larger than Duval was snoring beneath a blanket in the bunk next to the toilet. "Who's that?"

"My bunkie? I don't know. Some dyke from up your way. They're holding her under investigation for something. She'll probably hit the compound this week. All she does is sleep."

Miranda studied her staples. The laceration spanned from her left temple, across her cheekbone, hooking her nostril and slashing between her nose and mouth before terminating in a crusty incision an inch below her right earlobe. "I'm sorry this happened to you. In some ways, I feel like it's my fault."

"Come down here to this flap," said Duval.

She glanced over at Daniels and Vanessa before squatting in front of the door.

"Where the fuck is my dope?"

Miranda blinked. "Excuse me?"

"Ain't no fuckin' excuse," she hissed. "I got a kite from Kim saying you grabbed my shit off my bunk when they took me to medical."

"Would you had rather I let the guards find it?"

"So you did grab it?"

"Of course," said Miranda. "I've got it on me right now." She leaned to the side and dug a finger into the elastic waistband of her blues.

"What the fuck are you doing?" Duval hissed.

"Giving you your stuff. Half of it, at least."

"Stop that! If the guard in the bubble sees you reaching in your pants, you're gonna end up back here with me . . . and I need you out there."

"Really?" said Miranda. "Because you don't sound very needy to me. You sound rude."

"Look at my face." She pointed at the staples. "Would you be in a good mood if you had all this going on?"

"Well, hopefully Kim apologized in her *kite*. If I could take back New Year's Eve, I would."

"Eh, it's not your fault. It's nobody's fault. She's just a jealous psychopath . . ."

The blanket rippled in the bunk behind her. A huge foot, almost as big as Dixie's, shot from beneath the wool.

". . . but I love that crazy bitch." Duval shook her head. "Hey, remember when you jumped on that poor girl in transport?"

Miranda rolled her eyes, nodded.

"That shit was so funny. Rocky kept yelling *beat her ass Miranda!* Kim ain't the only crazy bitch I fuck with."

"That would be offensive coming from anyone other than you." Miranda smiled.

"Now look at you—a law clerk trainee," said Duval. "I've been on the boss about hiring you. Did he tell you that?"

"He did. Thank you."

"I know how bad you wanted the job. I came through on that tip, at least."

"You're always coming through, Duval. You have since the first day I met you."

She glanced back at her sleeping cellmate. "Well, now I need you to come through for me."

Miranda swallowed, waited.

"Don't worry about the two hundred dollars you owe me. Keep the dope too. Just promise me you'll look out for Kim, same way I used to hook you up when you were back here. Remember how to do it?"

She nodded, a little miffed about having to share with a woman who tried to slice her face. "I'll do my best."

"I know you will," said Duval. "One more thing . . ."

Miranda leaned closer to the flap.

"I need you to bring me my jack."

"Okay," she said, then, "what's a jack?"

"Shh!" She glanced back at her bunkie again. "My phone. I need you to bring me my phone. In the back of the law library, there are hundreds of books on the shelves. You're looking for *Federal Supplement 825*. It's a dusty old hardback from back in the day that no one ever looks at. The pages in the middle are hollowed out. My jack is taped inside. Get it and bring it to me."

"The whole book?"

"No," she said, "not the whole damn book. We can't have hardbacks no way. Just hide it in some caselaw and bring it the next time you come back here. But hurry. They're gonna ship me as soon as they take these staples out."

"Federal Supplement 825."

"You got it. Right between 824 and 826. Don't let me down Red."

"Have I ever told you how much I detest that nickname?"

She smiled her tragic smile. "Couple times."

Suddenly the blanket behind her peeled away and a thickset black woman stumbled to the toilet.

Is that . . . ? Her inner narrator's voice filled her head. *It can't be . . .*

"You good?" Duval frowned through the flap. "You're all pale and shit, like you just seen a ghost."

Miranda continued to gawk as the woman stood over the toilet and urinated like a man, noisily breaking wind before flushing and staggering back to her bunk. She was snoring again within seconds.

Duval shook her head. "I know . . . I got some bad ass luck, right? 1500 bitches at the annex and I get the only one that's manlier than me for a cellmate."

Vanessa and Daniels hurried back down the tier. "We gotta go. There's still nine people in quad two we need to see, and I don't want to get stuck in here for count."

"Tell Kim I love her," said Duval.

Daniels rolled his eyes and slammed the flap.

Miranda stood and squinted through the plexiglass a final time. "What's her name?"

"Who?" He shoved his keys in his belt.

"The woman in there with Duval."

"Oh, she just came on the county van. Had a *keep away* at the reception center. She's got one of those crazy names. Nevada something." He turned and headed for the stairs, then paused. "No, not Nevada. Nebraska . . . Nebraska Jackson."

EPILOGUE

The *Inmate Law Clerk Training Manual* was 15 chapters and over 150 pages of allegedly dry reading that opened with the three branches of government and meandered its way through the various types of law, collateral attacks, extraordinary remedies, appellate procedure, federal habeas corpus, civil rights complaints and, finally, clemency.

Miranda soaked up every word.

Grateful for the opportunity and determined to master the subject matter, she read the thick packet from beginning to end three times on consecutive days. The notes she scrawled were unnecessary, more to do something with her hands than to concretize the curriculum. By Thursday afternoon she could almost quote the entire module without pulling up screenshots in her mind. By Friday she was itching to take her first test.

She leaned back in her chair and massaged her neck, still a little nauseated from the sizable piece she snorted in the bathroom. She closed her eyes and let the library sounds wash over her—Yani flipping pages of a *Florida Law Weekly,* Vanessa explaining federal time limits to a woman from Q dorm, the hair-netted kitchen worker clicking and scrolling through caselaw on the computer, and beneath it all, the silence . . . beautiful, sacred, atmospheric silence.

So what are you going to do about Duval? Her inner narrator's voice exploded in her mind. *You've been procrastinating all week.*

She sat up straight and looked across the room. Behind the counter, a maze of law books—hundreds of them—lined the shelves. Somewhere, down one of those rows, Duval's gutted Federal Second awaited her. All she had to do was grab it. The problem was that Mr. Silva's office window provided an unobstructed view into the law library.

She glanced back at her boss. The soft glow of his twin computer monitors reflected from his glasses. His mask concealed most of his craggy face. Was he watching her? It was difficult to tell. But surely a flash of blue would hook his attention, if her flaming red hair didn't.

How do you know that? Her inner narrator pressed. *There are well over a thousand blue uniforms on this compound. He sees them every day. Maybe he's desensitized. Maybe he doesn't care if you walk back there and grab a law book. Isn't that what law clerk trainees do?*

She didn't feel like a law clerk trainee yet. She felt like a guest in Vanessa Hackett's world. It seemed presumptuous—if not outright suspicious—to wander the aisles alone. Especially during her first week of work. Once she aced a few tests . . .

There's no time for that and you know it. Duval will probably be on the next bus out. She's been a good friend to you—generous with her canteen, lobbying for you to get this job, forgiving your debts . . . She's the reason you're high right now. She asked you for one thing. Now get up, walk back there, and find it.

Miranda sighed and pushed back her chair. It was clear that her drug tolerance was increasing. A few weeks ago, it took a tiny sliver of Suboxone to muffle the voice in her head. Now, a half strip was apparently no match for her relentless inner narrator.

Quietly, stealthily, she slipped behind the counter and headed for the books. Row upon row of stuffy volumes towered over her and snaked around her, garnet and gold dinosaurs with rulings reversed and remanded or affirmed, their spines tramp-stamped with *in memoriam* inscriptions, tributes to forgotten judges and legal scholars from a bygone era.

She hurried past the *Southern Reporter*s and *Statutes Annotated,* her pace quickening as she came to the *Federal Reporter*s. Finally, on a splintery wooden shelf in the back, she found what she was looking for.

"What are you doing?" Vanessa's cold voice split the silence.

Miranda flinched. "Oh! You scared me." Her nervous laughter felt contrived. "I was just looking for caselaw on women who accepted plea agreements while going through postpartum."

"In the Federal Seconds?"

"Well, I'm not sure where to look." She scanned the volumes on the shelf . . . 825 was bottom right, three from the end. "Most of the cases I've read so far deal with women using postpartum as a defense in trial. Not as a basis for an involuntary plea."

"And you're just flipping through random books hoping to find this needle in a haystack?"

Weak, said her inner narrator. *Weak and illogical. You're going to need to do better than that. She is clearly on to you.*

"Well, really I was just familiarizing myself with the anatomy of caselaw. How the narrative is arranged, from the synopsis to the ruling . . . and stuff."

"Stuff." Vanessa scrutinized her.

". . . You know, while I looked." Miranda added.

"Hackett!" Mr. Silva called from his office. "I've got two more grievances on my desk claiming we're denying access."

Vanessa ignored him. "Most people just search caselaw on the computer."

"That was my next step," said Miranda.

"Hackett!"

"Coming!" She turned and made her way between the shelves. When she reached the counter, she paused and looked back. "I can show you how to search caselaw on LexisNexis. This will only take a sec. Why don't you wait for me at a computer?" Vanessa flashed a frosty smile, pulled on her mask, and disappeared around the corner.

She chewed her lip inside her mask as the clerk's footsteps faded. Then she quickly knelt down and wrenched the heavy book from between its neighbors. She lay it on the floor and flipped to the middle.

The hollowed space was right where it was supposed to be, but there was nothing inside. A few paper shavings. She ran her finger along the rough perimeter of the cut rectangle and looked out across the library. From Mr. Silva's office window, she could see Vanessa watching her. Her glacial smile told Miranda everything she needed to know.

She held her gaze for a pregnant moment before closing the book and returning it to the shelf. Then she stood and made her way back to the open training manual on the desk. She had a test to study for.

ACKNOWLEDGEMENTS

Damn. So many people to thank. We've come a long way since *Consider the Dragonfly,* which didn't even have an acknowledgements page. But before I begin rattling off the names of loved ones, I want to acknowledge you, the reader. The world has no idea who Malcolm Ivey is. So far our home appears to be more *Banned Reading List* than *Bestsellers List.* That's pretty cool in its own right—makes me feel like Pat Conroy. But I expect it to change sooner or later. Possibly with the release of this novel. No matter what happens, I will always look back on these lean years with nostalgia . . . when you and I were celled up like two old convicts in the box telling war stories after *lights out.* I appreciate your time, your support, your friendship.

Special thanks to Marlene Sullivan, Judy Sullivan Peters, Teresa Rhodes, Deborah Hinton, Meg Nelson, Sheena Law, Tristan and Dara Stokes, Brittney Knapp, Amy Elliott, Marcia Ensminger, Jane Shimkowski, Greg Holland, The Mattson Family (Chad! Life begins . . .), The Sieferts, Joker Trevino, Patrick Odom, Eurel Maddox, Josh Bonilla, Jacob Gaulden, Ernest Davis, artist Jonathan Page, chain-gang poet laureate Chris Malec, to the ageless Lester Wells (wrongly convicted in 1983), Harry Tipton, Nicholas Tapout Warren, Robert Chevy Floyd, Archie Crews, Dylan Mancil, Korey Cole, Vontae Lang, Mark Hale, fellow writer Eric Rivera; to my good friends Marcus and Kelly Conrad, and Janet Zimmerman;

to my nieces Melanie, Sarah, and Caroline Collins, Eloise and Penny Mae Rhodes, Ms. Juniper Sponaugle; to my newest nephews Troy and Henry Scout, and the rest of my massive family which has grown exponentially since I last breathed free air. If you don't see your name here, check the other novels—*READ* the other novels—you might find more than a mere shout-out in the acknowledgements. I've dropped breadcrumbs in every book.

Mafia level favors to my homegirls Marlo Knapp and Sheila Jenkins—mothers, hustlers, legends, friends. The last time our paths intersected, we were all lost in the world. May we never lose our way again. Thanks for being my boots on the ground.

Also, to my brothers and mentors at the law firm— Trevor Davis, Roderick Ward, and Teddy Stokes. All teenagers when they were sentenced to life in the '90s; impulsive, impressionable, their brains not yet fully formed. Now men in their forties, self-educated and self-rehabilitated in a system that offers very few programs, they wait and they hope.

Can't forget my people 2060 miles away—Leah Skates, Avery Goosebumps, Sgt. Maj. Nicolas, and Bob the female lizard. Watching you grow in pics and videos over the years has been one of the great privileges of my life.

To the sweet little old lady at the end of the street who has sat at her computer and winced her way through every fist fight, facial slashing, F-bomb, and overdose on these handwritten pages (not to mention the real-life trauma of seeing me mauled by police canines, enslaved by addiction, stapled together in ICU beds, and sentenced to decades in prison) . . . It's almost over Momma! Just a couple more Christmases.

Finally, to my best friend Shonda Kerry—teammate, dreammate, and cofounder of Astral Pipeline Books. There's a million things I could say right here but none rub closer against the truth than this Jason Isbell lyric: "*. . . home was a dream, one that I'd never seen, till you came along.*" Thanks for riding with me. The Universe is clearly rigged in my favor. You're proof of that. We are waveform.

Turn the page for a preview of

The Law of Momentum

The third Miranda McGuire novel
by Malcolm Ivey

coming soon
from Astral Pipeline Books

PREVIEW

She was first on the kiosk after the evening count. She left her inmate ID in the chair to save her spot. There was so much to tell her dad—about the law library job, the 3.850 motion she was drafting, the stimulus money she was sending . . . She wondered if he was still living in a tent beneath the underpass. The special withdrawal form required an address. Her fingers danced across the metal keyboard as the dayroom noise melted into the background.

"Hey law clerk trainee McGuire." Throkkie leaned over her shoulder and rested her chin in the crook of Miranda's neck. "Why are you going all Trump on the caps lock?"

"Huh?" She stared at the screen. "Oh, because there's no right-hand shift on this stupid keyboard and it was slowing me down."

The officer pounded on the glass. Every head in the dayroom turned. He used all four fingers to point, his hand slashing down like a karate chop. Then he turned his palm upward and made a *come here* motion.

"What a dick," said Throkkie. "Anyone who wears a hat like that is a first-rate dick in my book. I think he's calling you."

"Definitely not." Miranda resumed typing. "I've got my mask on."

"Shit." Throkkie felt her face, pointed at herself.

His hat bobbed up and down.

"Ugh . . . I'll be back."

Miranda finished up the message and read over it once to check for errors—there were none—then, impulsively, she looked into the kiosk camera and snapped a pic. Normally, she hated taking pictures, but her dad requested one in his last email. It wasn't nearly as awkward with the mask covering two thirds of her face.

Studies have shown, her inner narrator broke in, *that the wearing of a mask makes you sixty-six percent less hideous . . .*

She just hoped he wouldn't notice her pupils.

"Excuse me. Don't you work in the law library?"

She logged off and rose from the chair. A small, sharp-featured woman watched her from over the rim of a dirty coffee cup. There was something familiar about her face. Miranda couldn't place it at first, but then it came to her: confinement, the rec cages, the woman who was talking to herself.

"I just started this week."

"Hmmph. Well then I doubt you'll be able to answer my question, but . . . do you know if Tallahassee is going to be voting on any new laws that might send us home early this year?"

She remembered someone asking Duval a similar question on the night Kim slashed her face. She also remembered being appalled by her friend's rudeness.

"That's a good question," she said. "I'll have to look into it."

The woman cocked her head and appraised Miranda with pawnbroker eyes. "You think you're gonna be any good at lawyering?"

"I think so."

"Maybe you could help me then." She took a swig of coffee and launched into her story. "I got arrested for burglary and grand theft four years ago. I ain't do the shit but try telling the police that. They lock me up and gimme a five-thousand-dollar bond. Costs five hundred to get out. Nobody I know has five hundred bucks just laying around. So I sit in the county six months before I go to court. Here they come with a deal—probation."

"Did you sign it?"

"What do you think? Hell yeah I signed it! I got two kids. But now I gotta pay money every month. They violated me the first time for moving without telling them. I didn't *move*, I got evicted. So they let me back out. Then I missed a couple payments when we were living in the shelter . . ."

Tasha looked up from the chessboard and caught her eye. She pointed at her ear and circled it a few times. Dixie glanced over her shoulder and smirked.

"Then I get a job at Whataburger, and a trailer, and here comes my cousin with her no-good boyfriend. Turns out he's got a warrant. When they kick my door in to arrest his stupid ass, I get violated for 'sociating with a felon *and* coming into contact with law enforcement. They gimme five years for that. No trial or nothing. Don't seem right . . ."

It *didn't* seem right. "Let me do a little research and I'll get back to you, okay?"

"I would surely appreciate it."

Throkkie stormed back into the dayroom, glasses perched atop her mask, clutching a yellow piece of paper. "Can you believe Sergeant Dipshit wrote me up for that?"

"Hell, I believe it." The woman walked away muttering. "I don't put nothing past the State of Florida . . . Come on vacation, leave on probation, come back on a violation . . ."

"Who was that?" said Throkkie.

Miranda shrugged. "She was asking some legal questions."

Throkkie balled up the paper and tossed it in the garbage can. "Some stud on side two was calling for you when I was at the window."

"Me?"

She nodded. "Big mean-looking musclebound chick."

"How—how do you know she wants me?"

"You're the only redhead named McGuire I know."

With a deep exhalation, Miranda turned and made her way out of the dayroom.

Throkkie followed.

The guard was still bent over the desk doing paperwork when they arrived. "Asshole!" her friend whispered. "Who writes CCs in 2021 anyway?"

Miranda was about to ask what a *CC* was when she spotted Nebraska across the officers' station on the other side of the glass. She was leaning against the wall, her thumbs hooked in the elastic of her blues. She smiled and threw up her hands when they made eye contact. *What's up?*

"That's her," said Throkkie.

Nebraska began speaking in sign language, her right hand twisting, pointing, cupping as she blasted through the alphabet, transmitting her covert message.

Miranda shrugged and shook her head, then looked at Throkkie.

"Lemme guess," said her friend. "You can't sign."

"I need to learn."

"Yeah you do. It's like Prison 101. Who is this chick anyway? Is she the one you were telling me about? Duval's cellmate? The one who testified against Amethyst?"

"Amity," said Miranda. "Yes, that's her."

Throkkie pushed her glasses up, leaned forward, and signaled Nebraska to start over.

Again, she took off, her fingers moving with blinding speed as she glared at passersby who dared to sneak a peek at the message she was relaying.

"Whoa." Throkkie held up a hand. "Slow down. I can't read that fast."

Nebraska's brow creased and her nostrils flared as she paused and took it from the top, emphasizing each letter, poking at the air, punctuating every word with a look that said *did you get that, stupid?* She had to stop every now and then when the guard looked up from his paperwork. At one point, Throkkie glanced at Miranda then turned back and shook her head. This seemed to be a trigger for Nebraska who reverted to her initial breakneck pace, glowering through the window as she barked orders with her right hand.

In the end, Throkkie used sign language that even Miranda could read—she held up both middle fingers and thrust them toward the glass.

Nebraska stared daggers at them before turning and storming off.

"Are you crazy?" said Miranda.

"No." Throkkie put an arm around her, guided her toward the bathroom. "But you're way too tense. How long since you got high?"

Miranda shook free of her grasp. "What was she saying?"

"She said Duval told her to get five strips from you. Nice try, right? I told her to fuck off."

"Yeah, I saw that part," said Miranda. "I wish you would've injected a little more diplomacy into your response. Especially since you were speaking on my behalf."

"Well, she was lying." Throkkie adjusted her glasses. "And she testified against your friend."

"I know," Miranda sighed. "But she's extremely volatile. And scary. I watched her bash a woman's head against the concrete in the county jail when I was pregnant with my son . . . over the television!"

"We don't need to worry about that. At least not for the next fourteen days." Throkkie smiled. "Side two went on quarantine this afternoon."

"Great," said Miranda. "Maybe I can take a couple law clerk tests before I die a violent death."

"Wait. Did you just make a joke? I think that's the first time you've made a joke since I met you."

Miranda shook her head. "I don't find anything humorous about this situation."

"Relax," said Throkkie. "I wouldn't let anyone hurt you."

She glanced at her *Dungeons and Dragons*-playing friend, all five feet and one hundred pounds of her. There was no need to state the obvious.

"Why are you looking at me like that? Don't let this size fool you . . . I bite hard."

Miranda swallowed and surveyed the dorm, her eyes coming to rest on the law books stacked on her bunk. She just wanted to study. But there always seemed to be an obstacle.

"Plus," her friend winked at her, "we've got Dixie on our team."